"Stay on the lead lap and we got a fighting chance," Jodell told the car. "Anything can happen at the finish, girl, if we're still around for it."

Jodell tried to pick up the pace, to stave off the inevitable as long as he could and hope for a caution to put them back even again. Now he could easily see the blue '43 Ford looming in his rearview mirror, running only a straightaway behind and clearly gaining. Jodell adjusted his line in the corners, trying to find some more speed, gritting his teeth as he thought of the beating the tires were taking trying to keep the heavy car from going the way it wanted to go. But he tried not to think about that. He breathed in the sounds and the smells of the race and tried to think of nothing else but keeping the car at speed and on the track.

D1593128

Follow all the action . . .
from the qualifying lap
to the checkered flag!

Rolling Thunder!

#1 White Lightning
#2 Road to Daytona
#3 Race to Glory
#4 On to Talladega

Forthcoming from Tor:

#5 Young Guns

Rolling Thunder

STOCK CAR RACING

ON TO TALLADEGA

Kent Wright
& Don Keith

TOR®

A TOM DOHERTY ASSOCIATES BOOK
NEW YORK

NOTE: If you purchased this book without a cover you should be aware that this book is stolen property. It was reported as "unsold and destroyed" to the publisher, and neither the author nor the publisher has received any payment for this "stripped book."

This is a work of fiction. All the characters and events portrayed in this book are either products of the author's imagination or are used fictitiously.

ROLLING THUNDER #4: ON TO TALLADEGA

Copyright © 1999 by Kent Wright & Don Keith

All rights reserved, including the right to reproduce this book, or portions thereof, in any form.

A Tor Book
Published by Tom Doherty Associates, LLC
175 Fifth Avenue
New York, NY 10010

www.tor.com

Tor® is a registered trademark of Tom Doherty Associates, LLC.

ISBN: 0-812-57509-1

First edition: January 2000

Printed in the United States of America

0 9 8 7 6 5 4 3 2 1

"Racing is life. Everything else is . . . waiting."
—Paul Newman, in the motion picture *Le Mans*

BY A NOSE OR BY A MILE...

A steady, distant rumble threatened the approach of a mighty storm, but strangely, the sky was a deep, clear blue. There was not a thunderhead in sight.

A stampede maybe? The drumming could have easily been the roar of the hooves of a hundred breakaway horses, maybe spooked by lightning or a sudden gust of hot wind. That could be the reason the ground trembled and that the birds had long since flown away.

But no, this was not horse country. Dairy cows, maybe, or beef cattle, but not horses.

Whatever the thundering noise was, thousands of people had apparently abandoned their cars to check it out. They had made their way inside an endless chain-link fence and to the other side of some towering mounds of dirt to investigate the din, to solve the mystery. And now those very same people contributed their own share to the commotion. Their screams and yells only added to the continual barrage of noise, like a hundred-thousand-voice choir all singing a different song.

There were bleachers that climbed up long red-clay banks several stories high, forming an almost oval corral. Few of the people actually sat on the benches, though, as they mostly stood to better witness the harnessed storm that raged down there before them. But the only lightning was the flash of brilliant sunshine off the windshields of better than three dozen galloping race cars, and the only horses down there on the track were captured beneath the hoods of those swiftly circling automobiles.

The cars ran in packs, each clump of them mostly side by side, clearly racing hard for position whether they were near the lead or back there among the also-rans. The spectators were a loud swirl of color all the way down the front stretch as the cars flew past them on their way to the track's first hard, sweeping left turn.

In the middle of the oval, the infield was a shifting sea of humanity, of partying fans of all types, some with long hair and some with short, some with shirts on and some not, but uniformly white-skinned beneath their sunburns. Many of them were only marginally paying any attention to the hard-fought battles being waged out there on the track that encircled them. To most of them, after several days of drinking, the hurtling race cars weren't the only things that seemed to blur and swim before their eyes. Dozens of Confederate flags blew lazily in the hot breeze, suspended from makeshift poles, CB radio antennas, or the tailgates of pickup trucks. The atmosphere was like that of a state fair, a noisy carnival, and the spectators in the infield seemed especially carefree, happy, mostly oblivious to the inherently dangerous struggle that was going on out there on the track.

That was certainly not the case, though, along the

sliver of asphalt in the infield that was known as "pit road." Those who stood tensely on top of or behind the low wall, among the toolboxes, equipment, and discarded tires, were not even close to being carefree. Everything was on the line now. There were only thirty laps left to go. Crunch time. There was prize money up for grabs for practically every position and the next few minutes would determine who would claim what portion of it.

But it wasn't just the money. These teams, the drivers, the crews, all had come here to get the victory. To prove who was the best at building and preparing a car, and then who among them was superior at driving one of those machines the fastest he possibly could for whatever the duration of the race might be. Money made it possible to afford to race and it was a convenient way of keeping score. And it made it worthwhile to come and run the race, even for all those who wouldn't hold the point when the checkered flag ultimately waved. But it was the will to win, to finish first, which actually drove them.

And that's what drew most of the assembled crowd, too. To see for themselves which of the competitors would be the first to finish and what he would do in the process to try to get there ahead of the others.

Right now, the race's leader was almost two seconds ahead of the three-car pack that fought amongst themselves for second place. That trio was in a furious battle, swapping positions back and forth with each lap, and the crowd was watching the give and take with great interest. As with most tracks, the majority of the spectators here were knowledgeable, as appreciative of the subtle nuances as they were of the broader, more obvious moves.

As the race played out, the crewmembers standing along the pit wall were, to a man, bathed in sweat, as much from the tension of the competition as from the all-consuming heat of the day. It was clear that the outcome of the race would be in doubt until the bitter end, that success or failure could ride on one small bobble, one minor move.

Joe Banker was sweating right along with the rest of them as he stood there on the narrow cement wall, spinning around like an ice skater doing a slow-motion pirouette, one eye on his driver, the other on the stopwatches in his hand. He was a tall, athletic man, with dark eyes and hair and an air of almost childlike mischief about him. But at that moment, he was all business, timing Jodell Bob Lee's car. Lee happened to be his first cousin as well as the race-car jockey who was driving the Ford that was currently fender to fender with Richard Petty and Buddy Baker in the tight skirmish for second place.

And there was renewed hope now for something even better than second spot for Lee's car.

The tires on the leader's race car were beginning to wear away, to make him finally vulnerable. But that advantage would be lost if the three of them who were trailing didn't quit racing each other as if it was the last lap already. The smart thing to do would be to catch up to the leader and his gimpy tires. Then, with him passed, they could settle this thing amongst themselves. But so far, there was no agreement among the three competitive drivers on this point, or on much of anything else at all.

As long as they stayed back there, though, kissing fenders and swapping side-panel paint, David Pearson was going to lead this race all the way to the checkerboard-floored Victory Lane. And Petty, Baker, and Lee would have to divide up what money was left over for second through fourth places while they watched Pearson take the trophy and the kiss from the beauty queen and the truly big payday.

Under his breath, Joe Banker kept urging his driver to break clear of the other two race cars and make a run for the lead. Petty and Baker had the same intentions, though, and the cars to back them up. Joe could only keep clicking the buttons on his stopwatches, comparing the times of his cousin's Ford and those of the other Ford, the one that Pearson drove and that was leading the race. The interval between them had been shrinking for a while, but lately it had been holding steady as the three racers behind Pearson chicken-fought among themselves.

And the laps continued to wind down steadily as they always seemed to do.

"Come on. Come on!" Joe half whispered, wishing his car onward as if it was somehow deliberately holding back.

The huge man standing on the wall next to Joe Banker read his lips and nodded. Bubba Baxter looked every bit as broad of beam as any one of the cars out there on the track, and nearly as powerful, but now he danced nimbly along the narrow wall as the three cars rumbled past, stepping like a surprisingly graceful but highly inflated ballerina. Like Joe, he spun around deftly as he studied with a practiced eye the line their car took as it roared around the track, whether it went high or low, the path it took through the corners, and how it held its position with the other cars.

Bubba Baxter had been going racing with Joe Banker and Jodell Lee since the very beginning. He'd been a key cog in the team since the hot, dusty Sunday afternoon they had first spun their wheels on a rough track scraped out of a converted cow pasture on the Meyers farm not far from Chandler Cove, Tennessee, the place they all still called home. Called home even though they spent far more time in motels, in garages and racing pits, or in the cab of the tow truck headed in the general direction of a racetrack somewhere.

"Take the high line, Jodell," the big man said out loud, throwing in some serious body English as he tried to drive the car around the track for Jodell. He was certain that the other two drivers were holding up their car, that they had enough left in the Ford to run down the leader if Jodell didn't heat the tires up too much while he scuffled with those other two cars.

Buddy Baker rode along in front of Jodell, sliding lower to the inside, hugging the bottom of the track. Richard Petty's Ford was running side by side with Baker, looking to get past him on the high side.

Inside his own car, Jodell Lee had a wide grin on his handsome face, his features a confirmation that he and Joe Banker were, indeed, blood kin. Right now, he was hot, dirty, sweating, aching all over, his mouth full of tire grit, his eyes stinging from the perspiration that seeped in around his racing goggles, and his head throbbing from the continual tension and noise.

But he was happy as a man could be.

Jodell Bob Lee dearly loved being in this position, challenging good drivers in strong cars, but with a strong car under him as well. He kept sticking his car's snout right up on the back bumper of Baker's racer, hoping to be able to give him enough of a push that they could clear Petty and finally make it a two-car fight. One on one, Jodell was certain he could get a good run on the Cotton Owens–owned Dodge, make it past him, and then go looking for David Pearson and his Ford with the worn-out tires.

Jodell got a glimpse of the signboard Bubba Baxter was holding up for him in the pits. "20," it said. Twenty laps to go. He would have to do it soon if he was going to try to move up. There would be no glory, no money, in passing anybody on the cool-down lap!

Baker drove deeply into turn three, nosing his car past Petty. It was clear the veteran driver had decided that he too needed to make his own move quickly. But by steering so aggressively into the corner, his car pushed upward ever so slightly, opening a sliver of racetrack near the bottom for Jodell to try to scoot into. There had been a time when Lee might not have recognized the opportunity that had just been presented to him. But a combination of experience and instinct made the hole look a hundred feet wide when it finally opened up.

He pounced like a leopard on a gazelle.

Even then, the fenders on the two cars rubbed briefly as they made contact before Jodell was able to safely get through and past the other two racers. Petty had seen the same bobble as Baker's Dodge pushed up the track in front of him. He tried to jump downward to the inside, to follow Jodell past. Coming out of the fourth turn, Baker and Petty still ran side by side but Jodell had moved away from them, already setting his sights on the lead car.

Joe Banker breathed a sigh of relief and studied his stopwatches intently. Jodell was picking up a tenth of a second per lap. Pearson's tires were fading fast. There was no doubt that Jodell was quickly catching the leader. Getting by him, he knew, would be a different story yet.

"How are the times?" Bubba yelled over the roar of the cars' engines as they passed the pits down the front stretch.

"A tenth or more a lap. We'll catch him for sure," Joe replied with certainty.

"Catching him and getting by him are two different things. Pearson's as smart as an old fox. He'll have saved enough of those tires to give us a run to the end," Bubba observed, but he never took his eyes off Jodell Lee and the blue Ford as he talked.

"Our boy's smart, too. He knows how to take care of the tires."

Bubba nodded his agreement, wiped the sweat from his face with an oily rag, and watched their driver dive into the first turn.

Jodell was flying like the wind. He had already managed to put a dozen car lengths between himself and Petty and Baker, that two-car duel now nothing more than a moderately interesting vision in his mirror. Jodell wouldn't try to watch any of that, though. The next battle was in front of his windshield, and it was coming up quickly. He would surely catch Pearson within the next ten laps or so. And that would leave him ten or less to somehow get past him and into the lead.

Out of the turn, he gave the gauges a quick glance, saw the needles were where they should be, then jammed his foot to the floor one more time as the car built speed down the long, straight backstretch. Then, in seconds, he was near the third turn. With another quick glance in the mirror, he was out of the gas at his mark, a scuff on the outside wall where someone had popped the spot in practice sometime in the last couple of days. He allowed the car to drift into the turn and then was back on the gas as he powered through the center of the corner.

It was all a matter of concentration and maintaining his rhythm, doing the exact same thing he had done hundreds of times already this race, scores of times in practice the last couple of days, once during qualifying. But now there was no one to get in his way, and the rear end of the lead car was coming closer and closer to him with each lap. When he had finally closed right up on Pearson's Holman-Moody Ford's rear bumper, when he could clearly see Pearson's eyes watching him in his own mirror, Jodell caught a glimpse of Bubba's sign indicating ten laps to go.

"Ten laps. Please be enough," he whispered, and it

sounded so much like a prayer that he almost added, "Amen."

He had caught Pearson. Now the truly tough part began.

Jodell followed directly in the tracks of the car in front of him as they circled, content to ride there for a lap or two as he tried to cool his tires. He knew there would likely be only one shot to make the pass and the car would have to stick to the track in the turn when he did.

Ahead of him, Pearson was hugging the inside line of the track, leaving no room to get by him the most direct way, the most obvious way, on the inside. As each lap ticked off though, Jodell kept taking a peek, trying to find an opening. But each time he even thought about trying to dive underneath, Pearson would seem to anticipate the move and slam the door shut before it was ever actually opened.

Jodell could only stay tied to his bumper, all the while looking through Pearson's windshield to see if there was any traffic ahead he might could use as a pick. But the track ahead was clear. Where the heck was everybody else? There might as well have been no one else in the race now but Lee and Pearson.

Okay, so there would be no help from slower cars. Jodell would have to find a way around the leader all by himself.

"All right, Mr. Pearson. I'll just have to out-drive you, I guess."

He started working on the car in front of him in the corners. Pearson would pinch the car down tight, taking the inside line away. Jodell would have to get out of the throttle or risk running right up his tailpipe. He tapped Pearson's rear bumper with the nose of the Ford several times, as gently as anybody could at a hundred and sixty miles per hour.

Back on the pit wall, Joe Banker was beginning to

wonder whether Jodell had enough power to get by Pearson. As they crossed the line with five laps to go in the race, the two cars were still running close enough that Jodell seemed to be hitching a tow from Pearson. Joe had let his stopwatch drop and hang from the shoestring around his neck, its gradation not nearly fine enough to figure the time difference between the two cars any longer.

"Take him high! Take him high!" Bubba screamed over the roar of the cars as he held up his board with the large "5" chalked on it. He waved the·sign board as far out toward the track as his giant arms would reach.

"Come on! Take him! Take him!" Joe pleaded, waving the clipboard where he'd been writing down the cars' times, as if that slight a wind would be enough to shove Jodell on past the leader.

"He ain't gonna let go of the bottom. Jodell needs to take him on the outside." Bubba said, punching Joe on the shoulder and pointing as the cars raced through the first turn.

"We're running out of laps. Whichever way he goes, he's got to do it right quick. That Pearson's tough as whit-leather when the race is on the line."

Bubba suddenly stopped dancing and stuck out his jaw.

"He'll take him." The big man narrowed his eyes and smiled. "Joe Dee's just cooling the tires down and settin' him up. That's what our boy is doing."

Bubba went to work with the chalk and scribbled a big four on the signboard. He wanted to count every lap down to the end just in case Jodell had missed the previous signboards. He did not want to risk him miscounting the laps and making his move too late.

Like Jodell, Bubba and Joe relished being in this position. Aw, being out front was better, but competition like this was what they actually raced for. There were few other things in life as invigorating as being in position to use skill and a fine-tuned machine to claim a win even as the laps were winding down to the instant of truth. Victory Lane was within sight. And they knew they had the car and the driver to get them there.

Winning. That's why they raced. Second place? Last place? What was the difference between the two? It was obvious in the way Jodell Lee drove a race car that there was no substitute for finishing first.

And Joe Banker shared his first cousin's lust for victory, if not his confidence. He tended to get more and more nervous as the races wore on. He built and tweaked the engines and he, of all people, was well aware of the myriad of parts that might suddenly shatter, break, or drop loose, taking a car from sure victory to a smoky "did-not-finish" in the blink of an eye.

Now, with less than five laps remaining, Joe was feeling the strain. Each time their car went past, he listened intently to the engine, trying to hear the slightest burp in its roar. With each trip by, he was certain he could make out something amiss in the growl of the motor, something that would certainly cause an oily, fiery explosion beneath the hood a few more feet on down the track.

"I think I hear a skip," Joe suddenly exclaimed as Jodell zoomed by. "You hear it, Bub? A miss in the engine?"

Bubba ignored him. He had suffered through the late-lap jitters with Joe Banker plenty of times over the past ten years. Sometimes he was right. Usually it was sheer paranoia.

"Did you hear me?" Joe asked as Bubba held up the sign, signaling four laps to go, all the while disregarding the almost certain catastrophe that was about to befall their race car. "I think there's a miss in the motor."

"I heard you," Bubba growled, finally acknowledging

him as he wrote a "3" on the sign in preparation for the next pass-by. "Have some faith in your motor, Joe. You worry too much."

"I ain't worrying. We need a win."

"Then have a little faith in your own cousin."

Then the big man turned his back to watch the finish.

He saw Jodell dive down to the inside of Pearson as they came off turn two. He was trying to get alongside him as they raced toward the end of the backstretch. Of course Pearson anticipated the move and cut down, effectively blocking the inside line as he tried to make his car as wide as possible.

Jodell held his position, though, and the cars almost touched. At the last instant before they slammed together, Jodell yanked the wheel of his Ford to the right, swinging the car back to the outside. He drove her deeply into the turn on the high side getting his left fender up almost even with Pearson's right-side door.

The lead car was forced to stay down as they hit the center of the corner. Jodell was able to keep the RPMs up in Joe's "missing" engine and with its awesome power at his disposal, he managed to pull up dead even as they exited turn four. The fake to the inside and the swing to the high side of the track had worked. Coming down to the start/finish line with three laps to go, the two race cars flashed across side by side, neither driver showing the other any quarter.

The huge crowd was standing, cheering them on, showing enthusiastic appreciation for such close, clean racing. Even the folks in the infield had abandoned their parties long enough to watch the epic struggle playing out around them. This was, after all, what most of them had paid several days' wages each to come watch. Side-by-side racing at a hundred and sixty miles an hour! And in cars that looked an awful lot like the ones they had driven to the track that very day. While most of them had their favorite drivers or car makes that they preferred to see win, a close race settled in the closing laps was still better than seeing their favored driver win by several laps in a boring runaway.

Just then, in the first turn, the two cars rubbed together as they hit the slight bump at the entrance to the corner, each one wiggling, threatening to take a sudden route to the wall. A quick puff of smoke rose from the spots where each tire touched the sheet metal of the other car, leaving big black donuts in the paint as evidence. The fans howled with delight as the drivers expertly kept the cars headed straight after the precarious touch in the turn.

Pearson gained a slight advantage through the center of the corner but Jodell was able to get a better run coming up off the turn. He pulled out in front by a nose. Down the backstretch they raced, Pearson stubbornly trying to push his way back out in front. He hugged the inside line, pulling ahead slightly once more as Jodell rode high through the turn.

But once more, Joe's motor answered Jodell's call. He was able to keep the engine revved all the way through the turn and once again eased inches ahead coming out of turn four.

Side by side they went down to the line again, the cars once more bumping together slightly as each driver fought to hold his position. As they raced across the line to begin the next to last lap, Jodell was out in front by no more than a bumper's width, but that was enough to give him official credit for leading that lap. Jodell was able to pull out by half a car length before they hit the turn. But one more time, Pearson found the power and tire traction to get back up alongside him.

The tires on both cars smoked slightly going through the turn. Each of them was in desperate need of a fresh set of rubber all the way around. The worn tires made it hard for either driver to hold his line in the turns and they bumped together yet again, but this time harder.

Jodell Lee kept an iron grip on the steering wheel as he struggled to push the car out in front while keeping it under some kind of control. He tried to ignore the cramp in his left arm, the ache in his right leg, the searing heat in the floorboard that was surely blistering his heels. Next to him, David Pearson was fighting just as hard in the cockpit of his own racer to maintain his inside position.

It would not have surprised either man then to hear the concussive explosion of a tire, or the telltale boom of an engine erupting in their faces. They both knew they were pushing their machines to the edge. It was asking a lot of them to hang together for another lap and a half of such brutal torture.

Yet Jodell Lee was still grinning, loving the close-quarters racing with someone of the caliber of David Pearson. He ignored the vibrations and the smells of his race car. He visualized finding the checkered flag, crossing beneath it first. He rammed his foot to the hot floor once more as he came off turn two and felt the obliging car surge out in front once again as they raced in tandem for the white flag.

Meanwhile, in the infield, a pretty blond woman stood nervous guard over a brood of small children who were playing in the dirt at her feet. She tried to watch the nerve-wracking duel on the track at the same time because one of the combatants was the man she loved, her husband. Catherine Holt Lee finally scooped up her two kids, a boy and a girl, and dumped them into the rear of the station wagon. Joyce Baxter, Bubba's wife, collected her own boy and girl and sent them tumbling in behind their playmates. The children had long since gotten used to racetrack noise and flashing race cars and bizarre behavior by normally sane grown-ups near the end of races.

But frankly, they preferred playing in the dirt or wrestling with each other, and as soon as they landed in the car a vigorous match broke out in the carpeted rear quarters of the station wagon. They were oblivious to the close finish about to take place out there on the track. But now, their mothers had shed their shoes and were already standing up on the dropped tailgate, watching every move.

"Lord, I hope they don't wreck up each other and both of 'em lose," Joyce moaned as she watched the two cars bump into each other as they skidded through a corner on their terribly worn tires.

"Me, too. Whoa! That was close!"

Catherine had already crossed her fingers then crossed her arms over her chest in her usual end-of-the-race good-luck stance. But she was having a hard time standing still on the tailgate. She was jumping up and down, willing her husband to safely make it around the track one more time.

The two cars stayed side by side through the third and fourth turns, swapping the lead several times, but with Jodell again pulling out by half a car length coming off the corner. Catherine was certain he was finally going to make a clean pass and pull away. She jumped even higher and squealed.

"Easy, girl," Joyce cautioned. "We haven't got this thing won yet. And if you keep jumping up and down like that, you're going to make the kids seasick."

The white flag waved as the two drivers set off on a final-lap scramble for the win. The crowd's excitement washed over the track, carried by the hot wind. All eyes were on the two cars as they plowed side by side into the first turn for the final time this day.

Jodell had seen the white flag waving in the flagman's

hand and he tried to nudge his car out in front as they had approached the start/finish line. He also saw the "1" on big Bubba's signboard. He had led the lap by a fender but that meant absolutely nothing as both drivers charged headlong down into the first turn. This would be the only lap that counted. The only one that paid money. The only one those screaming fans would remember when they went back to their homes and jobs on Monday and described the frantic finish for their friends who had not been fortunate enough to have been here to witness it firsthand.

Somehow, Jodell got three quarters of the car out in front of Pearson's Ford as he set his line down into the corner. He could hear the tires of both cars scream in protest as he and Pearson yanked their vehicles through the curve. He gripped the wheel even more tightly, trying to hold onto the bucking car. The bald tires barely gripped the surface of the track and it felt as if he was once again driving on an icy, dark road back in the Smoky Mountains, his car loaded down with white liquor.

"Last lap, baby. Last lap. Hang with me. Please hang with me."

Now Pearson was pushing harder still, trying to pull back even, and driving the car much deeper into the corner than he had been before. His tires, heated from the side by side jockeying over the last several laps, had no traction at all when he cut the wheel. The car pushed upward on the track, banging hard into the side of Jodell's Ford. A quick puff of blue smoke marked the spot where the right front tire of Pearson's Ford had rubbed off a slice of the painted-on number from the side of Jodell Lee's door.

Jodell felt the bump, heard the screech of the contact. The car was already dancing around, on the raw edge of breaking loose, and now it began to get away from him for sure. He twisted back and forth on the steering wheel, trying to keep the car under control without losing his momentum. He had flashes of other races, times he had been certain he had won, only to have a move by another driver take him out, or a tire blow, or something in the engine go sour and leave him with nothing but broken equipment and dashed dreams.

But this time, just as he was certain that the car was about to get out from under him, he managed to gather it back up without ever easing up on the throttle. Somehow, he was able to keep her headed straight down the track.

Straight for the finish line.

Pearson never got out of the gas either, using the side of Jodell's car as a bumper to keep his own car under control. By the time Jodell had slid high up the outside groove toward the wall with the impact, Pearson had edged back out in front.

Jodell gritted his teeth, hammered the gas, and got a tremendous run off the corner. Pearson did his best to pinch him against the outside wall but Jodell held his position. The cars touched once again as Jodell nosed up alongside him. Jodell stubbornly pulled even again in the long run down the back straightaway as they raced off into the third turn.

Joe, Bubba, and the rest of the crew stood watching the cars race through the final turns. To a man, they were holding their breath, none of them saying a word, their contributions to the race already long since made. All they could do now was watch and hope.

Catherine and Joyce were still on the tailgate of the station wagon full of kids, still screaming, yelling, waving, and trying to will Jodell past Pearson for the win. Across the infield, thousands of other fans were doing pretty much the same thing, for one driver or the other. Everybody would get his money's worth today.

Jodell had run as hard as he dared into the third turn. Pearson had given him plenty of room as he got his own car as close to the white line on the inside as he dared. He had the inside wheels down so low they were almost on the flat part of the apron that ran around the inside of the corner.

Both cars sailed through the center of the turn still perfectly even. Nearly five hundred miles of driving and not a blamed thing had been settled!

"Come on, Miss Becky. Give me just a little bit more," Jodell pleaded with the car as he kept his foot hard on the gas pedal. He always called the cars by a different woman's name each race, never wanting to tempt fate by giving her a name he might have used before.

He could tell his car had again pulled out in front slightly as they exited the final corner. The high line was allowing him to use the torque of the motor to his advantage, but Pearson was not giving up. Since he was on the inside of the track, he had a slightly shorter run to the flag, and, as they raced along in front of the final stretch of grandstands filled with cheering spectators, he clearly intended to get there first.

Jodell could already see the checkered flag in the hand of the flagman, waving high over the start/finish line in a beautiful figure eight. Everything else was pushed out of his mind and he was hardly aware that the cars were practically in a dead heat as they flashed to the line.

Jodell tried to push his foot through the floorboard in an attempt to get that extra fraction of power out of Joe's motor. Then, he was dimly aware that his Ford seemed to have nosed out in front as they crossed the line painted across the pavement.

But it was close. Lord, it was close! He only hoped the officials saw it the way he did from the best vantage point of all.

"Wheeeeeyeeeew!" Jodell yodeled, releasing at once in one long scream all the tension of the last twenty-five laps, of the last ten years of racing. "Beautiful job, Miss Becky!"

Finally he let off on the gas and sucked in a deep breath of the superheated air inside the car. Only now did he become fully aware of how torrid it was inside the cockpit of the race car, of how badly his arms and legs and butt ached, of how completely exhausted he was. But as he kicked the shifter out of gear and allowed the Ford to roll along under its own built-up momentum down the backstretch, he realized that he didn't mind the discomfort at all. He reached over and unbuckled the window net, then pumped his fist in the air outside the window, acknowledging the supportive acclaim from the still-standing crowd.

They had won. Thank the Lord, they had won!

David Pearson pulled up alongside and gave Jodell a thumbs-up. He'd been in enough close races to know he'd been licked at the line in a contest that could have gone either way. Jodell gave him a wave back, confirming his appreciation for the good, clean race to the finish David had given him. Either of them could have wrecked the other practically anytime during the last dozen laps. And the remaining car would have had a better than even chance of continuing on to win the race. And the men knew that not a single driver out there would have blamed either of them if he had clobbered the other one. They each knew the little bumps and rubs he had given the other driver were nothing more than good hard racing. And that come next week and another race, they'd go just as hard again, then pat each other on the back when it was all over.

For a while, only the fans that had been directly even with the start/finish line knew for certain who had actually won the race. For the rest who had been watching from up and down the straightaways or in the infield, it was an exciting finish that could have gone either way. They could only tell that both cars zoomed across the line in a finish too close to call.

But Jodell Lee would pull his Ford into Victory Lane while David Pearson simply steered his own race car toward the garage, ready to load her up and head for the next race. Bubba, Joe, and the rest of the crew were still doing a victory square dance all the way down the pit road, much to the amusement of the other crews. They understood the jubilation. It was the team's first superspeedway win in almost three years and the crew was ready to celebrate the long-awaited victory.

Catherine and Joyce were still hugging each other, doing their own victory waltz in the dust of the infield. While the kids had wrestled in the car, the women had watched breathlessly as both cars crossed the start/finish line side by side. But there was no way for either of them to tell which had crossed that line first. To them it had looked like a dead heat.

"Did he win? Can there be a tie?" Catherine had asked frantically.

"I don't know. They were so close I just couldn't tell." Joyce had jumped off the tailgate to try to hear the station wagon's blaring radio. "They're saying something about a photo finish. That it was too close to call."

"We better get over there to the pit just in case he did win."

"You go on, Cath. I'll round up the kids and get things squared away here."

And then Joyce heard the announcer on the radio say that Jodell Lee was the apparent winner pending a recheck of the photos of the finish. That's when the impromptu dance had broken out.

Joyce and Bubba's oldest child, a girl named Rose, was the first to climb out and join in the jig. Then out came Catherine and Jodell's son, Bob Jr. He was a few months older than Rose and was quick to join the celebration when he heard his daddy had won the race. His baby sister and Bubba's younger boy simply stared out at them from inside the car, wide-eyed, watching the silliness going on with their mothers and siblings. They were not yet old enough to be accustomed to how crazy their mothers acted sometimes when they came to these big, loud places.

Jodell slowed the car as he passed the crew and they all piled on for the short ride into the winner's circle. He could hardly see around Bubba's bulk and the car listed dangerously toward the side where the big man rested. Joe Banker sat on the roof, blowing kisses to all the girls he could spot in the crowd. Johnny Holt, Catherine's brother and the crew's lead tire changer, sat half in the passenger-side window, whooping and yelling at the top of his lungs.

Jodell shut the engine off, rolled to a stop, and took a towel someone kindly offered him to wipe the sweat off his dirt-streaked face. He paused for a minute to catch his breath before he began to unbuckle his safety belts. Then, he felt strong arms reach in the open window and help to pull him outside.

It was Bubba, of course, and he yanked Jodell outside the car as if the driver was one of their kids, not a tall, muscular man. Jodell tried to wave to the cheering crowd but Bubba had him wrapped too tightly in a bear hug and Joe and Johnny were trying to join in the smothering embrace, too.

"Yeah, it was a tough one," Jodell said into a microphone someone had thrust in front of his face. "I didn't know if I was going to be able to get by David or not. Man, he was tough!" He listened to his voice echoing across the speedway as he took a swig of a soft drink that someone had handed him. "But whether we win by a nose or by a mile, it's still a win. And a mighty sweet one, too."

Suddenly, Catherine came rushing out of the crowd, ran up to him and gave him a gigantic hug. The gathered crowd cheered lustily as she followed up with a long victory kiss. Meanwhile, Joe laid a smooch of his own on the beauty queen that was supposed to be delivering the winner's kiss to the driver, along with the trophy. But she didn't seem to mind. And Joe Banker certainly didn't.

By the time the crowd and the media had wandered away and the crew had finally carried their celebration back toward the pits, one person was missing from the party. Bubba Baxter had long since wandered away, anxious to get started on the job of packing up and getting everything loaded back onto the truck.

"Hey, big man!" someone shouted at him as he worked away. It was a familiar voice: Richard Petty. "Why aren't you over there celebrating with all those other cats you hang out with?"

"Oh, hey, Richard. Good finish today." Petty had ended up outdueling Buddy Baker for third. "I got lots to do. We got another race in a couple of days, in case everybody has forgot. There ain't no time for us to be playing around. The boys can have their fun. Me, there's just too much work to get done."

"You're right, but you ought to savor the wins, though. 'Specially big ones like today's. But I reckon if it was me, I'd be passing up the party, too."

Petty slapped him on the back, congratulated him again, and moved on down the pit road in the direction of his own truck where the crew was finishing up loading the car and equipment. And where countless fans would be waiting for their autographs and a second or two of time with him.

Bubba watched him go, then went back to work. It'd

be dark soon and he wanted to be on the road before it got too much later.

Winning was wonderful. Make no mistake about that. That's why they ran the races, after all. There was plenty of glamour about the sport, too, what with the fans, the flashbulbs, the color, and Bubba enjoyed it all. But there was plenty of hard work to get done before they went back out and tried to do it again. And a lot of that preparation fell on the broad shoulders of Bubba Baxter.

The big man wouldn't have had it any other way. And now, while the rest of them soaked up the glory, relished the win, relived the final laps for the media and the fans and anybody else who would listen, he would do what he usually did after a race, win or lose.

Go right back to work and do what had to be done.

Catherine and Joyce had their own packing up to do. Moving themselves and four kids to and from races was like loading and reloading a circus train. They finally got everything and everybody stowed in the big station wagon and then started the six-hour drive back toward home. But they didn't complain. They usually only got to attend the races that were within driving distance from East Tennessee and they refused to miss any of those if they could help it.

Over in Victory Lane, Jodell and the car were standing still for the photographers, even as the inspectors raised the hood and began to tear down the motor to make sure everything was legal. Joe kept a close eye on the inspectors in between photos and getting all the vital statistics he could from the beauty queen. He knew the victory wasn't actually theirs until the car had cleared inspection. Not officially anyway.

Finally, he received the thumbs-up and a nod from the inspector then got the car and the engine in pieces back from the officials. Bubba was waiting there impatiently then to claim it all, to begin to get the car onto the trailer, and get ready to be on his way.

He surprised Joe when he told him he was hitting the road and that he would see them the next day.

"You not going to the party, Bubba?" Joe asked him.

One of the companies that had sponsored the race was pitching a post-race celebration and the winning driver and crew were expected to make an appearance for more glad-handing and back-slapping. Joe Banker usually managed to make such events regardless of where they finished in the race. A party was a party, for goodness sakes! And he certainly wasn't going to miss one where he would be one of the guests of honor. And besides, his new friend for life, the beauty queen, had never been to one of the post-race parties before and he was looking forward to escorting her there and introducing her to everyone.

"Naw, y'all go on," Bubba told him and Jodell. "I wanna get this horse in the barn tonight so I can get back to work on her first thing tomorrow. That is, if y'all want to run her next weekend with a motor in her."

Bubba nodded back toward the trailer where the car quietly rested, her engine in pieces from the inspection, the sheet metal of her body ugly, dented and scraped up from all the slamming and banging she had taken all afternoon. She really was a sorry sight by now, not resembling a race champion at all, and that bothered Bubba Baxter. He liked for their cars to be ready to go at any time should a sudden stock car race break out.

"This win's been a long time coming," Jodell joined in. "You need to stay and celebrate. We'll be home by early afternoon tomorrow. You get home at three or four in the morning and you won't be any account for anything tomorrow anyway."

"Don't worry 'bout me, Joe Dee. Y'all go on and have a good time and pop a top for me."

"You sure? You want Johnny to ride with you and keep you awake?"

"Uh-uh. He'd rather go with y'all and have a good time. You know me. I like to race and win but I don't cotton too much to all that partying no more. I guess I'm just gettin' too old."

"Thirty ain't old!" Jodell was thirty himself. So was Joe. Neither thought it was anything approaching ancient. "But suit yourself. I'll try to get these lug nuts up and moving early so we can get back in time to still get in a decent day in the shop."

With that, Bubba said his good-byes, climbed up onto the running board, and swung himself into the truck cab. He fired up the engine, gave a wave out the open window at what was left of the crew, and slowly steered the truck and its tow toward the crossover gate that led out of the speedway. The traffic had thinned considerably by then and he was able to pull straight out onto the highway. Before long, he was cruising along at a good clip, singing quietly to the sounds of a country song that came crackling in over the AM radio.

He loved Jodell and Joe and Johnny as surely as if they had been his own brothers. But sometimes it was good to be by himself for a little while. During race season they were together constantly, usually sharing motel rooms, the cab of the tow truck or the follow-car, or the space beneath a jacked-up race car. And in the few months in which they didn't race two or three times a week, they were usually at the shop in Jodell and Joe's grandpa's old barn back in Chandler Cove, working elbow-to-elbow on the cars. Heck, he spent far more time with the boys than he did with his own wife and kids. And there was never time to simply be by himself.

He missed the rest of the crew when they weren't together. But sometimes it felt good to be alone, facing a dark stretch of highway and several hours of precious solitude. It gave him time to think. To plan what he wanted to do with the cars. To sing along off-key with the radio if he wanted to without Joe cuffing him in the back of the head and telling him to quit making "dying coyote sounds."

He checked the clock on the dashboard. It was even later than he thought. That was about the only drawback to winning a race. It took so long to get away from the media, the fans, the inspectors, and then to get things loaded up to clear out. It would be three, at least, before he got to the shop. Three-thirty or four before he got to his own bed and Joyce. But that was still better than three tomorrow afternoon if he had stayed for the party and then the inevitable tussle of getting Joe and Johnny awake and headed for home. If he could even find them after the party, that is.

Another hour passed and Bubba caught himself fixating on the white dotted line that led down the center of the highway. He knew better. With only an occasional car coming to meet him from the other direction and with the steady drone of the truck's motor, he would hypnotize himself and be asleep and off the road in no time if he wasn't careful.

Maybe it would have been a good idea after all to have Johnny Holt ride back with him. But he would have had to hear him complain and moan all the way back to Tennessee about missing the party and all the women who would have been there specifically to meet him. Joe Banker had taken Catherine's brother under his wing and had shown him much of what he knew about cars and engines. But he had also introduced him to the joys of the parties that often broke out along the stock car racing circuit. A natural mechanic anyway, and with an equally natural outgoing personality, Johnny had taken easily to Joe's tutelage in all areas.

Bubba shook his head, yawned, then reached into the glove box and retrieved a can of soda he had hidden there. He had planned to stop at an all-night café he knew about just over the border into North Carolina. The soda would have to hold him until he could get food and coffee there, and he was already deciding what he would order, picturing what all he would ask for on his burger.

He cranked the radio a little louder and took a long swig of the fizzy, lukewarm pop. He hadn't realized how dry he was from the long day's work. The drink reminded him of the years when a soda bottler had sponsored their race team and, in addition to money, they had gotten for free all the product they wanted to drink. Then, when the bottler had finally been sold to one of the major companies, they had lost not only the sponsor but also the bottomless well of soft drinks. Replacing the bottling company as a sponsor had not been that difficult, but Bubba still missed the free soda pop.

He noticed than that a light rain had begun to spatter the truck's windshield, leaving big smeared holes in the dust from the racetrack that was still left there.

"Great. That's really going to help," Bubba said out loud.

Not only did he face at least five more hours of night driving on bad roads, but it apparently was going to be in the rain as well. He took another swallow of the soda, shifted in the seat to get more comfortable and leaned forward so he could better see the road through the sweep of the busy windshield wipers.

Then ten more miles down the road, as he topped a rise in the highway, there was a crossroads dead ahead in his lights. And there beside the roadway, leaning into the rain and wind with his arm outstretched and his thumb in the air, was a single, sorrowful hitchhiker.

Bubba wasn't as generous offering rides anymore as he once had been. There had been a time when he would never have passed someone trying to catch a ride, and especially in bad weather. But times had changed. There were some rough characters out there these days, many of them drug-addled. And he was towing a trailer that held a mighty expensive race car and thousands of dollars worth of tools and equipment to keep it running. There were plenty of folks who would put a knife in a man's ribs and make off with a load that valuable if they got half a chance.

But it was raining, and the fog on the windshield indicated it had gotten colder out there and the blustery wind almost certainly had a bite to it. He didn't hesitate at all. The brakes squeaked softly as he pulled to a halt next to the man. Bubba reached over, flipped the latch on the passenger side door of the truck, and shoved it open for the hitchhiker.

"Hey, stranger, need a ride?"

"I'd feel mighty appreciative if you could spare one."

"Hop on in, then, and stow your stuff behind the seat there."

"Much obliged, my friend. Looks like it may start raining after while."

Water dripped off the man's felt hat and he looked fairly soaked already. Bubba flipped the heater on.

"How far you going tonight?"

"All the way across the country eventually. But nowhere in particular. I'm just doing a little sightseeing."

"Well, you certainly picked a fine night for it."

"I'd planned to make it to the Appalachian Trail by nightfall and spend the night in one of their lean-tos, but my rides played out and left me stranded when it got dark."

"I'm going as far as south of Bristol or thereabouts.

You're welcome to ride as far as you like."

"Thanks a lot. I'll ride as far as you'll let me." The man took off his hat and freed a mop of long, red hair from beneath it. Hippie or not, he still seemed safe enough, with a friendly face and soft, direct eyes. But Bubba renewed his intention to keep an eye on the stranger. "I probably can't find the Trail in the dark and rain and I expect the accommodations would be full by now anyway in this weather. I'm usually pretty particular about who I bunk down with."

The man smiled then and it, too, seemed peaceful.

"Well, you may just as well settle in. We got us a lot of road ahead," Bubba said, shifting the truck up into high gear as he got back up to speed.

They rode for a while in silence, with only the radio holding up its end of the conversation. The stranger eased out of his poncho and carefully shook the water onto the floorboard, then he settled back again. He was clearly glad to be in out of the rain. And Bubba was appreciative of the company, even if it was some long-haired stranger.

But before long, he was feeling drowsy again. The cost of the ride for the stranger was going to have to be some conversation to keep Bubba from dozing. He was about to ask the man his name, where he was from, but the stranger spoke first.

"Hey, pal, I didn't catch your name."

The man must have seen him nodding, his eyelids falling.

"Baxter. Bubba Baxter. But my friends just call me 'Bubba.' "

"Pleased to meet you, Bubba. Call me Billy."

"Well, Billy, it's good to meet you."

He took one hand off the wheel and reached over to politely shake the stranger's outstretched hand. The man looked into Bubba's tired eyes.

"If you don't mind my saying so, you look pretty tired, my new friend."

"Been a long day. We were up about sunrise gettin' ready to head for the track and I don't remember stopping to rest all dang day."

"Track? Then that's a race car on that trailer back there?"

"Yessir."

"And you drove in a race today?"

It always surprised Bubba that everybody in the world didn't know there was a race being run on a particular day. And especially the one this day, one of the big ones on the circuit.

"Sure did. At least Jodell Bob Lee did. He's the driver on our team. That's the Ford I'm towing back there."

Bubba pointed with his thumb back toward the trailer. Billy seemed impressed, as if he might actually have heard of Jodell Bob Lee.

"So how'd y'all do in the race?"

"We won!" Bubba said, brightening appreciably. "Beat David Pearson to the line in a squeaker of a finish. It was one fine race!"

"Sounds exciting. I've never been to a big-time race."

"You ought to go to one, Billy. There ain't nothing better in the whole wide world than seeing them big old cars running so close and so fast and the ground pounding with all the horsepower and the smells and tastes and all. Shoot, ain't nothing like it that I've ever seen."

"You don't say."

Billy was clearly amused at how animated Bubba had suddenly become. He had seemed to be just another stoic mountain man when he had first climbed into the truck. The almost silent ride so far had only seemed to confirm that. But the big man had immediately seemed to come alive when he began talking about racing.

"You ought to watch my buddy Jodell drive. Ain't

nobody that drives any prettier than he does. He can do things with a race car that nobody else on this planet can do," Bubba stated with obvious pride. "And that goes for Richard Petty and Cale Yarbrough and all the rest of them, too. Jodell is the best there is."

"I always thought it was the cars and not the driver that really won the races. If you got a fast car and if you stayed out of a wreck, then just about anybody could drive to a win."

"Hah!" Bubba erupted into a deep belly laugh. "Not hardly! It's a team. You got to have a good car, that's true. You can't run a nag and hope to win a horse race. But you got to have a good crew, too, and a good driver. We got all three. Joe Banker's a whiz at building engines. That's Jodell's first cousin. And Johnny Holt is gettin' to be about as good as he is. Johnny's Jodell's brother-in-law. I know a thing or two about setting up a car to run, getting the suspension and the tires right and all. But I ain't no kin to Jodell a'tall. Just growed up with him and played some high school ball with him is all. And like I say, Jodell's the best. He was running moonshine for his grandpa before he was even old enough to get a driver's license. He's gotten away from more revenuers than Carter's got pills."

"Y'all used to run moonshine?"

"Jodell did. He was the fastest driver anywhere around. They still talk about some of the things he did in them old cars loaded up with moonshine, the folks up there in those mountains do. He never got caught, you know. No sir! Not even close. He ran 'shine right up to when we got going good in racing. Heck, our first race was in Jodell's granddaddy's 'shine car. We busted it up good in a wreck in that race and nearly got our butts busted by Grandpa Lee."

Bubba smiled at the memory then broke into laughter when he remembered how scared Jodell and Joe had

been after that race. Jodell had scatted away from revenuers for years on dangerous mountain roads without
ever losing his nerve. But Grandpa Lee had put the fear
of God into the boy.

"So what made you start serious racing?"

"It was hard to make a living farming on those old
rocky hillsides back home. That's why a lot of them
made and sold whiskey. But the moonshining business
was about gone and then Grandpa Lee died and that was
it. Jodell decided to try to make a go at racing and see
if we couldn't make a living and he brought me and Joe
in and before we knew it, there we were, running against
the Pettys and Joe Weatherley and Junior Johnson and
all of them."

"So how'd y'all ever make it to the big time? I would
suppose that would take some serious money."

"An old bootlegger loaned us some of the money we
needed to buy a race car and we pooled all the rest of
the money we had between us and went out and bought
one. We hauled it down to Darlington and ran it in the
Labor Day race. Luckily, we won enough prize money
to get us back home and there we were, in the racing
business."

"Looks like you've done well," Billy said, nodding
back toward the trailer that followed the truck.

"You start winning races and things can change in a
hurry. Or if you don't finish in the serious money, things
can go to pot on you in no time, too. There's a bunch
of them gave it a try and went back to the dirt tracks
and bull rings when their stake ran out." A sad look
crossed the big man's features, a look that was clearly
visible to Billy, even in the dark truck cab. "And some
of them, like Little Joe Weatherley and Fireball Roberts,
didn't make it out alive, even though they were on top
at the time." The big man was quiet for a moment,
clearly remembering something, somebody. He was

much less animated when he spoke again. "But we've done okay so far. Better than okay." Bubba stopped once more and rubbed his stomach. It had been making odd noises the last few miles that were audible even over the road noise. "Say, you wouldn't be hungry would you? There's an all-night café just up the road here a ways. I could use a bite to eat and a stretch of the old legs."

"Now that you mention it, Bubba, I could use a bite."

"I had a few hot dogs before I left the track, but they're long gone," Bubba remembered wistfully. Six hot dogs. And a double order of french fries.

Bubba Baxter's eating habits were legendary among the other racers. He constantly reminded them that he was a big man, that he had to eat to keep his strength up. And his strength was almost as legendary as his appetite. Although he was kidded constantly for his love for food, everyone knew there was no better friend to have in a scrape or altercation than big old Bubba Baxter was.

Just then, Bubba spotted the dim glow of the café's neon lights up ahead, shining like a watery beacon in the dreary night. The rain had grown to a downpour by then and the café's parking lot was virtually empty as he swung the truck and its tow off the highway. The two men hopped out and sprinted across the gravel lot toward the front door, sidestepping mud puddles.

"Counter or a booth?" Billy asked when they stepped inside.

"I think I need a booth. I need to rest these tired bones on something a little more substantial than a barstool."

"I think I'll second that," Billy answered as he led the way to a booth along the back wall.

The place was empty except for a pair of lovers huddled together in a corner booth, and the pretty young waitress behind the counter. She flashed a friendly smile their way as they stomped in and went to fetch them

some menus. The cook must have been in the back.
There were dish-washing noises coming from back
where the kitchen probably was.

"Place looks pretty dead," Billy said, looking around
the room. "I hope that doesn't speak to how good the
food is here."

"Naw, it's just late. I'm glad it ain't crowded. Means
we can eat and get back on the road. We still got better
than four hours ahead of us and I don't want to drive all
night."

"What can I get you to drink?" the waitress asked with
another smile as she placed the plastic-covered menus
in front of them. She seemed happy to see them, to see
anyone on such a nasty night.

"How about the biggest, coldest, wettest iced tea you
got?" Bubba asked her as he surveyed the offerings.

"Same for me," Billy said.

She stepped back behind the counter to get their
drinks, took their orders, and then headed off to the
kitchen. Just then, a series of headlights flashed against
the back wall of the restaurant as at least three cars
pulled up outside. Billy and Bubba watched as they
screeched to a stop and disgorged a mob of tough looking young men, all in dirty jeans and with long, unkempt
hair. They were pushing and shoving at each other and
making so much noise they could be heard inside the
café, even over the kitchen noises and the love song the
couple had playing on the jukebox in the corner.

"This might get interesting," Billy said, nodding toward the door.

"Lord, I hope not. I just want my iced tea, my cheeseburgers, and my piece of pie, and to get back on the way
home."

Bubba watched out of the corner of his eye as the
long-haired, ill-clad bunch shuffled in, eyeing the place
and obviously looking for trouble. They kept up their

loud sparring and several of them were clearly either drunk or high or most likely both. They immediately began rearranging the booths, dragging the tables and then the heavy booth seats together so they could sit in a bunch against the far wall of the place and keep an eye on everything else going on.

Bubba deliberately paid them little attention, refusing to allow the jerks to ruin his meal. Besides, not many folks who were sober and in their right mind dared to mess with someone of his size and obvious strength. He could only assume this pack would have sense enough not to either, so long as he stayed out of their way. Still, he had to wonder about the look on Billy's face. It wasn't exactly fear. It was more like determined dread, as if he smelled something bad and knew he would be the one who would eventually have to clean it up.

"They're just a bunch of skied-up thugs," Billy finally said. "I don't understand their type but I've certainly seen my share of them since I got back. Let's hope they mind their own business."

But Bubba had lost interest already in the swarm of loudmouths, and he was so distracted by the smells and sounds from the kitchen that he didn't even think to ask Billy where it was that he had gotten back from. The arrival of his dinner was imminent and that was what was really important.

When the young waitress finally set the plates of food down in front of them he was ravenous, and he attacked the burgers and fries with such ferocity that Billy sat back in his chair and watched wide-eyed. The arrival of the entire Vietcong army would not have distracted the big man from the meal.

The waitress grinned.

"Can I get you gentlemen anything . . ."

"Hey!" one of the new arrivals yelled rudely across

the restaurant. "Can we get some service over here for a change?"

She made a face, rolled her eyes, then said, "Excuse me, fellows. This bunch comes in here sometimes but it looks like they're even a little bit more obnoxious than normal tonight."

Then she started toward where the motley crew had now claimed one entire side of the café as their own territory.

"Any day now would be fine, if you don't mind," another one of them yelled at her before she could even get across the room. His words were slurred.

The couple in the corner booth had come up for air, had taken stock of the situation, and had quickly scooted out the door. Bubba and Billy tried to ignore the uncivil bunch as they rained crude remarks on the couple. The sooner they could finish their meals and be on their way, the better.

The commotion did subside for a bit after the waitress had managed to get all their orders down and taken them to the kitchen. She came back out to refill Bubba and Billy's iced tea glasses, all the while ignoring the newly increasing volume and foul language that flew from where the new customers swarmed.

"Hey! Sweet thing!" one of them yelled at the waitress. "You gonna stand over there and flirt with Fatboy and Red or are you gonna get our food out here?"

"It'll be coming right out," she answered calmly with a dismissing glance their way.

"Well, how about some more water over here? Can't you see these glasses are empty?"

"Just hold your horses. I'll get you some more water."

She fetched the water pitcher from behind the counter and headed their way.

"You gettin' smart with us?" the loudest one hollered across the room, then said something ugly not quite under his breath that set off a giggle among his friends.

"What did you say?" the waitress asked, stopping, the water pitcher still in her left hand but her right hand in place on her hip to show she wasn't going to take any guff from him.

"You heard me," he said, and used the curse again.

Bubba calmly placed his paper napkin next to his half-finished burger and started to get up. Billy put a hand on his arm and nodded for him to stay seated.

"Let's see if she can handle it, Bubba Baxter."

The girl did seem to be holding her own. She glared hard at the scraggly bunch as she spoke.

"I don't have to listen to any of your nonsense, and neither do any of my other customers. Hold it down and behave or I'll have to ask you to leave."

Suddenly, a couple of the young men stood and let fly a few choice words, clearly daring the waitress to do anything about it. Now, she had a worried look on her face as she backed up toward the kitchen, apparently looking for some help from the cook. But then, several more of the thugs were up, moving toward her, mumbling something about getting her out of the way and getting their own food.

Bubba could take no more. He climbed out of the booth, turned and stretched his huge frame out to its full height, then strode to a position between the waitress and the three disheveled toughs who were headed her way. He spoke slowly, deliberately.

"The lady is only trying to do her job and does not have to put up with you and your language. Now, I would suggest that you all just get on up and ride right on out of here before you get yourselves into some serious trouble."

"Hey, hillbilly," the one who seemed to be the leader spat. "Why don't you get up on your tractor and head on back to the farm before you bite off more than you can chew? This ain't none of your business, Fatboy."

Bubba Baxter's expression never changed.

"You just made it my business when the bunch of you ganged up on this young lady. And where I come from, we don't use language like that in front of ladies. I suggest you apologize and be on your way now."

One by one, the rest of the group had stood up behind the three who had been threatening the waitress. Bubba quickly took a count and came up with a dozen of them in all. They were plenty brave since they certainly had the numbers. The leader kept talking as Bubba edged a bit closer. He was now only a few feet away and had situated himself between them and the door outside.

He had no desire to get into a melee with a whole mob of jerks, most of them brave on drugs and drink. Besides, they were in the middle of nowhere, the law likely a good long drive away. Since this was their territory, the law might take their side anyway. It happened sometimes. And who knew what weapons the so-and-sos might be toting and be crazy enough to actually use.

But dadgummit, they were wrong. And they shouldn't be allowed to get away with treating the girl the way they had. He had to convince them to leave, and to leave without a fight. And he had to be willing to accept the consequences if they didn't.

But he saw then that a couple of them had moved to either side of him now and several of the others had stepped up to back up the leader, who was still spouting off. His words blurred, his monologue had become mostly a long list of curses and filthy language.

Bubba held up one big hand to tell him to stop.

"I think we've heard enough from you already, buddy. Now why don't y'all just get on out of here now before there's trouble?"

"You gonna make us, Farmer John? If you ain't too fat to fight, that is."

"To tell you the truth, I don't think that is something you want to find out," Bubba said, squaring up his stance.

That's when one of the jerks who had moved closest made a dumb mistake. He suddenly took a wild sucker punch swing from the side, aiming at Bubba's head, obviously trying to land the first blow. But he missed the big man by at least a foot when Bubba took one step backward and easily ducked the fist. And before the guy could even regain his balance to throw another round-house, Bubba sent him flying backward with a massive right hand to the jaw. He was likely out cold when he hit the restaurant floor like a sack of wet mush.

Then Bubba tensed, waiting to see if any of the rest of them wanted to give him a try.

A couple of them apparently did. They rushed Bubba together, attempting to double-team him. The big man didn't flinch. A quick uppercut and a hard right cross sent both of the men staggering backward. Then here came two more, another couple more behind them, and still more after them, approaching in waves. Bubba realized at once that he had his hands full.

As soon as he had taken care of a couple of the guys, some more had recovered and took their place. It seemed like an endless line of them, all going for his face, his legs, and his back, like a swarm of angry bees. They were merely a nuisance one at a time but downright dangerous in a bunch.

It seemed that no matter how hard he hit them, they would bounce back up and come at him again. The drugs and alcohol had made them tough, foolhardy.

It finally took four of them together to do it, but they managed to pin Bubba's massive arms behind him, and then two more wrapped themselves around his tree-trunk legs and tried to tackle him. Bubba gave a mighty heave, trying to loosen them, but just then, the man who had

seemed to be the leader came running from all the way
across the café and launched and landed a vicious punch
to his jaw.

The room seemed to suddenly get darker. Bubba felt
dizzy, his knees beginning to buckle. For the first time
ever in a fight, he felt a twinge of fear, that he might
actually be in serious trouble with these so-and-sos.

He shook his head to clear the grayness that was
creeping in from the corners of his vision, then gave
another mighty heave, trying to loosen the grip the pair
of thugs had on his arms. But then, emboldened by his
first connected blow, the leader apparently decided that
Bubba needed another slug. He reared back, ready to
launch a boilermaker from somewhere way behind him.
There was nothing Bubba could do, not even duck. He
braced for the impact.

But in mid-swing, the goon's fist stopped cold, a half
foot from Bubba Baxter's chin. Somehow, Billy had
slipped into the melee while everyone had forgotten
about his even being there. He had caught the man's
arm mid-swing, then he deftly twisted it up and behind
him before the man had even realized what had happened. Then, there was an ugly cracking sound as Billy
jammed the arm upward hard, pulling the man completely off the floor. Before he even landed again, Billy
gave him a good hard kick in the groin with his knee,
then tossed him aside like so much garbage.

Next, Billy spun and grabbed one of the ones who
held Bubba's arms, chopping quickly to the kidney and
then to the throat with the heel of his right hand. The
punk let go of his hold immediately and stumbled backward, holding his back and neck and fighting for breath.

Two more came at Billy from behind, but he seemed
to sense they were there, whirled, and lifted a boot high
enough to kick the nearest one squarely on the side of
the head, expertly dropping him in his tracks as if he

had been sledgehammered. Billy made another three-hundred-sixty-degree spin, faked a kick at the next ducking attacker, and then caught him directly in the solar plexus with the knuckles on the fingers of his right hand in a pure, effective judo blow. All the air left the man's lungs instantly and he crumpled into a heap, trying to breathe.

Now Bubba was able to pull away from the others who held him and went to work, too. He and Billy, as a team, quickly turned the fight their way. Though still heavily outnumbered, it was clear the big man and his red-haired friend had won the war. Bubba chased the last of the ones who were still standing out the door while Billy collected the several that lay writhing on the floor and sent them lurching after their buddies, coughing, sputtering, spitting out blood. Billy had taken only one punch and it had left a small mouse beneath his left eye. Bubba had already forgotten about the blow to his jaw.

No one noticed that the leader, the first one to have fallen, had now climbed back to his feet and stood, leaning against the counter, an ugly switchblade knife unfurled in the hand of his good arm, making a move toward Billy's unguarded back.

"Look out!" Bubba warned. "He's got a knife!"

Billy deftly stepped away from the lunging move that, if successful, would have sunk the blade deeply into his back. In one smooth move, he grabbed his attacker by the arm, gave a quick twist, and the man did a full flip in the air, landing smack-dab on his back. The knife went skittering harmlessly across the floor.

Bubba grabbed the man's shoulders and Billy took his feet. They tossed him out into the muddy parking lot like so much dead wood, then dusted their hands as if they had been handling something dirty and unpleasant.

"We better get out of here before the cops show up,"

Billy said, giving the last injured thug a quick kick in the butt as he threw him out into the rain.

"Shoot, Billy, we ain't done nothing wrong," Bubba protested. He still had the best part of a cheeseburger left on his plate on their table. About the only table left upright in the place.

"Those yahoos may have been from around here. You want to explain to a cop who started what when he might be one of them's cousin? You know how some of these mountain folks stick together. Besides, they may be on the way to get something more deadly than a knife."

"All right. All right." Bubba gently gathered up the sandwich in his two hands as if it was something precious and fragile. Then he spotted the waitress just crawling out from behind the counter, a cast-iron skillet in her hand, just in case there was more trouble. "Gosh, we're sorry, honey. We made a mess of the place. Can we help clean it up?"

"Don't worry about it. You've already cleaned up the real mess. That bunch has been in here causing trouble before. They got themselves a commune or something up the road but it's just an excuse to gang up and act tough. They get stoned then come down here and harass folks sometimes, but that's because nobody's ever stood up to them before the way y'all did."

Bubba paid for both meals despite the protests of the waitress and then followed Billy out the front door. A few of the toughs were still sitting in the only car full of them that was left in the lot. They licked their wounds and warily watched the two men who had just whipped them and all their buddies. Bubba made one threatening step toward them and they quickly shut and locked the car's doors, cranked up, and screeched out of the lot.

Back on the highway, they were hardly a mile down the road when they met a police car, heading back toward the café with its lights flashing.

They had traveled another five miles before Bubba finally spoke.

"Where'd you learn to fight like that, friend? You even scared me for a second back there."

Billy smiled slightly in the dim light from the dash. He looked out the window for a moment before he answered.

"Well, Bubba Baxter, I received a degree in 'fightology' from Uncle Sam. And then two tours of on-the-job training in Vietnam." He turned and grinned at Bubba. "That little fracas back there wasn't much to speak of, really. But I'm glad it turned out the way it did. Some of 'em only got their feelings hurt. If they had pressed the point . . ."

The man's voice trailed off. Bubba didn't want to think what Billy could do if pushed too far. His moves had been effortless, natural, and artistic. There was no doubt he could do deadly damage if need be.

"Well, I'm much obliged to you for taking my back the way you did. It wasn't necessarily your fight."

"Looked like you were holding your own 'til they ganged up on you and had you pinned."

Bubba sat up straight in the seat, trying to ignore the ache in his jaw where the one good punch had landed.

"Aw, I expect I could have come out okay in a little while. I was on the verge of gettin' loose when you stepped in. I'd just been playing with them up to that point."

"I know you were, big man. Sorry I spoiled it for you. But I knew you didn't want to hog all the fun."

Then they both burst into uproarious laughter.

It was past three in the morning when they finally rolled into Chandler Cove. The rain-slick streets were empty as they rode through the middle of town. There had been no more sleepiness for Bubba. Probably still keyed up from the excitement at the café, the two of them had talked the entire way. And they were still talking when Bubba backed the truck and trailer up to the shop door.

Billy had offered to get out on the highway coming into Chandler Cove but Bubba would have none of it.

"You ain't gonna get no ride way out here this time of night," he had argued. "Come on and bunk down on one of the cots in the shop. We use 'em when we pull all-nighters sometimes working on the cars, and I can say from experience it's way better than the ground for a mattress and a rock for a pillow."

Bubba decided to sleep in the shop, too, since he would need to have the car unloaded and be ready to start work on it when Jodell, Joe and Johnny got there in the afternoon. He determined he might just as well baby-sit it all night and be ready to go to work rather than go home and have to turn right around and come back after sunup.

Sure enough, he slipped out early after only a few hours sleep, and was busy unloading the truck and trailer when the noise woke Billy.

"Sorry I disturbed you," Bubba apologized.

"No problem. But I believe I'd pay ten dollars for a cup of coffee."

"I'll get some going in the shop. Grandma Lee'll probably have us some breakfast down here directly anyhow. She's never failed me yet."

They had just finished pushing the engine-less race car off the trailer and into the shop when Jodell and Joe's grandmother walked down from the house with a basket full of biscuits, sausage, eggs, and homemade fig preserves. She didn't seem surprised at all to see a stranger helping Bubba.

"Pleased to meet you, Billy," she said when Bubba introduced him. "You Baptist, Methodist, or Presbyterian?"

Billy didn't hesitate.

"I was baptized in Soldier's Branch just up the road from New Bethel Baptist Church up close to Charlottesville."

She nodded her approval. And then not so subtly prompted him to brag some more on her cooking. Billy had passed Grandma Lee's ultimate test and was more than welcomed to have a second buttered biscuit smothered with preserves.

"You want me to give you a lift out to the highway?" Bubba asked, once Grandma had gone on back up to the house.

"Maybe later. It looks like you got plenty of work to do before your buddies get here." He looked around at the parts, tools, tires and other equipment that were scattered around as if there had been some sort of explosion. "Look, Bubba, why don't you let me help you finish up here before I go? It's the least I could do to pay for the ride and the roof over my head and all the good food."

And without another word, the two of them pitched in and, side by side, they got busy once again, doing what had to be done.

The two men finished all they could do and then found themselves some shade under the big chestnut tree that grew high and broad next to the shop. They talked for a while but the late night and the lack of sleep and the gentle warm breeze finally swept them both under. They were dead to the world when Jodell and the rest of the crew finally pulled up about mid-afternoon.

As they spilled from the car, it was clear that they were, to a man, suffering the effects of the late night before. Jodell was first out and he hobbled over to the cool shade and slid down next to where Bubba leaned back against the tree trunk. Johnny Holt crawled from the backseat and stayed on his hands and knees for a while, until he found the strength to stand and make his own way to the shade before he collapsed again. Joe Banker was still wearing the same shirt he had worn to the race the day before. He kept his hands pressed over his ears, his face screwed up in agony as he uncoiled from inside the car.

"What's that infernal racket?" he moaned.

"Birds, Joe. Them's birds singing," Jodell announced.

"Make 'em stop, Jodell."

Joe kept walking right on into the shop without stopping, as if his momentum, once achieved, was too much to overcome. None of them seemed to notice the stranger leaned back against the side of the tree trunk opposite Bubba.

Bubba had finally pulled his baseball cap up from over his eyes to watch the sorry sight of their arrival.

"Well, y'all certainly are a mess. Did you come on straight from the party or did you check right out of jail or what?"

Jodell rubbed his eyes with his fists like a tired two-year-old on the verge of tuning up and crying.

"I want you to know that we've been working hard most of the night making sure that race sponsor was happy. Then we got up at dawn to get on the road to get back here to help you so you wouldn't overdo it. And Lord, if we don't get here and catch you gettin' forty winks in the shade like there wasn't a thing in the world to get done."

"A man needs a little nap every once in a while," Bubba said, pulling the cap back down over his eyes to shut out Jodell's barbs.

"Well, I sure don't want to disturb your sleep, Bub. I reckon me and the boys'll just have to unload the trailer and truck," Jodell said with mock disgust.

"Jodell, you know I wouldn't be sittin' here if we hadn't done got it unloaded and everything put away. We was just takin' a little nap while we was waitin' here for y'all to get back. And sleepin' off all that fried chicken Grandma fixed for our lunch."

"Fried chicken?" Johnny Holt raised his head from his knees only long enough to say the two words, then he dropped it again.

"What about the motor parts?" Jodell asked.

"We got everything settin' in there on the engine table waitin' for Joe to get here and put them all back together again."

"I don't know if he'll be doing much piecing back together today. He didn't turn up until we was just about ready to roll out of town this morning. I don't think he's doing too well right now. Are you, Joe?"

Joe had stepped back out of the barn/shop. He had his eyes shut tightly against the bright sunlight. He had forgotten to tuck in his shirt and zip up the fly of his jeans, too.

"All I need is a couple of aspirins and a nap. Or a couple of naps and an aspirin. I forget which."

"Why don't you stretch out on one of the cots in there before Grandma sees you and puts two and two together?"

Joe seemed to be thinking for a moment, maybe deciding if he could make it all the way back inside the shop to a cot. Then he slowly turned and disappeared inside once again, still with his eyes shut, feeling the way with his outstretched hands.

"I don't know about that boy," Jodell said, shaking his head. He leaned back on his elbows then and gave Bubba a long look. "What in the world happened to the side of your face?"

"Huh?"

Bubba rubbed his jaw and noticed for the first time that it smarted when he touched it.

"If I didn't know any better, I'd say you done gone a round or two with Sugar Ray Robinson."

"Aw, that," Bubba said sheepishly. "We accidentally

got mixed up in a little old scrape on the way home last night."

"Scrape? We leave you by yourself for a few hours and you go off and get yourself into a free-for-all. Looks like somebody got in at least one good punch. And your friend don't look much better." Jodell acknowledged Billy's presence for the first time as he gazed at the bruise beneath his eye. "You gonna introduce us or am I gonna have to guess who he is?"

"Oh. This is my buddy, Billy. I was giving him a lift when we stopped at that diner . . . you know the one in the curve on the highway . . . and he helped me dish out a little bit of education to some folks that needed a dose of it in the worst way. He helped me all morning getting everything in place."

Billy leaned over, tipped his hat, and offered Jodell his hand.

"I'm Billy Winton, Jodell. Pleased to meet you. Bubba's told me a lot about you and Joe and the rest of 'em. Oh, and congratulations. I hear you won yourself a race yesterday."

"Yeah, we got ourselves a big one. One we needed in the worst way." Jodell lay on his side in the grass and propped his head on his hand. He studied the stranger for a moment before he asked his question. "So where you heading to, Mr. Billy Winton, if it's any of my business?"

"Tell you the truth, if I knew, I'd probably already be there. Like I told Bubba, if I found a place that felt right, I'd probably drop anchor and stay there. Meanwhile, I was figuring on getting a good look at this country of ours before I did."

"Where you from, then?"

The way Jodell asked the question, it didn't seem to be nosey at all. And Billy didn't hesitate in his answer.

"Born up near Roanoke but I've been all over the

country in the last year. Since I got back from an all-expenses-paid trip to Southeast Asia compliments of the taxpayers of the U. S. of A."

"I imagine you have some stories to tell."

"I expect I do. Two tours with the Air Cavalry. But I try not to remember any more of it than I have to in my nightmares."

"That's got to be tough. But I guess it's good to be back home. To the States, anyway."

"That it is. But it's a complicated time, Jodell. Sometimes I think there's more craziness here than I ever saw over there. All the rioting and fussing and fighting amongst ourselves. You don't need to cross the big water to see a mean, vicious war, it don't seem like. And I'm not so sure folks get along any better here than they do anywhere else on this old lopsided planet."

Jodell nodded his head. The stranger was right. It was, indeed, a complicated time. The men were quiet for a minute, considering Billy's words. Johnny snored softly. Bubba eventually broke the silence.

"Billy's pretty good with a wrench, Jodell."

"You don't say." Jodell had brightened up immediately.

"I had to keep him from going to work on that motor. You know how Joe hates for anybody else to lay a hand on his engines. But he sure told me how he'd put it back together and make it work."

"How'd you learn about cars, Billy?"

"My dad was a mechanic. I guess I was born with 10-W-30 in my veins. I worked at a garage while I was in high school so I could put together about the hottest '57 Chevy anybody in the west part of the state had ever seen. I won myself a drag race or two before I tore the car all to pieces one night when the guy I was dragging got squirrelly and took us both into the ditch. I was trying to save up enough to get her put back together when I got drafted."

"Fifty-seven Chevy, huh? What size engine you have in her?"

And then they talked cars for awhile. Apparently what Billy told Jodell impressed him mightily.

"Billy, I don't know if you're interested in staying in one place for a few days or not, but we could use another wrench for awhile. It doesn't pay much but we'd have a place for you to stay and I think you've sampled Grandma Lee's cooking already. We've got to get this car back together, then we run Bristol in a couple of weeks. But before we do, we need to bang out all that body damage and rebuild the other car . . . well, you see we got things we need to get done around here and all we got ourselves are some old sore tails to try to get 'em done with."

He nodded toward Johnny Holt who had slowly toppled over and now lay curled up on the ground, sleeping as soundly as he might have at home in his own bed. Bubba Baxter was grinning broadly. He had had every intention of suggesting just such an arrangement to Jodell and Billy. Jodell had beaten him to the punch.

"Well, that's mighty nice of you to offer, Jodell," Billy said. "But I wouldn't want to be in the way."

"You get in the way, we'll run you off. But I like a man who appreciates good, fast cars. Why don't you stay around for a few days and give it a try. No rush and it might prove interesting to you. We've got ourselves a pretty good racing shop going here and we expect to get some more wins like yesterday."

Bubba winked at Billy and gave him a thumbs-up.

"Well, okay. I reckon I can quit being a tourist for a few days."

"You want to see the country, you stay with us,"

Bubba jumped in. "From Riverside to Daytona. We go everywhere."

"And right now," Jodell said, "we're going into the shop and get to work."

He stood, still a bit unsteady, and gave Johnny a nudge with the toe of his shoe. Apparently dreaming of a pit stop, he came awake mumbling something about "four tires" and "gas ready." The other three men laughed and made their way toward the barn-turned-race-shop.

As they walked, Jodell pointed out where they planned to soon start digging the foundation for an addition onto the side of the shop. That is, where they were going to dig it whenever they found enough time to get started on it. With all the tools and equipment, the three cars to work on inside the barn, and another wrecked car in a shed out back, they had long since outgrown their facilities.

They set to working, paying no attention to Joe Banker as he slept peacefully on one of the cots.

"Billy, this sport is changing quickly," Jodell said as they hammered next to each other on the Ford's sheet metal. "We won yesterday but we got to run to keep up. We don't keep an edge, we'll get left in the dust." Jodell stopped pounding for a moment. "And one thing you'll learn about me, Billy, is that I race to win. I'm not interested in second. That's the same as losing to me. I race to come in first, not just in the money." There was no mistaking the set of his jaw, the look in his flashing blue eyes. Jodell Lee was damn serious about winning races! "We've been halfway looking for another permanent member of our crew. Bubba and me both are pretty good judges of character. You done passed his test, I reckon, and I'm willing to give you a few days to impress me. If you work out and want to try for it, that permanent crew job could be yours."

Jodell explained that there was no dearth of young men willing to help out at races within a few hours' drive from Chandler Cove. Or they could come over and devote a few hours in the shop after their day's work. But when it got right down to it, with wives and kids and car payments to meet, they couldn't afford to give up the security of their day jobs, time with their family, and some semblance of home life, all to run away and join the circus. Sometimes they would have to be gone for several weeks at a time and most weeks meant Wednesday through Sunday night away from home at the very least.

Billy Winton smiled and shook Jodell's hand.

"Much obliged, Jodell. I certainly don't have any family to consider and I don't have a clock to punch either. Let's see how it goes."

"Fair enough, Billy. Fair enough. Now could you hand me that chisel on the workbench behind you?"

They set to pounding on the car again. Despite the din, Joe Banker never even rolled over on his narrow cot.

I t was only a couple of weeks later when they found themselves convoying across the Cumberland Plateau and down the other side of the mountains to Nashville. The Fairgrounds Speedway there was awaiting them. It was a circle a little over half a mile around, and Jodell was anxious to get back to one of his favorite tracks.

They were dragging along behind the truck a good race car, one with which they had won several times before on similar tracks. With that knowledge, they were excited about the prospects for the race. But there was more. They were also looking forward to a side trip to downtown Nashville, to the Ryman Auditorium to take in the Grand Ole Opry.

The caravan rolled out of Chandler Cove early Thursday morning. Bubba and Billy were in the truck, towing the race car. Riding in the trailing car were Johnny Holt and Joe Banker, along with two men who often helped crew the car when the trip was not too far from Chandler Cove, Clifford Stanley and Randy Weems. At the mention of Nashville, both Clifford and Randy had jumped to volunteer to go and help out. Nowadays they didn't get to work as many races as they would have liked, but they still tried to help out on the shorter trips and at the key stops on the circuit, like Daytona and Charlotte.

There was some history with Clifford and Randy. They had made the trip to Daytona for Jodell's first run there in the superspeedway's inaugural race in 1959. That had been their first trip out of the mountains, and watching the hillbillies take in the big water, the girls at the beach, the monstrous track, all had produced several days of pure entertainment for Joe, Jodell, and Bubba.

Catherine, Joyce, and Jodell followed the other two vehicles over to Nashville in the station wagon. As she often did, Grandma Lee was keeping the whole flock of kids, allowing them all to be able to get away together for the weekend. Even though she was getting up in years, she maintained that the kids kept her going and sincerely seemed to enjoy having them with her. Since Jodell and Catherine lived in the house they had built not far from her own house and the shop, and since Catherine still worked part-time for a lawyer in town, then their two kids stayed with her almost as much as they did at home anyway.

About the only thing Jodell didn't like about racing was that he was forced to be away from the kids far more than he wanted. They went with them whenever it was feasible, but this trip was different. He was looking forward to spending the weekend with Catherine in a town they had come to love since they had first started going there to race years before.

They rolled into town about the time everyone was quitting work for the day and the traffic was thick on

most of the highways out of town. Many of the cars they
met or passed waved and honked their horns when they
saw the car number painted on the doors of the tow truck
and realized what rode beneath the tarp on the trailer
behind.

Race fans. God love 'em!

They got settled into their motel on Murfreesboro
Road. Bubba would pick the spot for dinner. But before
they could even get unpacked, Joe had gathered up all
the other guys, Billy Winton included, and they had
taken off for parts unknown.

"We're going to do some sightseeing," Joe had announced with a wink. "I want to show the boys some of
the museums and art galleries here in Nashville."

"I think I know what kind of sights you're looking
for," Catherine chided.

"We're gonna see the homes of some of the country
music stars," he had said with a mostly straight face.
"Maybe try to find out where Porter Wagoner lives so
we can drop by and say hello."

And then they were gone.

"Wonder what they're getting into?" Bubba mused.

"No telling," Jodell answered, a bit of a worried look
on his face. "I hope old Billy is up to hanging with the
likes of Joe Banker when he's out on the town. And to
babysitting Clifford and Randy. Them boys still act like
they just fell off the hay wagon sometimes. Bet you half
my share of the race purse they come home without
Joe."

"I know a sucker bet when I hear one," Bubba responded with a crooked grin.

Since early in their racing exploits, Joe Banker had
been more than willing to take advantage of the parties
and women and wild times that seemed to spring up
wherever the racing circuit landed that particular week.
He was indefatigable. Somehow, he could manage to

stay out all night and still show up and run a race as if
he had been in his own crib all the evening before. And
with his movie-idol looks and winning personality, he
seemed to have no trouble attracting female companion-
ship along the way.

He had learned at the feet of the masters: Joe Weatherley and Curtis Turner and some of the other drivers
who seemed more a part of a rolling circus than a band
of big time racers. But, like them, Joe was as serious on
race day as he was wild and carefree with his partying
the rest of the time.

"Well, you know my primary concern," Bubba said.

"Where we gonna eat?" Jodell answered without hesitation.

"Where we gonna eat?"

"I don't know, Bub. I'm not all that hungry and Catherine said she just wanted a pack of crackers or something, so I thought we'd just not eat tonight," Jodell
teased, a serious look on his face. But then he saw the
painful look across the big man's brow and he cackled.

"Now don't be messing with me. You know I tend to
black out if I don't eat regular. I've got to keep my
strength up."

"Hold your horses, partner. You know I'm kidding.
Catherine wants some barbecue, so I thought we would
go to that place you like so much. What's the name of
it?"

Barbecue and the fixings was Bubba Baxter's number-
one favorite meal, followed closely by steak, biscuits, or
anything else someone could fit on a plate.

"Charlie Nickens! How could you forget such a truly
wonderful place?"

"That's it. Charlie Nickens. I just hope they'll let you
back in after the last time you were there."

"Why do you say that?" Bubba asked defensively.

"You don't remember last time we were there you

almost fell into the pit when the cook lifted the screen to slice you off some meat?"

"Naw, I did not! I was just trying to get me a good whiff of that heavenly smell and make sure he carved off the best part of that big old shoulder and I slipped on something."

"All right, all right. But this time behave yourself. I like that place too and we don't want to have the whole crew banned from there."

And that was the Lee's and the Baxter's first night on the town in Nashville.

It was middle-of-the-day hot as the cars worked their way through the first practice session the next day. There were cars all around the track running laps, some feebly feeling their way, others boldly, proudly showing their best.

For Jodell Bob Lee, the frustrations from the race they had run the previous weekend still lingered like a bad headache. And it had been especially galling since that disappointing outing had followed by only a couple of weeks their big superspeedway win. He'd gotten himself wrecked on only the twelfth lap of the race when the transmission locked on him suddenly in the middle of traffic. And it was even more humiliating since they were running at what might could be considered his "home track," just up the road from Chandler Cove in Bristol. And that meant he was listed as being in dead last when the race had continued on and finished without him.

"Dadgum Bristol!" he had exclaimed as he kicked the crumpled fender of his Ford. "North Wilkesboro. That's our home track from now on, boys."

It was farther away from Chandler Cove, but North Wilkesboro was far kinder to Jodell Lee and his team. He always seemed to run much better there than he did

at the track at Bristol, only thirty or so miles from his
home. For some reason, whenever he tried to run at
Bristol, he would inevitably find himself caught up in
someone else's wreck, have the oddest, most obscure
part on the car break, or simply miss the setup just
enough that they faded all race long. Once he didn't even
make it to the start when he got kicked hard from behind
by some eager rookie and that had sent him straight
into the fence as the cars were coming out of turn four
to take the green flag.

But he still loved the place. It just seemed that some
kind of black cloud hovered over his car as soon as the
green flag dropped. Or sometimes even before. In almost
twenty starts at the place he had never even made it into
the top ten.

Nashville? That had been a very different story, even
though the tracks were very similar in size and layout.
Jodell always seemed to run well here, even if the fin-
ishes didn't always show it. They had brought the same
car they had raced so briefly the week before. The transmission had been the thing that had gone belly-up that
time. Jodell had changed clothes and been sitting in the
pits, drinking a soda, watching the rest of them duke it
out by the time the crossed flags in the hands of the
flagman signaled the halfway mark.

He loved the high banks and fast speeds of Nashville.
It was much like driving on a big speedway except for
the shorter turns and straightaways. Sometimes he could
actually forget this was nothing more than a short track.
About the only thing he didn't like about it was the
unique pit road, but he wasn't alone in that opinion. The
pits at Nashville were a source of frustration for everybody running there.

A quarter-mile track that looped around inside the
center of the half-mile track served as pit road. Cars
would enter the pits as they went into turn one, after

passing the start/finish line. The car would then zoom its
way down the quarter mile track until it found its pits,
got serviced, then exited the pits through the quarter-
mile track's turn four. That meant he would have to
cross the start/finish line again, for the second time that
lap. This system of pitting had led to its share of scoring
controversies and post-race fistfights over the years as
the scorers would sometimes accidentally double-score
a lap on a pit stop.

Jodell squinted into the hot sun as he pulled the car
out of its spot in the center of the infield and steered it
back out onto the track. Bubba and Billy had just finished changing a couple of springs while Johnny had
crawled beneath the car to check on the new transmission they'd bolted in before they left Chandler Cove.

Jodell eased into the throttle, carefully gauging the
feel of the new springs beneath him. He stayed down on
the apron of the track for a ways before finally gunning
the throttle going down the backstretch. He allowed the
car to roll into turn three, giving her head enough so that
she drifted up slightly in the center of the corner. Then,
coming out of turn four, he opened her up and set sail
down past the mostly empty grandstands.

He caught the Ford Torino driven by Richard Petty in
the center of turn one and settled in on his back bumper.
The two of them cranked off several laps, running nose
to tail, as Jodell studied the line Richard was taking
around the track. As far as he could tell, the two cars
seemed evenly matched as they raced together for a
spell.

Richard finally peeled off and took his car into the
pits. Jodell let him go, staying out to try a few different
lines around the track. The car seemed to prefer the
higher line, the groove that circled out toward the fence.
Jodell ran off a couple more laps, making certain his feel

for the track was accurate, then headed into their pit so
he could check the times with Joe.

He cut the Torino's powerful engine as he came out
of turn four toward the start/finish line and rolled to a
quiet stop near where Bubba stood waiting, holding the
heavy floor jack. The crew went to work immediately.
Jodell let down the window net, then started unbuckling
the web of safety belts. He tossed the helmet up onto
the shifter knob and then pulled his lanky frame out
through the window.

"How were they?" Jodell asked, nodding toward the
clipboard Joe was intently studying. All the scrawled
numbers on the sheets of paper were the lap times from
the run he'd just completed.

"Not bad. When you and Richard were running all
those laps y'all were within a tenth or less every time."

"The car felt good, I guess, but I was having trouble
holding it down to the bottom on the inside."

"You ran about a tenth better when you were running
in the next groove up."

"I thought so. It kept wanting to push out toward the
wall if I pinched it off too tight on the inside. The higher
up the track I run, the freer the car feels through the
corner."

"Do you want us to work on getting it better down
low or are you comfortable with the line you're running?" Joe asked, studying the times on the chart as if
they were the vital signs of a critical patient. He also
moved his lips as he read through the notations he'd
made about the line the car had run each lap. "You the
guy that's got to keep the thing on the track, cuz."

"Let's dial it in where we're running. I can hold it
down tight for a lap or two if I have to, but if we get a
track full of slow cars I'll have to be able to pass on the
outside or ride along behind them for the whole dang
race."

"You're right about that. We're gonna swap out the springs one more time like we talked about. We'll hurry so you can get a feel for them."

Jodell wanted to stretch his legs before climbing back into the car so he ambled down the pit stalls to where the Petty crew was working on their car. He spied Richard standing by one of the toolboxes, drawing a drink out of a water cooler. His brother, Maurice, was buried under the hood, working on the engine.

"What do you say there, Chief?" Jodell asked. Everyone called Maurice "Chief." He gave the man a friendly pat on the back as he walked by.

"Hey, Jodell," Maurice answered without even glancing up from his task. "You were looking good out there."

"So was your old tall, skinny brother."

Richard motioned toward a stack of paper cups. Jodell grabbed one and held it under the spout of the water cooler while Petty held the spigot open.

"You were scattin' pretty good, Richard," Jodell said after a big swallow of the icy water. He nodded toward where Chief labored beneath the Ford's hood. "Y'all got motor trouble?"

"Naw! Old Chief ain't never satisfied with 'pretty good.' He's got to look for more or he'll bust."

"I know what you mean. Bubba's the same way when we're trying to set the car up. I tell him it's fine and he agrees with me then goes to twisting or winding on something else. He's swapping out the springs again now."

Both men grinned. Most any race crewman worth his salt would crank away until the last instant, looking for an edge, until the driver finally pulled the car out of his reach to take it out and race it. Jodell wiped his face with a bandanna from his back pocket.

"Richard, you heard anything else about that track they're building down there in Alabama—Talladega?

We'll be racing there in a month and a half and I can't find out much about the place."

"I heard Big Bill France telling somebody that things are coming along real good. They're building it at an old air base. They say it's gonna be something else but I reckon we'll have to see it for ourselves when we go down to run the place."

"I can't wait to see it. I love to run Daytona, so I'm looking forward to getting down there and seeing what the old Torino will do."

"Same here. From what I've heard, it'll be almost identical to Daytona but longer. They say it'll be even faster."

"I don't see how we can go much faster than we already do," Jodell said, shaking his head at the thought of circling a track any faster than they did at Daytona.

"Well, don't be surprised if what some of these cats are saying is true. This place is going to have some high banks and it's plenty long."

The two men were quiet for a moment, considering the possibilities, sipping their cool water.

"Well, I got to go run some more laps. Bubba dived under the car as soon as I pulled in and I better go see if he fixed it or tore it up."

"Better check he didn't get hungry and take a bite out of one of your tires," Richard said with a chuckle. He held a rag under a stream of ice cold water from the cooler, ready to wrap it around his neck once more.

"See ya, Richard, Chief."

Bubba and Billy were still underneath the car, hammering and beating on something with a vengeance. Johnny Holt was under the hood, making some minor adjustments to the engine timing.

Billy came crawling out from under the car, covered from top to bottom in grease and dirt, his face streaming sweat, his long red hair escaping from his cap. Jodell smiled down at him and tossed him a rag.

"Bet you weren't expecting all this glory and glamour when you signed on for this job, huh?"

"Hey, I will gladly take all the grease, oil, and gasoline you can pour on me. It's a far sight better than the mud, muck, and mosquitoes I got in my last job," Billy said, swiping at his face, his teeth bright white against the sweat and grime when he grinned. "And so far, nobody has taken a shot at me, either."

"Some folks don't know how much hard work it takes to win."

"From what I've seen so far, it's directly proportional. The harder you work the more likely you are to win. I plan on having this car where you can win every week."

"That's music to my ears," Jodell said smiling. "Speaking of which, you going to go to the Opry with us tonight? We've got enough tickets."

"Yeah! I can't go out every night and try to keep up with your cousin over there. I wouldn't mind something a little more sedate at all."

Bubba slid out from under the car, stood and set a hand full of wrenches on its roof. He reached back to dust off the seat of his pants.

"All right there, Joe Bob. You can take her out and give her another whirl and see how she behaves."

"You got it done that quick?"

"You bet. Old Billy here is a whiz with a wrench. We've been needing somebody like him for a long time."

Bubba retrieved the wrenches from the car's roof and waited for Jodell to climb in the car so he could help secure the window netting. The nets were one of the innovations that had resulted from a series of tragic accidents that had claimed their good friends, racing legends Little Joe Weatherley and Fireball Roberts. Weatherley had struck his head on a wall when his car crashed at Riverside, California. Fireball's fiery wreck a few months after that at Charlotte had led to the mandatory fuel cells. They had made the sport safer, but regardless of the improvements, it was still dangerous. A driver could get hurt badly, and especially at the phenomenal speeds they were running at the big, fast tracks like Daytona and Charlotte. And that was what was already of concern to the drivers and crews as they anticipated the opening race at the new Talladega track.

Jodell buckled up the belts and pulled on his helmet. He could remember when he had run races with a football helmet on, or an old miner's hat. This, too, was a much safer way to race.

Johnny closed the hood and signaled for him to fire up the car. He shifted into reverse and gunned the engine. Clifford and Randy both had to jump to get out of the way as he backed the car out, then he pulled forward out onto the track, getting to speed as quickly as he could.

Jodell only ran off a few quick laps. The car was not tracking as precisely as he wanted in the turns. He was having a bit of trouble maintaining his line in the corners and had to wrestle with the wheel in the center of the turns. He found he had to keep yanking on the wheel to overcome the car's tendency to push up toward the outside wall. After a few trips around the track, he headed back toward the pits.

"She ain't right," he hollered to Bubba over the grumbling of one of the other racers revving his engine. Bubba stepped closer to the window trying to hear what his driver was reporting. "Something y'all did on that last adjustment just doesn't feel right."

"Let us string the car and check it out. Just hold tight."

Bubba began barking out orders to the others like a drill sergeant. He sent Randy and Clifford to check the air pressure in the tires while he and Johnny set about "stringing" the car. Billy watched fascinated as Bubba and Johnny took a string and ran it along the side of the tires, checking the toe-in on the car.

"I never would have thought to do that," Billy remarked. "You boys got plenty of tricks up your sleeves."

"You don't always have the time or the place to put a car up on a rack. You got to make do. Everybody has been doing this kind of stuff for as long as I can remember."

Bubba pulled the string tight along the edge of the tire, then leaned down and eyed it, seeing how it lined up. He seemed satisfied with what he saw and waved at Johnny to roll the string up.

Clifford walked up then with the air pressures.

"We're a little high in the right front. I dropped a couple of pounds out of it."

"Well, well," Bubba said, scratching his chin with his thumb and forefinger as he thought for a moment. "I think we better send him out and have him run a few laps and then check those tires again. They might be the problem."

"That is a good idea. Me and Randy seen a lot of the other teams struggling with their tires. The track just seems to be eatin' them up."

Bubba stepped back to the car's driver's side window. Jodell waited patiently with an arm resting on one of the rollbars and the other propped lazily on the lip of the window. When they were making short runs and quick adjustments to the car, it didn't make much sense for him to keep climbing in and out of the car all the time. That was especially true when they had the luxury of bringing to the track a full crew that was familiar with the car. Other times, when they relied on a pick-up crew, Jodell would have to come in, unbuckle, jump out, help make the changes, then hop right back into the car to go

out and make a couple more laps to check the results.
That certainly slowed progress.

"She stringed out okay, but Clifford said you might
be having a little trouble with the right front tire. He let
a couple of pounds of air out to see if that would help."

"You sure? It didn't feel right."

"Some of the other teams are having trouble with the
tires so we need to be careful. Go out and make a good
run and we'll tell you when to come in based on the
times. We need to check the tire wear and see if that's
the problem."

"Let me run some hot laps and then get in a rhythm.
I'll watch for the signboard. Give me some times."

"Will do, but now you pay attention to the right front.
We don't want you to push it too hard and get into the
fence," Bubba advised.

The deep roar of the engine when Jodell cranked it
up could be heard all across the infield and the pit area.
He pulled back out onto the speedway, quickly bringing
the car up to speed. He'd had enough laps now in the
practice so that he didn't hesitate to take the car out and
see exactly what it would do with the changes.

The push in the car was better but it still was there.
He ran the next several laps hard, testing several lines
around the track, trying to get a feel for what the car
needed so he could report to Bubba and Joe and the rest
of the crew. That was the value of a driver who understood the dynamics of a car. He could tell from the
slightest gee or haw that something wasn't quite right.
And he could also recognize instantly when the car was
set up perfectly. Otherwise, there could be much wasted
effort and even then, the race car might not be the best
it could be for the contest.

Sailing down the front stretch, Jodell glanced to his
left and saw the towering figure of Bubba Baxter, holding the signboard out by the wall. Joe Banker stood there

next to him with his stopwatches in his hands.

Jodell glanced at the board as he went by and saw "75" scribbled on it. That was not good. Not good at all. They had been running in the thirty to forty hundredths of a second range in the earlier laps he'd made with Richard. But that had been before they had changed the springs. If the times didn't pick up then they would have to go in a different direction altogether. Yet they had all been of one accord that the spring setup they had now was best.

He focused hard as he ran through turns one and two on the next lap. He concentrated on being as smooth as possible through the turns. In the center of the corner, he felt the car again want to push up on the track, to seem to be drawn toward the outer wall as if tugged by a giant, unseen hand. It was better than before but it still was enough to cause him to lose a bit of precious momentum right there in the center. That would cost him serious track position if he were side by side with a fast car, and there was no way he could win a race if his car behaved this way on race day.

Jodell steered out of the turn and allowed the car to drift out toward the fence, then felt the slight bump where the track crossed the tunnel entrance to the infield. Hard in the gas still, he headed off to the next corner, setting the car up to take the middle line. He hoped that she would run a little freer through that turn. He felt the weight of the vehicle set down on her springs as the momentum pushed her down into the banking. Then they were through turn four and racing back down past the grandstand on his right and the pits on his left.

A quick glance at Bubba's board gave him the time of the previous lap. He had written "70" this time. The next lap was a "65," then it stabilized between sixty and sixty-five.

The longer he stayed out the more he disliked the new

spring setup. The car simply didn't feel as good beneath him as she had on the earlier runs. High, low, wherever he tried to put the car on the track, there was just nothing like the bite she had had before the change. Jodell could reliably tell how fast the car was without Joe's watches, and only he knew how hard he was pushing and driving to even achieve that. When he came in this time, they would have to try to take the car back in the other direction.

Finally, Bubba flashed the signboard for him to bring the car on in. He ran one last hot lap before slowing coming out turn four, then brought the car down to the pit area. As he slowed, Jodell was already going over the list in his mind of the changes he wanted to make this time. He had to get the car right before the practice session was over. Qualifying was ahead and it was essential that they started toward the front.

Over the next hour they worked quickly to change out the springs, putting back in the set that had been on the car earlier. While the crew worked under the car, Jodell ticked off a list of other minor changes he wanted Bubba to make before they went out for the next run.

Joe was busy timing the faster cars practicing out on the track. Jodell was always amazed at how his cousin could operate the watches and still get all the times written down on the clipboard.

"What are we going to need?" Jodell asked. He was referring to the speed it would take to claim the pole position for the race.

"A thirty at least. Some may be able to get down into the high twenties. The way Richard and some of them are running, they might get down into the teens. If they do, they'll be hard to beat."

"I could run with Richard before, but he was mighty quick."

"Well, he picked up another tenth to a tenth and a half

on the changes they made for those last laps he ran," Joe said as he watched one of the cars going by on the track.

"Yeah, he was picking up while we were backing up. I think we know where we need to go now, though."

"The pole would be nice, but if we can put her in the top ten then we should be fine for the race. The way this place is using up tires, running smooth is going to be better than running fast, I'm thinking."

Jodell gave his cousin a sharp look. He always wanted the pole. Always. He didn't want to concede anything to anybody. But he knew Joe was right.

"If these guys go out and drive too hard, they'll burn the tires right off the rims. But if we set up right, I think we could still get the pole."

Jodell walked back over to the car to check on the progress of the changes they were making. It was certainly nice to have this much help at the track so he could actually focus on driving and getting a feel for the car. With Randy and Clifford here to help, they actually had six men who were intimately familiar with the race car, not counting Jodell. He had always known what an advantage it was to the other well-staffed teams but he could appreciate it more now as he watched his crew work so well together.

Finally Bubba signaled for him to get back in and take her out to see what they might have accomplished. They only had thirty minutes of practice time left and he didn't want them to waste a minute of it. In a flash, Jodell was back inside the car, backing it up to head out onto the track, once again sending a couple of his crewmembers scrambling when they were too slow in moving out of his way.

He gunned the engine and quickly brought the car up to speed, anxious to see what the changes had done to the handling. The first corner he took at speed felt almost too good to be believed. He smiled broadly, but decided to wait until the next turn to confirm it.

Beautiful! The push he had been feeling in the corners was completely gone. The car no longer seemed to be eager to head its nose toward the outside wall. Now it soared through the turns as if it was on a set of rails.

This was fun. Jodell Lee liked nothing better than piloting a race car when it was set up perfectly, when it handled so well it almost drove itself. Of course, to Jodell there was no such word as "perfection." He was already thinking of another change or two the car needed and he'd only run two laps so far. The car wasn't right until it sat in victory lane at the end of the day, being mobbed by fans and the media. And even then, Jodell Bob Lee would most likely be thinking of a few other tweaks he would have liked to have made so he could have won by a wider margin.

The cars on the track circled noisily through the balance of the practice session, their roar reverberating through the neighborhood that surrounded the state fairgrounds and track. Scattered through the grandstand were a couple hundred fans, braving the humid July heat, anxious to watch their favorite drivers.

Then, ultimately, the racers sat lined up on the pit road, ready to go out and make their qualifying runs. For racer and fan alike, it was a beautiful sight. All the shined and polished cars, still unmarked by combat, tuned and tight, ready to go out there for their first test to see who was the fastest. Slowly, one by one, the line grew shorter as the cars began to roll out and take their qualifying laps.

Jodell Lee and his Ford were among the last in line. The wait was killing him. He hated to be last at anything.

Richard Petty finally pulled out onto the speedway to take his lap. Most everyone in the pits watched him because they knew that his Ford was likely the car to beat for the pole if not the race itself. The Petty crew stood confidently watching as Richard ran his lap.

Sure enough, it was a blistering turn. When the public address announcer rattled off his time, there were gasps from many watching. Over eighty-four miles per hour! It was going to be a tough speed to beat. Several of the crews that had qualified already immediately put their heads together, trying to decide on some way they could find some more speed between now and the race.

Car after car went out after Petty but nobody could come close to his time. Jodell stood by his own car talking quietly with Joe.

"That's going to be a hard speed to beat, Jodell."

"Yeah, but if that last change we made works and if I don't get too scared to let it all hang out in the corners, then we just might get him."

"Yeah, and if wishes and buts were candy and nuts, we'd all have a merry Christmas. You just stay out of the wall or we'll be hauling what's left of the car back to Chandler Cove when the rest of them are racing tomorrow. We don't need to win the pole to have a chance in the race."

"Don't worry about me wrecking it. Remember I have to help fix it when I tear it up. But I *am* going to push it for all I can 'cause I really think we might can get him."

"That's why you're the driver." Joe said, smiling.

They yelled then at the others to come help push the car up to the line. It was almost their turn to go. Jodell zipped up his driving suit and wiped his sweating face one last time with the small towel he had thrown over his shoulder.

As the cars in front of him started to move out, he climbed in and quickly buckled up. He pulled the helmet and goggles on, ignoring everything else that was going on around him. He hardly noticed when Bubba reached in and checked the belts as he always did. All he was thinking was how he was going to go out and beat the track for that one, solid qualifying lap.

Then, almost before he realized it was time, the official at the head of the line waved him off. He hit the starter button and felt the rumble of the engine coming to life under his feet. He eased off on the clutch and the car rolled off to take the warm-up lap. He ran the car straight up into the banking of the first turn as he tried to build as much momentum as possible before coming back around to take the green flag that would signal the beginning of his qualifying lap.

Then, there was the flag, waving up ahead of him.

He flashed under the starter already at full speed and rumbled off into turn one as hard as the car would go. He prayed that the tires would stick as he ordered the car to run right up to its limit through the turn. The tires screamed in protest but did their duty, biting down into the hot, slick pavement.

Out loud, Jodell yelped, "C'mon, Miss Dolly! Give it all you got!"

He shot out of the corner as if propelled by rocket power instead of internal-combustion engine. There, ahead of him, was the backstretch. He'd made it through turns one and two safely and smoothly and, he knew, quickly. Now, all he had to do was repeat the same effort in three and four.

He set the car up perfectly at the end of the straightaway and turned her down low, seeking the shortest route through the arc. The car stuck right along the bottom line of the track. His powerful arms held the wheel tightly, turning the car hard to the left, fully expecting at any instant that the rear end would break loose and send him spinning like a mad top.

But again, even though the tires whined and the right-side ones sent off wisps of smoke, the car held its line.

Joe stood on the pit wall, following Jodell and the hand on his stopwatch simultaneously, watching and smiling. It was going to be very, very close, provided Jodell didn't make a bobble in the last turn.

Bubba stood beside Joe, watching every movement of the car, just as he always did, whether it was practice, qualifying, or racing. He didn't need a stopwatch to know it was a quick time so far. Damn quick.

And Billy Winton made it a trio on the wall. The newest member of the crew had a slight smile on his grimy face as he watched the result of their hard work circle the track at a blistering speed. He slapped Bubba on the back as Jodell held on to roar out of the last turn and point the car's nose toward the checkered flag.

And that was it. In less than a minute, they had earned whatever spot they would have in the race the next day.

Inside the car, a broad smile broke out on Jodell's face as he coasted the car back around one last time. If it wasn't speed enough to put him on the pole for the race then it was going to be mighty close. He was confident that there was nothing more that he could have pulled out of the car, out of his own driving ability. That was it, all he and the Ford had in them.

As he rolled in to a stop in the pits, all the boys were whooping and hollering. They knew it was a good lap, too. But would it be good enough? They all waited anxiously for the time to flash up on the scoreboard.

The look on Joe's face told the story already. By his watch, Petty had nicked them by a hair. But until the official time came up there was no way to be sure.

As Jodell climbed out of the car, the official time was finally posted and announced by the track public address system. Petty had beaten them by a few hundredths of a second. Less than the blink of an eye.

Jodell broke out into a huge smile. Even if it wasn't the pole, it was likely going to put him on the front row next to Richard. And considering how far off they had been earlier in practice, it was almost as good as winning the race itself.

Still, though he would never admit it to the others as they celebrated the brilliant run, Jodell Lee was disappointed. Outside pole was okay. Getting beaten by hundredths of a second by arguably the best team in racing was nothing to be ashamed of. But he was disappointed nonetheless.

As he helped pack up and get ready for a relaxing night with Catherine and the others, he tried to put it out of his mind. But everytime someone congratulated him on the great qualifying time, it came back. Lord knows, Jodell Lee hated to finish anywhere else but first.

Then he noticed Billy Winton giving him an odd sideways look, as if he somehow suspected how Jodell felt.

"You okay, boss?" he asked.

Jodell hesitated for the briefest of moments.

"Better than okay, Billy. Outside pole. That's something else! Let's get things wrapped up here so we won't be late for the Opry."

And with that, they went back to work.

WORSHIPING AT "THE MOTHER CHURCH"

Each of them showed up outside in the motel parking lot one or two at a time as they got ready for their night on the town. The Friday night Grand Ole Opry was waiting and they did not want to be late getting there. All the Chandler Cove crew had grown up with the weekend radio broadcasts of the Opry as much a part of their lives as church or family. And after hearing it for all those years on the radio, the chance to actually go and sit in the Ryman Auditorium audience was something not be passed up.

They had tried before when the races had brought them to Nashville, but something had always prevented them from going. But this time, Catherine had ordered the ten tickets weeks before, once she was certain of who was going to be making the trip. Clifford Stanley and Randy Weems had talked of nothing else since they had found out about the excursion, carrying on like a couple of schoolgirls readying themselves for the prom, rattling on about what they were going to wear and who they hoped to see there and who would get photos of what. It had fallen Johnny Holt's lot to be their baby-sitter for the evening.

Finally they were practically all assembled and everyone else waited impatiently in front of the motel for Joe Banker. He was going to meet his date at the Ryman but still needed to ride over with them.

"Bub, your turn to go in and fetch him," Jodell finally ordered. "If he doesn't get his butt out here soon we'll never make the start of the show. They say people line up around the block to get in."

"Why me?" Bubba whined. Joe's primping had reached new heights lately, his new long, flowing hair-style alone could take an hour to brush, dry and style precisely the way he wanted it.

"Just because y'all don't care how you look don't mean that I have to look like I just crawled out from under a tractor, too," he would grouse.

"All right. I'll flip you for it." Jodell pulled a nickel from his pocket. "Call it!"

"Heads!"

Jodell uncovered the Monticello on the back of the coin.

"Tails. You lose! Now hurry. We don't get gone in ten minutes, we may as well stay here and listen to it on the radio."

While they waited, Randy Weems entertained everyone in the parking lot and half of South Nashville with his best off-key Ernest Tubb impression while Clifford Stanley broke into some semblance of a buck dance. The assembled Jodell Lee racing crew couldn't help but laugh, even as they hoped nobody around knew these two farm boys were actually with them. Randy was decked out in his best Sunday white dress shirt, broad striped tie, a new pair of wing-tip dress shoes, and a clean, freshly blued pair of 401-brand bibbed overalls. Clifford was similarly attired but he had chosen to wear his work boots instead. At least he had polished them and, everyone hoped, taken the time to clean the manure off them as well.

Billy Winton stood to the side, leaning against the fender of the pickup, and watched the two young men as they danced and sang, observing everyone's excitement as they prepared for this pilgrimage to what many termed "The Mother Church of Country Music."

Jodell stepped over and leaned against the truck next to him.

"Remind you of the 'Beverly Hillbillies' just a little bit?" he asked.

"They look pretty excited, all right. They don't get out much, do they?" Billy whispered, careful not to let them hear him.

"You should have seen them when they got off the bus in Daytona the first time they came down to help us with a race. It was the first time they had been more than a few miles from their farms. And you'll have to watch them when Ernest Tubb comes on stage tonight. They'd rather see him than the Beatles, the Rolling Stones and Elvis Presley all at the same time!"

Billy gave him a sideways glance but he was grinning.

"How much worse can it get?"

The two young men had now joined hands and were waltzing each other around the lot, singing a sad ballad at the top of their lungs.

Thankfully, Bubba showed up then, literally dragging Joe Banker along behind him. Joe struggled, trying to catch his reflection in the windows of each ground-floor room as they passed by. Brush in hand, he was still trying to sculpt his hair as Bubba towed him along by an arm like a fitful child.

"Got him!" Bubba said proudly, as if Joe was a large-mouth bass he had just netted.

"Load up," Jodell said, and they all found spots in one of the two cars. "We're already gonna be last ones there. Y'all know how much I hate that."

And indeed, they knew that was true. Randy and Clifford fought for "shotgun" in the front seat so they could be the first to get a glimpse of the Ryman Auditorium where the Opry was held. Joe fiddled with the rearview mirror so he could check the lay of his mane of hair.

Johnny, Randy, Clifford and Billy led the way in the first car with the rest of them following. Jodell didn't want to get rear-ended when they caught sight of the Ryman for the first time. As they made their way down Broadway toward downtown Nashville, the big red brick building suddenly came into view, just around the corner from a line of neon-lit bars and souvenir shops. As soon as they had found a place to park down the hill near the Cumberland River, Randy and Clifford spilled from the car like a couple of eager kids. They made off at a gallop back up the street and across Broadway toward where a long line of people snaked down the sidewalk and around the corner.

Billy held his ears as he climbed from the car.

"They didn't quit that caterwauling from the time we left the motel until we got here," he reported. "Anybody got an aspirin?"

"I told you the Opry is a big deal to them," Jodell grinned. "The rest of us, we've seen a little bit of the world. But those two? This is the biggest thing since the hogs ate grandma!"

"Huh?"

"Old expression," Jodell grinned. "C'mon. Let's go before they break line and we have to fight the whole danged Grand Ole Opry audience."

Joe Banker had already snatched his ticket from Cath-

erine and was gone without a backward glance, off to
look for the lady he had met that day at the track and
had immediately fallen in love with.

"Any bets as to when we'll see him next?" Jodell
mused.

"Gimme breakfast at the motel," Bubba said.

"I got dibs on in the morning at the track," Joyce
Baxter quickly called.

"I got lunchtime," Johnny Holt chimed in.

"I say ten minutes before we crank 'em up and . . ."
Jodell started, but he noticed that Catherine had stopped
walking and was standing there, her hands on her hips
and her lips pursed.

"Y'all quit making fun of him. He'll be at the track
in the morning and he'll be ready to go just like he
always is. Has he ever let us down yet?" she asked
sternly, seriously.

Jodell and Joyce looked sharply at each other. Catherine was usually the primary one who complained about
Joe's late nights, the way he showed up just in time to
get done what they had to do before practicing, qualifying, or actually racing. He had cut it dangerously close
a few times lately, seriously close to hurting their effort,
and she had expressed a fear to her husband and her best
friend more than once that his tomcat ramblings and
nighttime distractions would cost them dearly one day.

Maybe her surprising objection to their teasing now
was merely some wishful thinking. Maybe she was whistling past the graveyard.

"All right! We'll lay off him," Jodell said. "We got
us a show to go see. What about it Ernest? You and
Faron Young ready?"

They had caught up with Clifford and Randy at the
tail end of the line. Clifford was trying to put a roll of
film in his camera and it had unfurled, spilling down the
sidewalk. Randy was attempting to put a flashcube on

his own Instamatic and had already blinded himself twice in the process.

"We're ready to do a little 'Walking the Floor,' " Randy beamed and several in the crowd near them giggled at him.

"How 'bout a little pick-me-up 'fore we go inside?" Clifford asked with a wink. Then he dug into the pocket of his overalls and produced a pint Mason jar filled with some kind of clear liquid.

"Well I'll be," Jodell said. "Been a while since I've seen any of that stuff."

Clifford unscrewed the lid, took a sip, then passed the jar around. Randy and Johnny tried a few drops, then Bubba took a swallow.

"For old times' sake," he said as he wiped his lips with a shirtsleeve.

Jodell tasted the stuff, too, then passed the jar to Billy Winton.

"This will clean out your carburetor," he said with a grin. "Try a little sample of Appalachian history."

Billy sloshed the liquid around in the jar and took a sniff, like a connoisseur checking the bouquet of a fine wine.

"Hmmm. Smells like turpentine. You sure this stuff is drinkable?"

Bubba gave a big belly laugh.

"It ain't as fine as Jodell and Joe's granddaddy used to brew, but it ain't as bad as some they make nowadays."

Before he could change his mind, Billy put his lips to the jar's rim and took a tentative sip. He winced, swallowed, coughed, then followed the fireball with his thumb all the way down his gullet to his stomach, and then he coughed some more. Clifford grabbed the jar from his hand before he could drop it.

"Whew!" Billy hissed. "What would possess somebody to want to drink that stuff on purpose?"

The whole group erupted into laughter.

"Be careful. You'll hurt old Clifford's feelings," Bubba said. "Some of his kinfolk probably took lots of pride in that batch."

"I thought I had tasted some foul hooch in Vietnam. But I think you could strip paint with that stuff."

"You get used to it," Jodell offered. "You have to remember that we've all been raised on the stuff. I was helping Grandpa Lee at the still before I was old enough to go to school. I could count and stack Mason jars before I could add and subtract."

Billy Winton shook his head and coughed one more time.

"And here I was, thinking I was a man of the world. Since I met you folks, I've realized what a sheltered life I've led!"

The doors opened then and the crowd began to eagerly make its way inside. Randy and Clifford pushed ahead, trying to get to their seats as quickly as they could, as if the show would start as soon as they showed up. Actually, the Opry was a live radio show on WSM and it would start right on time, just as it had every Friday and Saturday night for decades.

As nonchalant as they tried to appear, though, this evening was exciting to the rest of the crew too, just as it was to Clifford and Randy. Most weekends growing up, they would all gather around the radio on Friday and Saturday nights and listen to the broadcast of the country music and comedy show that rode the air waves all the way across the state from Nashville. As kids, they had wondered how the music and voices could magically find their way up the hollers, to their houses, and into their parlors

Now it was hard to believe they were actually here, in the place where those mysterious radio waves origi-

nated. And that this hot, non-air-conditioned auditorium
was the home of all the stars they had listened to as
children. The auditorium was actually a converted
church, and it still held hard wooden pews and stained-
glass windows as evidence.

As they found their seats, they could see people setting up their musical instruments on the darkened stage
while others, people who appeared to be audience members just like themselves, were sitting down on pews at
the back of the stage, looking back out at the crowd. Just
as the announcer took his spot behind the lectern to the
left of the stage, Joe came rushing in with a pretty blond-
haired woman. He introduced her quickly to everyone
and then they breathlessly took their seats.

Catherine checked her wristwatch excitedly, then
reached over and touched Joyce on the arm, then Jodell,
and pointed at the time. Jodell nodded down the row,
toward where Clifford and Randy sat open-mouthed and
wide-eyed, taking it all in, gawking at the crowd, the
auditorium, the big advertising signs that hung behind
the stage.

Suddenly, the announcer spoke, kicking off the show,
introducing the first segment's host as the band struck
up accompaniment. As they watched, Roy Acuff, Cousin
Minnie Pearl, Stringbean, Grandpa Jones and the others
they had listened to from a distance for so long came
out onto the stage and performed for them. The songs
and commercials and even many of the jokes were the
same ones they had heard so many times before through
the static, but they laughed and cheered and applauded
as if it was the first time for each.

Randy and Clifford bobbed and clapped and hooted
happily, but everyone knew the evening would not be
complete until they had seen their idol, Ernest Tubb. It
was hot in the balcony where they sat, and they all
fanned themselves furiously, trying to stir up a breeze.

During a break, the two young men exchanged worried looks. Maybe Ernest was not going to be on this week's show. Maybe he was off on a tour somewhere or something. Someone nearby overheard their distress and told them something about his having gone to Vietnam to entertain the troops and that they didn't know if he was back yet or not.

But then, the sign on the stage indicated they were going into "The Martha White Flour Hour." The curtain rose on a big Martha White banner and the house band kicked off a familiar refrain.

And there he was, bending at the waist to be near the microphone, his white hat cocked to one side.

"I'm walking the floor over you . . ."

The deep baritone voice of the legendary Ernest Tubb filled the building and drifted out over the ether via WSM as he belted out the trademark song in his patented style.

Randy and Clifford might as well have been at a church revival as they stared reverently at the stage, mesmerized by the tall, swaying Texan. Catherine and Jodell looked at each other and smiled. Each knew what the other was thinking. No matter what else came of their racing venture, they had treated these two young men to something they likely would not have been able to do if they had not been a part of Jodell's crew. Just as they, themselves, had been to places they would likely never have visited, seen things they would never have seen, had they stayed in Chandler Cove to farm or work in the mill in Kingsport as most of their contemporaries had done.

Marty Robbins closed the night's show, as usual. He went out of his way to welcome the racers, their crews and the race fans. Robbins often competed in stock car races himself and was considered a decent enough driver. If it had not been for his music career, many thought he could have had some success on the circuit.

Then, rising from the piano and strapping a guitar around his neck, Robbins stepped to the front-stage microphone and launched into one of Jodell Lee's favorite songs.

"Out in the West Texas town of El Paso . . ." he crooned over the nimble guitar strokes.

In the lightning flashes from all the cameras, Catherine could see the smile on her husband's face. She squeezed Jodell's arm tightly and rested her head on his shoulder.

The cool night air outside the auditorium felt wonderful after the show. Joe and his date had bolted for some club in Printer's Alley while Clifford and Randy begged everyone to accompany them on down the street to Ernest Tubb's record store, the scene for the after-Opry radio broadcast at midnight. But Jodell and Bubba were both bushed from the day at the track and ready for bed, and they knew the wake-up call would come early.

Billy and Johnny would have to chaperone the boys to the midnight show, making sure they got home before sunup. They would need them tomorrow. Jodell could still hear Randy and Clifford loudly singing Ernest Tubb songs as they made their way down the street toward the store, and hear Johnny begging them to shut up. Billy ambled along behind as if he was not even a member of the loud bunch.

"You can take the boys out of the country . . ." Jodell said, smiling.

"You know we'll have to hear about this night from now on," Bubba said.

"Long as they don't sing!"

And they all laughed. But Jodell was already humming the melody to "El Paso" as they made their way back to the car. They were headed to a good night's sleep, then a good day at the track tomorrow.

And, God willing, a winning day.

S aturday morning found the whole crew—except for an AWOL Joe Banker—hard at work on the race car. The only remembrance of the night before was when Clifford or Randy would suddenly break into a spontaneous version of "Walking the Floor Over You." Now, though, they all mostly had their race faces on, busily getting the car set for the final practice.

Jodell kept glancing toward the pit gate, looking for Joe. He had a few changes he wanted done on the engine before the practice, now less than an hour away from getting started. But so far, his cousin remained missing in action.

Bubba and Billy were doing heavy, noisy work under the front end of the race car, banging away brutally with a sledgehammer. They were concerned that the right front fender might rub the tire if the sheet metal got pushed in a little on contact with other cars during the race. And there would be contact. Of that you could be sure. They were trying to bang out all the clearance they could manage.

Randy and Clifford were getting wheels ready so they could have the night's supply of tires mounted and balanced and stacked where they could get to them in a big hurry during the race. Meanwhile, Johnny Holt huddled with Jodell, trying to go over with him what they wanted to accomplish during these last precious practice sessions. But Johnny actually spent most of the conference trying to overcome the driver's mounting irritation. Jodell was growing more and more disgusted that his crew chief and engine builder was nowhere to be found and the race was rapidly approaching.

Still, the two men mapped out the changes they wanted to make and what they expected each adjustment to accomplish. And they talked about what Jodell would do out there on the track to experiment with those changes which they had made already.

Ten minutes before the practice was to begin a haggard Joe Banker came ambling up. His normally carefully combed hair was askew and he was still wearing last night's clothes. He ignored the pointed stares of Jodell and the crew and walked straight over to the cooler to fish around in the ice-cold water for a soda pop.

"Mornin', y'all," he said, cheerily enough, as he popped the tab on top of the can of soda.

"Mornin'? Look at the sun. It's more like afternoon. Where the heck you been?"

Jodell didn't try to hide his irritation.

"Hey, Bonnie had to go to work this morning and I like to have never got a ride to the track."

"You should have come home last night then. Or taken a cab. We needed you to set the jets on the carbs this morning. We got a race to win, in case you forgot why we came here in the first place."

Bubba stood by uncomfortably, shifting from one foot to the other, waiting for an opening to ask a question about the tires. The rest of the crew worked busily, trying to ignore the exchange between Jodell and Joe.

"It won't take me long to set 'em. I just got to get my heart started first," Joe said, took a deep swig on the soda, then belched.

Jodell looked at him sharply, a hint of a spark or two in his deep-blue eyes.

"We don't have time for you to adjust them now. The practice session's about ready to start and we've got to get out there and see what we can find out."

"Sorry, man. I tried to get here. She had to wake her neighbor up to give me a ride in this morning." He took another draw on the pop and wiped a drop or two from his chin with the back of his hand. "What's eatin' you anyway, Jodell? Something's bothering you, why don't you just go ahead and say it."

There were flashes of lightning from his eyes now, too.

"Look, we're trying to win a race here today and you're lettin' your cattin' around get in the way of us gettin' the job done." He gave his cousin a hard, sideways look. "I think you need to get your priorities in order before it costs us more than it has already. We got too much riding on this car for you to mess it up with all your carrying on."

Now even Bubba Baxter pretended to be working so diligently that he couldn't hear what was being loudly spoken not ten feet away.

"Okay, okay. I don't see what business it is of yours what I do on my own time. Anyhow, I'm here now and ready to go and all you want to do is fuss. Calm down and we'll get it done."

Jodell stood there another ten seconds, deciding if this was the time or place to push his point. He finally turned

away. There'd be time later. Right now they had to concentrate on running this race.

They set about making the last of the changes. Jodell
decided to go ahead and let Joe jet the carburetors after
all. He figured it would be more valuable to see how the
car felt in race trim with the motor set up the way they
would run it in the race itself. His irritation and the sharp
words exchanged between the two cousins still hung
over the car like a dark cloud, though.

Joe went to work under the hood but Jodell noticed
the way his cousin's hands shook, likely from all the
drinking the night before and the late hours he had been
keeping since they had hit town. Still, he worked expertly and efficiently, jetting the motor for maximum
efficiency to match the day's weather conditions.

As he worked, Joe muttered to himself under his
breath. This had been one of the few times that he had
actually been this late to the track on race day since
they'd started their quest a dozen years before. Sure, he
enjoyed the parties and the young ladies that were so
numerous around the circuit. But Jodell Lee didn't have
a monopoly on wanting to win races. Winning was important to Joe Banker, too. He lived and breathed racing
and it hurt him to have his dedication questioned, and
especially in front of the rest of their crew.

Heck, he had actually slowed down some since the
days of Curtis Turner and Little Joe Weatherley and
Tiny Lund and their continual race-week parties and all-
night drinking sessions. Now it was usually only the
women who kept him out. It wasn't his fault he had
gotten caught without a ride to the track this time. That
the girl he had taken up with the night before lived all
the way out on Old Hickory Lake in Hendersonville.
Jodell didn't have to be such a jerk about it. He'd get
the carbs set. He always did. And he'd have the car
ready to win, too, also just like he always did.

The race cars finally began to roll out onto the track for the first practice session. With his crew still swarming all over the car and with Joe still elbow-deep in the carburetor, Jodell paced nervously, circling the Ford tensely, more than ready to be out there amongst them. He finally motioned for Johnny Holt to climb under the hood and help Joe get things buttoned back up. Then he pulled on his driving suit and climbed into the car and began buckling himself in so he'd be ready the instant they finished.

Out on the track the other cars were already counting off laps, experimenting, learning, while Jodell sat idly, impatiently tapping the steering wheel with his fingertips. Finally, Joe signaled for Jodell to fire up the Ford's engine and he jumped to do so, anxious to be on his way.

The motor rumbled to life. He let it idle for a minute or so as Joe stayed under the hood, looking things over. Then he gunned it a time or two while Joe and Johnny watched and listened, their heads cocked sideways. Joe finally pulled the hood down and latched it in place with the hood pins. Jodell shoved the car up into gear and steered out toward the track.

As he rolled slowly round the raceway, warming the car up, he tried to push the harsh words he had exchanged with Joe from his mind. It was time to focus on getting the car ready to race. To run fast, he would need his head clear of distractions and to concentrate on beating the track itself, not reliving the confrontation.

Jodell accelerated the car down the backstretch, pushing her now, ready to run his first hot lap. He pushed her deeply into the third turn, feeling the new tires bite into the track, sticking on the surface the way they were supposed to do. There was a slight squeal of protest from the tires as the car hugged the bottom line of the pavement. He sawed at the wheel, positioning the car for exiting turn four, and jammed his foot to the floorboard as he sped down past the front grandstand where some fans already had gathered to watch their favorites practice.

Billy Winton stood beside Johnny Holt on the wall, both men watching Jodell carefully as he built speed and circled the track. For once, Bubba Baxter was not there with them, in his usual spot, keeping an eye on the car all the way around all the time it was out there. Instead, he stood face to face with Joe Banker, over near the big upright toolbox. The two men appeared to be involved in a heated discussion. The noise of the practicing cars out there on the track drowned out their words, though.

Jodell ripped off a dozen or so very quick laps. He could feel the heat building inside the car, smell the hot rubber from the tires. It was an aroma he loved, though. It meant that he was able to push the car to the maximum, to heat the tires up with the speed he was attaining. And as the laps wore on, he fell into his rhythm, that point where he felt in tune with the car, its engine, the way she felt all the way around the track, and he forgot about everything else but the car beneath him and the next maneuver he would have to make to get around the course as quickly as he could. Slowly, surely, the car became nothing more than an extension of himself, as if he was actually willing the wheels to turn, the engine to slow and soar as need be to find its way around the course in one big hurry.

He couldn't help it. He felt his spirits soar, his heart pound harder inside his chest, and he let out a whoop of sheer joy. No matter how many times he steered a good race car around a course at speed, he never lost the visceral thrill of it all, the addicting intoxication that pure acceleration brought him.

Billy watched the car roll through the turn, learning all the time what to look for, and marveled once more at how adept Jodell Lee was at putting the car on the exact line necessary to maximize speed without careening to the wall, out of control. And then, he thought he saw a puff of smoke where there really shouldn't be any. He started to check with Johnny to see if he, too, had seen it, but Holt was watching another practicing car, trying to compare it to Jodell's lap.

Probably only smoke from the tires, he quickly decided. Jodell was pushing and they would be straining mightily to hang on. He watched even more intently through the next corner but he didn't see any smoke this time. He breathed again.

Back inside the car, Jodell was concentrating hard on hitting the correct line through each turn, the same line he would want to run in the race. He was now running with a pack of cars, all of them trying different lines around the track, looking for the fastest groove. Then, he caught a whiff of something that smelled like burning oil in the overheated air inside the cockpit. He chose to ignore it, assuming it was from one of the other cars running so close to him on the track. It would be impossible to tell which one, though, and they immediately left behind the smoke if there had been any.

Bubba hopped up beside Billy on the inside pit wall just as Jodell passed in front of them. He followed the car around for a lap, studying it carefully with squinted eyes and tightly clenched jaw.

"How's he running?" he asked without taking his eyes off the Ford.

"Seems real fast. The car is handling good all the way around. He looks like he's having just a bit of trouble trying to get by the slow cars, but then this place looks like it's pretty tricky," Billy replied, clearly proud of all he had learned about racing in such a short time. He deliberately didn't mention the smoke. He had seen no more anyway.

"Good. I'll mark the board so we can bring him in in about five laps so we can check things over."

Bubba scribbled a giant "5" and an arrow on the signboard and held it up high over his head as Jodell came out of turn four the next time. He flashed the board as the car came flying by, then got it ready for the next lap. Billy glanced over and noticed that Joe Banker was now standing atop one of the giant toolboxes with his stop watches, timing every lap Jodell ran.

It looked as if the tension of the morning had finally, gratefully, evaporated. Everyone was now focused on the job at hand: winning this race. The car was clearly fast and Jodell was driving it hard. They looked as if they could easily be a legitimate contender for the win.

Billy looked back toward the car just as Jodell let off the gas for an instant heading into turn one. Once more, he thought he saw a slight puff of smoke, but again he couldn't tell exactly where it had come from. He turned to mention it to Bubba but the big man was busily scribbling on the signboard. He decided he would wait to say something about it when Jodell brought the car in, only four laps from then.

Back out on the track, Jodell got hard into the gas as the car cleared the hump over the tunnel that ran beneath the backstretch coming off turn two. Once more, he caught a strong odor of burning oil as he made the run down the short straightaway and again wondered which of the cars he was running with would soon have a big problem.

He feathered the gas going into three and set the car up to smoothly take the corner, just the way he had already learned was the fastest way through.

KABOOM!

A bomb exploded directly in front of him, beneath the hood of his own car.

But before Jodell Lee could even realize where the

detonation had come from, he knew he was in trouble. The rear end of the car broke loose from the track, sending the car spinning around as she lost traction from all the oil pouring out of the bottom of the fractured engine.

The suddenness of the engine letting go and the dizzying spin of the car left Jodell disoriented. The car looped around once, then twice, pirouetting crazily. Luckily there was no one directly behind him to come piling into him like a bulldozer. The car drifted out toward the railing and backed into the fence, but with all the smoke it was difficult for Jodell to even tell where he was on the track, let alone what, exactly, he had hit as he skidded to a backward stop.

"Whoa!" Jodell yelped when he felt the jolt of the contact with the outside fence. "What was that?"

But then, one look at the smoking, steaming mess coming out from beneath his hood told him what had happened. And he immediately ran the possibilities through his mind, even as he began to unbuckle his belts.

Surprisingly, he wasn't as concerned about the blown motor at first. The engine they could probably replace. There was a spare one in the truck. They never went to a race without one anymore.

The damage to the back end of the car was what most worried him for the moment. He knew he'd backed into the wall solidly and there could be severe damage back there, a wound that might not be so easily or quickly fixed. And especially when they had an engine to replace, too, before they could race.

He waited for all the other cars to come around before he reached up and unfastened the net over the window. Then he pulled his long, lanky frame out through the opening just as a truckload of track workers came rolling up. Jodell leaned uphill against the banking to steady himself and sidled around to where he could survey the damage done to the back end.

He could see that the fender was crumpled in on the back of the car but, at least at first glance, it didn't look as bad as he had feared. He could only keep his fingers crossed that what he couldn't see was just as inconsequential.

"By the time the race is over tonight you might be looking a lot worse than this, Miss Jolene," he said out loud to the car, ignoring the strange stares of a couple of the track crew.

He took one last look at the damage and then walked down off the banking, heading straight back toward where the boys all stood watching him from the inside wall. As he walked, he stepped through a stream of fluids that were leaking from beneath the front end of the car.

Jodell climbed up over the low pit wall, still holding the driving helmet beneath his left arm. He grabbed a rag and wiped the sweat off his face and took a long drink of cold water when Bubba handed him a cupful.

"What happened?" Bubba asked.

"Don't know. The thing just blew up when I got out of the gas going into three. It was like somebody threw a bomb under the hood. Boom! And that was it. Next thing I know, I'm backed into the fence."

"How bad is she tore up?"

"The back end is not too bad, I don't think. I didn't hit it that hard. It'll look a lot worse before the night is over if we can get her out there and run her in the race. Under the hood? I don't know. We got some work to do."

Bubba turned to the rest of the crew and began barking orders like a drill sergeant.

"Randy, you and Clifford need to get over to the truck and start pulling that spare engine out. Billy, you might ought to go and help them and make sure they don't get sidetracked or nothing. We got to get that motor changed out quick as we can so we can see what we got to do to the rear end."

By then, the wrecker was hooking up to their damaged race car and getting ready to snake it off the track and out of the way of the other practicing cars, now idling under a waving yellow flag.

Joe had not even been a part of the discussion. He knew what they would need to do. He was already over by the large tool chest, beginning to lay out the tools he knew they would need to get the job done, looking for all the world like a surgeon prepping the operating room.

Everyone knew that Joe Banker took it personally every time one of his motors blew. Nobody was blaming him now. These things happened anytime machinery was involved. Even perfectly prepared engines sometimes came apart and blew up. It didn't happen often to Jodell Lee, though. Joe Banker made certain of that.

"Man, the car was running almost perfect. We just needed to make a couple of little bitty changes and we would have been set," Jodell was saying.

"Joe Dee, we'll get this motor swapped out and still have plenty of time to make those changes. For once we've got plenty of help at the track and Joe told me yesterday that the backup motor is just as strong or stronger than the one we had in the car. We were only going to run that motor here and then tomorrow in Maryville, then we were going to rebuild it anyway."

"I know, but I don't like putting the car into the fence. I hope we didn't mess anything up underneath the back end," Jodell said, now beginning to worry even more about those possibilities.

"Where is that car? We need to get to work on it," Bubba shouted impatiently in Johnny's direction.

"Coming in on the hook over there," he yelled back, pointing toward the exit of the turn.

The wrecker slowly pulled the dead race car down

past the front grandstands as if she was on parade. Oil was still dripping pitifully from underneath the ruptured engine, leaving a dark liquid line on the track trailing all the way back to where the car had backed into the turn-three wall. Track workers were spreading compound to absorb all the oil she had left there and then spilled all the way back to where the engine had erupted in the first place.

Johnny stood ready with the jack stands while Bubba rested on the handle of the floor jack, still barking orders to the others so they would be ready to go to work as soon as they got the car off the wrecker's hook. Joe peered under the car, trying to see what was left of his precious motor. He would have to wait until they got it back to the shop at home to take it apart and try to figure out what had gone wrong, though. There was no time today for an autopsy.

The kid working the controls at the back of the wrecker let the damaged car down with a thump as he dropped the front end much too hard. Jodell could only cringe as he watched it bounce and he thought of how precisely the front wheels had been lined up before, what would be required to align them once more.

"There goes a couple more hours of work," he said dully. He shot a sharp look at the kid but decided it was no good to lose his temper now. He simply didn't have time for such a luxury.

Johnny set about loosening one side of the hood while Billy, fresh back from helping load the replacement engine on its stand, undid the other side. Joe immediately dived in, assessing the damage as he got into position to start pulling it out. The engine had thrown a rod out the bottom and there was oil leaking from several ruptures in the block. A heavy layer of oil covered everything inside the motor compartment. It was hard to believe there had been that much oil in the motor to start with.

"This baby is history," he stated sadly.

"That's okay. We'll slap in the other one and we'll be good as new," Bubba assured him, and then he put his arm around Joe's shoulder.

"I don't understand what happened. That motor was fairly fresh and we didn't have anything that was really tricky in it anyway."

"Hey, everybody blows one up every now and then."

"My motors don't blow up," Joe said, still shaking his head back and forth.

Randy and Clifford showed up with the new engine then. It dangled from a large chain on its stand.

Joe climbed into one wheel well while Johnny settled into the other and they both began unbolting the engine. Bubba had crawled underneath the car to start loosening the bell housing. Billy worked on the front end of the engine, unfastening the belts and hoses. The steaming water from the radiator had spewed everywhere and it was hard to get their wrenches to stay in place on the slick bolts.

Jodell could only stand there, the top of his driving suit tied around the middle of his waist, watching while Randy and Clifford began to prep the new motor, or glancing over at the other cars that were still roaring past on the track as they continued practicing merrily. It was unusual for him not to be grabbing a wrench and helping, but for once they had a full crew, most of them fully capable of doing anything that had to be done on a race car. He didn't have a place to work.

Then he felt a tap on his shoulder and heard a familiar voice before he had even turned around.

"Tore up a pretty fast race car there, son."

"Uh, well, it ain't too fast for the time being."

There, standing not three feet in front of him, was Marty Robbins. Jodell knew the singer was a regular at the track in Nashville and occasionally drove other races on the circuit, but he was still shocked to see him standing there in the flesh looking sorrowfully at what was left of the Ford's engine.

"I guess it'll live again if you have another motor. But I sure thought you were going to knock the fence down when you first started to spin. I've popped that very spot pretty hard on occasion," Robbins said with a broad smile.

Jodell was not easily starstruck. He was accustomed to the fame that came along with being one of the top Grand National race car drivers. His name was well known all over the South. But to be standing here, casually talking with a true star, left him practically speechless. The fact that Robbins was Jodell's favorite singer didn't help the situation.

"You're gonna need a new bumper, too," the singer said as he inspected the crunched-in rear end.

"I'll probably need more than that before I get out of here tonight," Jodell offered. Robbins had a way of putting him at ease, and he actually seemed to understand what Jodell was telling him. "I'll be lucky to leave here with all the fenders on it. Four hundred laps around here can be pretty tough on a race car."

"Tell me about it. I can knock all the fenders off the car in twenty-five laps on a Saturday night. Heck, the way I drive sometimes, I can do that in the heat races!" Marty said with a grin.

Robbins raced strictly for the fun and thrills whenever he could fit it into his busy schedule. He always tried to do the last show on the Saturday Opry whenever possible so he could run in the feature at the Nashville Fairgrounds Raceway. Sometimes, the feature event ran late and that had cost him victories when the night's card ran past the time that he needed to leave to make it to the Opry. It was torture for a driver to have to park a race car when he was leading a race, but Marty Robbins had done it before.

"Which would you rather do, sing or race?" Jodell asked.

"Aw, I don't know if I would call what I do racing or not. But I like to play around in a car whenever I get a chance. It just isn't as often as I would like with the schedule I have to keep."

"I know what you mean about the schedules. More than three nights in a row in my own bed is a rare pleasure," Jodell said.

"I'm with you. Listen, I hope you have a good race, Jodell. You're good out there and always have a good car. I really enjoy watching you drive. I'll get out of your way and let you get back to work," Robbins said, shook his hand, and then turned to go.

Jodell was stunned. He could not believe his favorite singer actually knew his name. Actually knew his driving and considered him to be a good racer.

A sudden thought occurred to Jodell and he spoke before he considered what he was doing.

"Say, Marty. Could you give me an autograph for my wife? According to her, you're number one. We were at the Opry last night."

He immediately felt embarrassed and blushed a deep red. What in the world was he doing acting like a common fan? But the Opry star stopped and turned back and had a pleased grin on his face.

"Sure. I'd love to." Robbins seemed genuinely honored to have been asked. "What's your wife's name."

"Catherine, with a 'c.' Here, let me get a pen and paper," Jodell said as he rummaged around in the top of the large tool box.

Marty took the offered piece of paper, scribbled out a nice note to Catherine, then handed the folded sheet of paper back to Jodell.

"You got another piece of paper, Jodell?" he asked.
"Sure."

Jodell handed him another sheet from the toolbox.

"I'd appreciate it if you'd return the favor," Robbins said, handing the pen and paper back to Jodell.

"What?"

"Your autograph? I'd sure appreciate it."

Jodell quickly scribbled his signature on the scrap of paper, then scratched out the car number beneath and circled it, the way he always did. Next, he wrote out the words, "Green flags forever!" as he sometimes did for special autograph-seekers. Then he watched as Marty Robbins read it, winked, flashed his grin again, wished him luck, and finally walked away.

"Just try not to autograph that wall again," he called back over his shoulder.

Jodell tucked the note to Catherine into his pocket without reading it and strode back over to where the boys were still wrestling with the blown engine. They were at last ready to hoist it out and drop the new one in to take its place. It took all of them to maneuver the heavy motor back into the engine compartment and get it set on its mounts. Jodell was glad to finally be of some help and he joined right in as they swarmed all over the car, bolting the engine in, hooking up the hoses, tightening the belts, and making sure everything was taken care of.

The last practice was over by the time they had finally finished. Bubba climbed through the driver's side window, took a deep breath, and fired up the new motor. The engine came to life with a healthy roar. Joe Banker smiled for what certainly must have been the first time that day. For Jodell, there was only a healthy sense of relief. Now he could finally start to concentrate on the evening's race and try to put the unsettling events of the day so far behind him.

Bubba backed the car away from where they had been working on it and drove it down to the truck. Clifford and Randy had already moved most of the equipment that wouldn't be needed for the pit stops. Once Bubba had pulled the Ford to a stop, they all pitched in, peering under the hood and on the ground beneath the car to check for fluid leaks and anything else that seemed amiss.

While they finished up, and once he was convinced there was nothing else he could do until it was time to line up for the race, Jodell went off in search of Catherine and Joyce. He found the station wagon exactly where they had said it would be, parked outside the banking of the third turn. They had clearly been working hard themselves, spreading out on blankets the large picnic dinner they'd spent much of the afternoon preparing.

"Hmmm. Something smells good," Jodell said as he spied the small grill the girls had set up, its smoke advertising something wonderful. He made a move to steal a burger from the grate.

"Don't be getting any ideas now," Joyce Baxter said, threatening him with a large spatula she was wielding. She was busy cooking the aromatic and sizzling hamburgers over the hot coals. Catherine was nowhere to be seen. "Nobody eats 'til it's all ready and we still have a while to go."

"I got to have something before Bubba gets over here or I might not get a bite. And besides, I'm gonna need my strength for the race tonight, you know."

He peeked beneath the red checkered tablecloth that covered one of the full picnic baskets.

"I warned you, Mr. Jodell Bob Lee! Out of there!"

Joyce once again brandished the deadly spatula.

"What's going on here?" Catherine asked as she appeared from the other side of the car.

"I caught your husband trying to sneak into one of

our baskets. I took care of him, though," she said with a final hack in his direction with the spatula.

Jodell gave Catherine a quick kiss, helped her with the big cooler she was dragging, then pulled himself up onto the hood of the station wagon. She offered him a large glass of ice water and he gladly accepted it. He knew he needed to rest now and to keep taking in plenty of fluids for the long hot night that lay ahead of him. It wasn't unusual for him to lose ten pounds during a race in such hot, humid weather.

As the girls worked on supper, he ran through a litany of the day's troubles, how he had almost ended their weekend early with the blown engine. And he noted how it had been heartening to have a full crew to accomplish the motor swap so quickly.

Then, he casually mentioned that he had just remembered something, that someone had given him a note to pass on to a Mrs. Catherine Lee should he happen to run into her.

Catherine looked up from the grill and gave him a puzzled look through the blue smoke. She couldn't imagine who, in Nashville, Tennessee, would be asking her husband to pass a note to her.

"Who would give you a note for me?" she asked suspiciously. What kind of practical joke was Jodell playing on her?

"I don't know. I didn't really get a good look at him," Jodell said innocently as he fished in his pocket for the piece of paper. "Here you go."

As he handed it to her, Catherine still had a wary look on her face. She cautiously took the slip of paper, carefully unfolded it as if something evil might spring out of it, and then read the words written on it.

She read them silently first, then out loud.

" 'To Catherine, my number-one fan. I sang 'El Paso' just for you last night. Marty Robbins.' Jodell Bob Lee!

Are you pulling some kind of prank on me?"

"No honey," he answered, now serious. "I met him today in the pits. He came by and introduced himself and we talked some racing."

"I can't believe it!" she squealed, then jumped up onto the hood next to him and gave him a big kiss.

"He actually wanted my autograph, too. Can you believe that?"

Catherine had to hear a recap of the whole conversation while Joyce finally relented and allowed Jodell to sample one of the hamburgers off the grill. Then he trotted back toward the tunnel to tell the others that supper was waiting. Whether it was the look on Catherine's face when she saw the Robbins autograph, the fact that they had apparently successfully bounced back today from a major setback, or simply the adrenaline already kicking in from the quickly approaching race, Jodell Lee suddenly felt a wonderful exhilaration.

He didn't stop jogging until he was all the way back to where the crew was finishing up with the race car.

J odell Lee zipped up his driving suit with a flourish and climbed into the race car as if he meant business. No doubt it was going to be as hot a night as they had experienced in a while, the humidity of the day not dissipating much at all since the sun had gone to bed behind the fairgrounds' grandstands. He settled into the seat, trying to get comfortable before he began to fasten up the belts. Bubba waited until his driver was ready, then he performed his usual pre-race ritual, helping him buckle in securely.

Billy had shaken Joe awake a few minutes before. Banker had been catching a nap on the ground in the shade of the big toolbox. He blinked his eyes as if he wasn't sure where he was, then looked sheepishly at his wristwatch as he stood and stretched. Somehow, he had managed to doze right past the time for the drivers' meeting and most of the pre-race ceremonies. Not even the National Anthem, sung by one of Nashville's newest discoveries, nor the twenty-one-gun salute to the servicemen in Vietnam had awakened him.

In Joe's stead, Johnny Holt had gone to the drivers' meeting with Jodell. On the walk over and back they'd already discussed most of the race strategy.

As Jodell was fastening the last of the straps, Joe butted Bubba out of the way and stuck his head in the window of the Ford.

"These okay?" Joe asked, shoving beneath Jodell's nose the clipboard on which the pit sequences had been written out in Joe's precise hand.

"They're fine," he answered without really looking at them. His cousin still looked half-asleep, disoriented. "Look, Joe. This is nothing new. It ain't like we ain't raced here twice a year for the last ten years or so, cuz. We could do these stops in our sleep."

"I darn sure almost did. I'm sorry, Jodell. I don't mean to let y'all down. You know that."

"You didn't let us down. We need you good and fresh during the race. Johnny can set the car up as good as anybody can, but when it comes to making changes during the race, keeping me on my toes, scramblin' in the heat of battle, there ain't nobody any better than Joe Banker."

He showed his cousin a broad grin that confirmed he had put the afternoon's harsh words behind him.

Then Bubba butted Joe right back, pushing him out of the way as he resumed making sure Jodell was strapped into the cockpit good and tight before the call to start the engines came and found their driver only half gussied in. Joe pulled Johnny aside and reviewed what had gone on at the drivers' meeting and what the pit strategy was that Jodell wanted to try. Jodell was right. It was the same plan they had used here a dozen times before and there was really nothing new from the meeting.

Billy, Randy, and Clifford busily stacked tires and laid out air hoses in their pit stall, making certain everything would be ready once the race began. They went over the carefully typewritten checklist Joe had issued to them the day before, making sure nothing was overlooked in their pre-race setup. Once the race started, there would be no room for errors or time for scrambling. On this track, a slipup in the pits during green flag racing could cost a driver several laps, and they could be hard to make up again out there where the war was raging.

"Gentlemen, start your engines."

The words crackled over the loudspeakers in the grandstands, and then the screams and cheers of the packed-in fans and the throaty roar of the assembled racers washed out their echo.

Bubba still had his head in the window when Jodell reached up and pressed the starter switch. The big man gave the belts one last tug then pulled out of the car, listening critically as the powerful race motor came roaring to life. All along the front stretch, the engines in the three dozen or so cars sounded like captured thunder and the ground seemed to tremble in response to their grumbling.

Bubba reached in to shake Jodell's hand then fastened the protective window net. Jodell pulled down the goggles on his helmet and wriggled around some more, trying to find the most comfortable position. By design, the snug belts limited his movement and there would be little opportunity to shift around once they came up to speed.

Then he stared straight out the windshield at the open track that spun out ahead of him. When he glanced to his left he could see the crew backing away from the "Petty blue" number 43 Ford Torino. To his right, he could now see that the crowd was on their feet, and he knew they would stay standing well after the start, until several green flag laps had already been run and the race had settled down to a controlled frenzy.

As was his habit, Jodell ran through his own mental checklist one last time. He had just gotten to the last item when the officials waved the cars off the starting line. He could already feel the sweat beginning to form on his brow, and more perspiration tickled him as it ran down his ribs and over his back inside his driver's suit. The heat radiating from the headers running underneath the floorboards had already begun to build in the car and he was more than ready to get some cooling wind whistling through the windows.

They quickly ran off the pace laps and the cars rolling beneath the flagstand finally got the signal for one lap to go. Jodell scanned the oil and water temperature gauges even more attentively than normal. That was a brand new engine out there in front of him and it had been installed under the intense pressure of time. Thank goodness, all the needles were where they were supposed to be. Now would be a terrible time to discover something wrong.

He stretched his arms one last time, flexing his fingers, rotating his wrists, shaking his hands, and getting ready. He tried to visualize the line he wanted to take as he and Richard Petty would race side by side down into the first turn after taking the green flag in tandem with several dozen snorting beasts bearing down on them from behind. He pictured in his mind how he would try immediately to get the upper hand on Richard so he would have nothing but clear track ahead of him until he could catch up with the tail end of the field and start trying to put laps on some of the challengers. As they circled, he found the landmarks along the way where he would brake and accelerate, and he noted once more the best

spot to turn to whip into the odd pit road, all as if he
had never seen this track before tonight.

In the pits, Joe Banker was having problems keeping
his mind on the upcoming race. His head throbbed, his
stomach rolled dangerously, and he was clearly still suffering the effects of the late night, the tardy arrival at
the track, and the frustration of the blown engine. He
had hardly eaten any of the picnic lunch and now even
that bite or two was threatening to erupt on him. As the
cars thundered by to take the green flag, he tried to shake
off his case of the jitters, to concentrate on what he knew
he had to do for the next several hours.

Billy Winton was outwardly calm as he stood with the
others in the pits, but he was still wide-eyed, excited
about the whole show, still getting accustomed to the
color and hoopla of big-time racing. So far he had no
regrets about postponing his tour of America, and he had
to admit he was enjoying being a part of the Jodell Lee
race team. Even when it meant backbreaking, knuckle-
scraping work beneath a blistering sun like the quick
motor change had that afternoon. It was good being part
of something once again, though, something that mattered; to partake of the camaraderie of a group of men
all pointed in the same direction.

The last team he had been a member of had slowly
dwindled away, casualties of war, as his platoon had
been claimed, one by one. He had vowed not to grow
as close to anyone else again as he had with those men.
But he had already admitted to himself that he was not
much of a loner, that his months of bumming around by
himself had not been nearly as satisfying as he had
thought they might.

He pulled up his blue baseball cap and tucked his long
red hair back up underneath so it would be out of the
way during pit stops. He marveled at the undulating
crowd that filled the grandstand across the straightaway

from where the circular pit road was located. They were clearly primed for action, and, he had to admit, so was he. This was all so far from Vietnam, from all he had seen and done there, and he was surprised at how therapeutic it had all been so far. He already loved these people whose lives had somehow accidentally gotten entwined with his own. He genuinely enjoyed their company and he already felt as intensely as they did the need to excel, to conquer.

And being here, in this colorful, loud place, and spending the last few weeks alongside these salt-of-the-earth folks had all been like a soothing salve on some slow-healing wounds Billy Winton had been carrying around for a while now. For the first time in a long time, he felt as if he was part of something noble, part of a family, part of a quest.

He smiled as he watched Jodell's car glimmer in the bright lights as it rumbled past, as the others in the crew scrambled, checking for yet another time the equipment and tires they had inspected a dozen times already, as Bubba Baxter grinned and winked at him. He could only hope they would keep him along for the ride for a little longer, allow him to be a full-fledged member of the club until he had completely healed and was ready to go on to whatever next awaited him.

Catherine and Joyce had found themselves seats in the packed grandstands where they could get a good view of the track. They had given up scoring the races after the kids came along, even though that had been their best way to stay in touch with what their husbands did. Nowadays, Catherine liked to watch and follow every lap and pretend she was actually in the car with Jodell, helping him drive. Everyone teased her that she was as bad as Bubba Baxter when it came to using body English while watching a race. Joyce was one of the few who could tolerate being near her during the action, and even she complained of the bruises she picked up, especially in a tight race with the laps winding down to the end and Jodell in contention. Catherine Lee would become a regular whirling dervish then, trying to help her husband steer and accelerate and pull ahead, all from her spot way up there in the grandstand.

As they rolled down the back straightaway for the final time, heading inescapably to the green flag, Jodell twisted the car's steering wheel slightly side to side, making sure he scrubbed the racing tires clean of any debris they may have picked up. He certainly did not need the tires to break loose as he made that first hard charge down into the first turn, the green flag waving behind him. He glanced out his side window at the Petty car, trying to anticipate when the pole winner would make his jump for the start.

Side by side, the two cars at the head of the line rolled slowly through the fourth turn, waiting as patiently as they could for the flagman to wave the pendant high over his head. Jodell sensed when Petty stomped on the gas as they both saw the flag begin to flutter at precisely the same time. The two cars raced off down into the first turn with both drivers trying to get to exactly the same spot in the turn. The field followed them through, a hundred thundering horses' hooves pounding on the hot asphalt, each and every one intent on taking away the spot of the cars that led.

Jodell got a good start, managing to stay beside Petty heading into the turn. But the inside line was ever so slightly shorter than the outside one and that gave Petty the advantage running through one and two. He nosed out ahead by the width of a bumper, but then Jodell was able to outpower him as they came off the fourth corner. He pulled back even as both cars roared down the backstretch and they passed beneath the flagstand in a dead heat, nothing settled in the first lap at all except that it was going to be a night of tight racing. And to back it up, the rest of the field stayed tightly bunched, side by side, too, with only a couple of cars lagging already.

Jodell ran Petty hard into the first turn again, trying to see if he could stay beside him as they finally managed to put a couple of car lengths' distance between themselves and those drivers who were following behind. But then, Jodell felt the back end of the car start to lose traction, forcing him to tap the brakes just a bit harder than he had wanted to do. That allowed Petty to get past him, so Jodell settled in behind him and followed, now tightly locked to the leader's back bumper.

"Plenty of time for that, Annie," he told the car. He sensed she was ready to run, to have her head to challenge for the lead, but a tangle with the fence on lap one or two would do nothing more than send them packing for Chandler Cove before the moon was even up.

Up in the stands, Catherine was trying to shove Jodell past Richard Petty with her own gyrations. And, as she and Joyce watched, the two cars began to pull away from the others, even as they stayed locked so tightly together they may just as well have been joined at the bumpers.

"Go on, Jodell! Get around him!" Catherine screamed, but all the time she knew exactly what Jodell was doing, biding his time, looking for an opening he could use to drive ahead for a while.

"Go! Go! Go!" Joyce screamed, standing on her toes to attempt to see over the heads of all the other people who were standing, cheering, and watching the same duel that they were.

Now, the field of cars was slowly starting to string out around the track with a half-dozen or so battles for position going on at any one time. And as they did, the crowd finally began to sit, even as they picked out the particular battles between their favorites that they wanted to watch. It was like a three-ring circus with too much going on at any given time to take it all in.

It was only when someone politely asked them to please sit down that Catherine and Joyce realized they were the only ones left standing in their section. They eased down into their seats.

"He looks good!" Catherine yelled in Joyce's ear, barely loud enough to be heard over the din. "I was worried about how he would run after they had to replace the engine."

"I don't think you have a thing to worry about. Give him a few more laps and he'll pass the 43 and take the lead. Just you watch and see!"

"I hope so!" she said and smiled broadly as the clamor of the cars' engines once again drowned her out.

Jodell and Richard Petty were clearly setting a blistering pace for the others to try to match. Jodell's Ford and the 43 car of Petty's were certainly fast, but it soon became clear that several others were equal to the task. Bobby Isaac and David Pearson and a few others seemed perfectly willing to come on up and challenge the leaders once they had gotten clear of slower cars that had been holding them back.

It didn't take long at all before Petty and Lee were lapping the least competitive cars that marked the tail end of the field. But that also cost them. Catching up to the slower traffic upset the line Jodell had been taking in the turns and that allowed the others to catch up. It also gave Petty a chance to start to pull away by more and more, gaining a few car lengths' more lead with each lap.

Bubba stood beside one of the toolboxes watching Jodell begin to fall farther behind Petty. He knew the traffic played a role, but he also saw that the car was beginning to slip up higher in the corners as Jodell tried to maintain speed through the turns. As the tires heated up and began to wear down, Jodell was having trouble keeping the car down low on the track. It was already costing him precious speed and track position to the leader and giving the others behind him a chance to now draw closer, within striking distance.

"We need some tires," Bubba told Billy Winton. "He's gettin' real loose. We need ourselves a caution flag."

"That Richard Petty is stout. And the 71 Dodge is flying, too," Billy yelled over the deafening drone of the engines.

"We'll get 'em," Bubba shot back. "We got all night."

Billy gave him a confident thumbs-up, but he had to wonder how much longer Jodell could continue to lose position and have any chance of making it up.

A few laps later, two slower cars found themselves in a skidding, screeching embrace, dancing each other directly to the wall. The flagman quickly grabbed the yellow flag and waved it over the field, slowing them down before others could join the smoky tango.

When Bubba spotted the caution flag, he hooted excitedly and immediately started barking orders, yelling for everyone to get to position, grab what he was supposed to grab, and be ready when Jodell wheeled in for the much-needed pit stop.

Petty was first in, leading the colorful parade of race cars across the start/finish line and then veering into the first turn of the smaller quarter-mile track that served as the pit road for the night's race.

"All right, gentlemen. Let's be ready and let's be quick," Bubba shouted as he watched the cars pass slowly in front of them, heading for the quarter-mile loop.

Before Jodell had even rolled to a good stop, Randy and Clifford headed around to the right rear while Johnny worked on removing the right front tire. Clifford dropped one tire by Randy and held the other one, ready to stick it on the studs for Johnny once he got the lug nuts off. Bubba slid the jack up under the side of the car and gave it several hefty pumps, raising the right side of the car off the ground just far enough so the old tires could be pulled off and the new ones put on.

Billy hoisted the gas can high in the air and dumped its contents into the spout on the left rear of the race car. The pace car was already coming back around the track, exiting the third turn, so they had to hurry. Bubba watched the progress the boys were making changing the tires, already set to drop the car down off the jack as soon as they finished. Randy fumbled briefly with the lug nuts but finally got them fastened on tightly. Bubba dropped the jack.

"Go! Go! Go!" Bubba yelled, as if Jodell could actually hear him inside the car, and the big man actually gave the Ford a hard shove to help him spin away with a screech and boiling tire smoke. Jodell knew to pop the clutch and stomp the gas as soon as he felt the jack drop the car. He was away instantly and working his way back up through the gears as he steered back onto the track safely ahead of the pace car.

While the others put away the old tires and swept up the pits, Bubba watched Jodell circle the small quarter-mile track and sway back and forth to heat up the new rubber. It had been a good stop. To beat the pace car, it had to be. With the extra distance to travel around the quarter-mile inner track while making the pit stop, it was difficult to do all that had to be done to the car and still not lose a lap, even with the fastest of stops. But if there was any kind of bobble at all, there was a good chance a driver could go a lap down.

Now, with the speeds down and less wind pouring through the window, Jodell was sweating copiously in the oven that was the cockpit of the race car. He sensed that the caution period had come just in the nick of time for him. He had felt as if his car had been skating around the track for the last half dozen laps or so and he that he was fortunate to simply keep Petty in his sights and keep the rest of the field behind him. He was grateful, too, for the chance to catch his breath and stretch his arms. The car felt powerful beneath him, exactly the way he liked it. It would be a shame if handling and tires ended up costing him the race when he had such a superior motor working for him this night.

When the green flag once again was shown to the field, they all charged off into the first turn. Most of the field had been shuffled by the pit stops and everyone bumped and banged his way through the turns before setting sail once again at full speed down the back stretch. Jodell fought hard to maintain his second-place position but he was already getting pressure from behind from both Isaac and Pearson. It was Isaac that kept giving him gentle nudges on the back bumper, reminding him that he was back there and was interested in going on past.

While the three cars wrestled for position, Richard Petty set off on his own, leaving them to settle things among themselves while he drove away. It seemed his Ford was perfect on this particular night. It appeared capable of running wherever he wanted to put it on the track. High, low, it simply didn't seem to matter. Not long after the restart, in a startlingly short while, he was already passing some of the other cars, putting them a lap down with what had to be discouraging ease.

Meanwhile, Bubba Baxter was on his hands and knees in the pits studying the tires they had just taken off the car on the pit stop. Johnny was spinning around the one they had claimed from the right front and it didn't look good at all. A clear band of cord ran all the way around the outside edge of the tire, the rubber practically worn away.

"Hey, Joe. Looks like we got a problem," Bubba yelled up to where Joe Banker was standing on the toolbox timing the cars.

"Huh?" he grunted, cupping his hand to his ear.

Bubba motioned for him to get down and come over to where he still squatted, and then he pointed to the worn tire.

"Just a second!"

He held the stopwatch in his hand, waiting for Petty to flash by. He clicked the watch, then pushed the button again the instant Jodell roared past, a good twenty-five car lengths behind. The hands on the watch told the story. The interval between the two was growing a few tenths of a second every time they passed by.

With that reality confirmed, Joe finally climbed down off the toolbox and walked over to inspect the tire. Johnny rolled it around for him so he could see how severely it was wearing.

"Whoa! That's bad. Another couple of laps on that baby and he would have been in the fence hard."

Bubba sadly nodded his agreement.

"There ain't no way that he would have made more than another lap or two before that thing would have blown all to smithereens."

"How many laps did we run before that last stop?" Johnny asked as he ran his fingers over the mangled tire.

"About forty-seven, not counting the pace laps," Joe said, checking the numbers on the clipboard he had laid on the ground nearby. "Yep. Forty-seven."

"Is that all?"

"Yeah, that's it. That caution flag saved us."

"Johnny, go see if you can get a look at some of the other teams' tires they took off that stop and see if they're wearing the same way we are," Bubba shouted. "What do you think, Joe?"

"I think we better start short-pitting him if we don't

get the cautions. I knew this old track would eat up the
tires but I never dreamed they would go that quick.
Somebody needs to tell him on the next stop to go easy
on that right front. If he gets to racing it too hard, he'll
blow it out for sure."

"You keep an eye on his times and I'll watch the car,"
Bubba said. Joe had to read the big man's lips. "If he
gets to racing too hard for too long, we'll just have to
bring him on in right then."

It didn't take Bobby Isaac long to get by Jodell and
then set off in search of Petty. He simply waited for
Jodell to push up into the center of the corner a little
higher than he had been running. Then, in a flash, he
was underneath him and had gone past him. Pearson and
another car or two followed not too long afterwards.

The farther Jodell got into the race, the more he noticed the front end of the car wanted to ride up toward
the outside of the track. He was wrestling with the wheel
hard as he entered the turns just to get the wheels to
follow the contour of the track. And inevitably, the more
he had to fight the steering wheel, the more distance
Petty, Isaac, and the others were putting on him. It was
frustrating but there was nothing else that he could do.
Nothing at all.

Johnny came back then from checking the tires of
some of the other teams. He reported that some of them
were actually having the same trouble they were while
others weren't. Bubba could have guessed who the ones
having trouble were. Their crewmembers had already
come by their pit, peering over the wall trying to get a
glimpse of Jodell's used tires, too.

"Everybody's got some wear but I didn't see anything
as bad as our right front," Johnny recounted as he tried
to catch his breath.

"The toe-in or the camber must be off. Probably from
when that kid dropped it off the wrecker this morning.

I knew I should have checked it closer!" Bubba said, clearly disgusted with himself. He popped his fist hard into his open hand

He was in charge of everything on the car but the motor and it was his responsibility to make sure everything was right. He had checked over the front end, stringing the tires with a piece of twine. Everything had looked okay, but now, when it was far yonder too late to do anything about it, it was obvious that the front end had not been checked closely enough.

"The bad news is I got a look at Richard's tires. They ain't worn at all. If he don't have trouble it looks like it might be a long night for the rest of us," Johnny said in what was clearly an understatement.

Luckily, they caught another caution period after another thirty laps or so. They brought Jodell in twice so they could change all four tires without losing a lap. While he had the car jacked up, Bubba signaled Jodell to watch the right front tire.

Jodell nodded his understanding. Because of the way the car had been handling, he had suspected as much.

The caution period provided only a temporary reprieve for most of the cars. The domination by the front five or six racers continued again, unabated, once the green flag was shown once more. It was not long before the lead cars were again lapping the cars at the back of the field with Richard Petty bulldozing the way for the others to follow him through.

Jodell was driving conservatively, now even more aware that he couldn't push the tires too hard. And try as he might, he was still losing a tenth of a second or more on every lap around the Nashville track. If they ever had to pit under a green flag, he knew they would lose any hope of finishing well. They would drop at least two laps or more. Having to short-pit to keep from blowing the tires gave up even the slightest chance of winning, since Petty could apparently run twenty or thirty more laps on a set of tires than they could. Over the course of the race, that alone would translate into miles of difference on the track.

Catherine and Joyce watched the drama playing out on the track with mixed emotions. Now a hundred and fifty laps into the race, they were thrilled that Jodell was still valiantly holding on to his position in the lead lap, even if it was primarily due to good pit work and lucky breaks that brought out the caution flags. On three occasions somebody had either spun out or had blown an engine just when Petty had Jodell within his sights, ready to put him a lap down. But each time Jodell had been saved by someone else's misfortune.

Even from where they sat, the two women could tell that Jodell was struggling with the car. It seemed to have a mind of its own, wanting to rebelliously drift upward in the turns instead of obediently holding onto the line its stubborn driver dictated.

"He just can't hold the car down," Catherine said with frustration. She took a sip of her Coke without tasting it. "It's pushing bad."

"I know," Joyce agreed. They had eavesdropped enough on their men at work that they felt they knew almost as much about the cars as they did.

"Richard is so fast tonight."

"His car seems to be perfect. But then, we're still on the lead lap. We haven't lost it yet." Joyce said, glancing at the scoreboard to confirm her statement. She had also adopted Bubba's never-say-die attitude when it came to racing. Like her husband, she refused to give up until the checkered flag had finally flown over somebody else besides Jodell's Ford.

Inside the car, Jodell was stifling hot and growing more and more frustrated, but he was still as comfortable as he could manage. He was working hard to stay mentally focused, honed in on the job of wrestling the car around the track as smoothly as he could. He knew his only hope for a good finish was to be as easy on the tires as he could but still maintain a fast enough pace to avoid getting himself lapped. It would be a mighty tall order to try to make up even a single lap on the likes of Petty or Isaac or Pearson the way they seemed to be running this night.

"Stay on the lead lap and we got a fighting chance," he told the car. "Anything can happen at the finish, girl, if we're still around for it."

But if he went one down he'd be running only for position money. And that would gall Jodell Lee like nothing else. He hated being an also-ran.

But Bubba's signboard told him a discouraging story each time he went past. The leaders were coming at him, and they were coming in a hurry.

Jodell tried to pick up the pace, to stave off the inevitable as long as he could and hope for a caution to put them back even again. Now, he could easily see the blue 43 Ford looming in his rearview mirror, running only a straightaway behind and clearly gaining. Jodell adjusted his line in the corners, trying to find some more speed, gritting his teeth as he thought of the beating the tires were taking trying to keep the heavy car from going the way it wanted to go. But he tried not to think about that. He breathed in the sounds and the smells of the race and tried to think of nothing else but keeping the car at speed and on the track.

Joe looked down at his clipboard to check the number of laps since the last stop. There was no way around it. They would have to do something quickly. He signaled for Bubba to bring him in for a stop in four more laps, even as he was thinking to himself that two more would be smarter.

Bubba saw that the lead car was closing in. He didn't

want to bring in his driver now and doom him to a certain loss. It had been a while since anybody had broken or tangled, and he had been half-watching a furious battle between a half-dozen lapped cars that was clearly a demolition in progress. Maybe, with any luck at all, they could get the caution they so desperately needed before they conceded the race to one of the others.

Bubba walked over to where Joe stood and pointed out the cars that were beating and banging on each other going into the first turn.

"If we can hang on for a few more laps those guys are going to cause a big wreck. Even if they don't, Richard or one of them is going to catch us in about seven or eight more laps. Let's just wait 'til we get lapped, then we can bring him in."

"I don't know if the tires can hold out that long, Bub."

"We should be okay. He knows to take it easy on them."

"Yeah, I guess you're right," Joe said, but it was clear he wasn't totally sure of the decision. Half under his breath, he tried to talk himself into believing it was the right choice. "He's been running pretty smooth. That'll only be about forty-four laps on this set and he's been taking it easier than he did on the set we started with."

Bubba caught the gist of what he was saying. He had already conducted the same argument with himself.

"We'll get a new set on all around and be good as new. There ain't but a handful of cars we have to worry about and with a new set he might be able to get his lap back anyhow," Bubba said, hoping he sounded as confident as he tried to.

He didn't like taking the tires to the limit, but he also knew they would have to stretch them as far as they could or their shot at winning this race would probably go right into the garbage with the jettisoned tires.

"Let's get ready. We'll be bringing him in for the stop

in a couple of laps," Bubba yelled at the crew. He could see the doubt in their eyes, too. They knew the score as well as he and Joe did.

Clifford grabbed up a pair of new tires while the others began to ready themselves. Bubba began to scribble "PIT" in big letters on the signboard. All the while, out of the corner of his eye, he kept watch on the group of cars he was hoping would create their caution, their salvation.

Those cars were racing hard, not really for position because it hardly mattered back there where they were. They were simply racing each other because that's what race car drivers did.

Just then, two of the dueling cars bumped together hard with a flash of sparks.

Bubba stopped his scrawling on the board long enough to straighten up and watch, to hold his breath, to hope. At the same time, he could see that Richard Petty was now only seven or eight car lengths behind Jodell's Ford. But he watched one of the cars involved in the getting-together begin a long slow slide toward the outside fence while the other one straightened and drove on.

Bubba's heart stopped. Unless the driver in the skidding car made a remarkable recovery, they were likely now to get the caution flag they so desperately needed.

"Caution! Caution!" Bubba pleaded out loud, as if the flagman could hear him and would heed his words. Sure enough, up in the stand, the flagman was already reaching for the yellow banner.

But then, somehow, the driver of the out-of-control car gathered it back up at the last instant, barely grazed the railing, and used the slight bounce off the wall to right the car and head it in the direction he wanted to go. He was immediately right back on line, headed the way he had been going before, likely seeking out the driver that had given him the shot so he could return the favor.

The flagman returned the yellow flag to its holder.

"Dang it!" Bubba shouted, stomping his foot in the dust. Then he bent down, reluctantly picked up the sign-board with its message of surrender, and looked around for Jodell, ready to wave it in his direction when he came past. Then he saw Billy Winton, hopping up and down and pointing frantically in the general direction of the third turn.

Jodell Bob Lee had been checking the mirror each time he came off the corner. Every time, he had seen the blue 43 getting bigger and bigger as it resolutely closed in. He had had no choice but to push the car harder and harder, trying to stay on the lead lap with Petty. He knew it would take a caution if he was to have any shot at all at winning and it was his job to delay Petty's pass as long as he could, simply to give something time to happen. Jodell knew he would have to stay on the lead lap to have any chance of beating Petty unless the 43 broke something or somehow got involved in a crash.

Last time by, he had seen Bubba writing on the pit board, likely getting ready to bring him in anyway. Lord, he hated to give in that easily! To go down without a fight.

His arms were beginning to ache from all the sparring he had been doing with the wheel. Sweat poured down his face, but he hardly noticed. He had to concentrate on keeping in front of the 43. He was already planning how he would try to block Richard when he inevitably would try to pass, likely as they dove down into turn three. He felt the car settle down as he used the brakes to set his line for the turn. The tires gripped the pavement as the car started to turn once more against its will. He gave the steering wheel a big heave, trying with all his might to get the car to the center of the corner. He still had his foot on the brake as the Ford drifted through the turn.

BOOM!

Jodell felt it at the same instant he heard it. The car jerked hard to the right and sailed straight toward the wall as if it was on some kind of a suicide mission. Luckily for Jodell, he still had his foot on the brake. The instant it would have taken him to pull off the accelerator and find the brake pedal would have been all it would have taken to allow him to plow full speed into the wall. All he had to do was push down hard on the brake. That was enough to scrub off a little more speed as the car made the sudden short but direct trip to the outside railing.

Richard Petty had been closing quickly on Jodell, already positioning his car for the pass. He clearly saw the right front tire blow out, and he could see the car heading straight for the wall. He had only a second to react, to do the geometry in his head so as to figure where the wrecking car would bounce once it had contacted the wall. He jammed the brakes hard and jerked the wheel down to the inside. Sure enough, Jodell Lee's car bounced off the wall and veered back down the banking toward where Petty was heading.

Richard played the careening car like a pool shot, goosed the gas, touched the brake, twisted the wheel, and just managed to slide by as Jodell's damaged Ford skidded harmlessly past where he had just been.

Jodell slalomed to a smoky stop down on the inside of the track as cars zipped by him on the outside. His foot had been knocked off the clutch with the impact with the wall and that had stalled the engine. He shook his head for a second to clear his thoughts, then did a mental check of his body to see if anything might be broken while, at the same time, he reached for the starter switch to re-fire the motor.

The engine burped once, belched black smoke out the exhaust pipes, then caught and turned over, perfectly willing to tug him to wherever it was he wanted to go. He shoved the shifter up into first, trying to move the damaged car off the lip of the track and head for the pits. The car moved slowly down the backstretch, trailing a shower of sparks and slinging pieces of rubber. It was all he could do to hold her straight as she limped along like a horse on a bum leg.

Back in the pits, the crew saw for themselves that they were finally getting the yellow flag they had prayed for, just not from the car they would have preferred.

"Boys, let's get the tools ready. She looks pretty banged up," Bubba ordered as he picked up the jack and got himself set to do whatever it took to heal the Ford and get it back underway. They could all clearly see the long trail of sparks spilling out from behind the car and the way the Ford was shuddering and shaking as Jodell tried to bring her around.

"Tires are ready!" Clifford yelled, but it was doubtful if anyone heard him. The other cars were already roaring down along the pits, thankful for the chance to come in. The noise was almost unbearably loud.

As Jodell came slowly down the front stretch, the extent of the damage was obvious to the crowd in the grandstands. The right front tire was not only flat but the wheel was cocked out at an odd angle to the side of the car.

Catherine covered her face with her hands. Losing was as painful to her as it was to her husband. Maybe more so because she felt not only her own disappointment but absorbed Jodell's agony, too. She couldn't bear to watch him as he limped to the pits, his night severely curtailed if not totally finished.

Jodell drove the battered car right on past the entrance to the pits and went instead to where they had parked the truck. There was little they could do to heal these wounds in the pits. It was going to take some surgery.

Bubba watched the car go on past the pit entrance and, even though the left side of the racer looked perfect, he felt his stomach fall. If he was heading for the truck, Jodell must know it's serious, not just a flat tire and some sheet metal damage.

"He's taking her to the truck. Let's bring all the tools we can. Looks like we got a lot of work to do."

He heaved one of the heavy toolboxes onto the wagon along with the jack. Johnny joined Randy and Clifford in stacking a set of tires and the jack stands onto the other wagon. Billy grabbed a handful of parts and they all took off for the garage as soon as they could safely cross the pit road.

Jodell parked the smoking car, sat there for a moment, and then dejectedly climbed out. The stench of burning rubber filled the air. He looked at the skewed front wheel and all the damage in the area and could only shake his head. Finally, he gave the smoldering tire a swift kick and then plopped down hard on the running board of the truck.

Somehow, the kick made him feel a little better. Not much, but some.

Bubba and the boys came galloping up then, towing the wagons, huffing from the run.

"Y'all might as well slow down. There ain't nothing broke that can be fixed in a hurry," Jodell said, shaking his head in disgust.

"Billy, grab those jack stands," Bubba said, ignoring his driver as he set the jack and raised the car up for a look-see for himself.

Billy placed the stands under the car while Randy grabbed the other pair and placed them under the left side. Johnny was already trying to take the still-smoking wheel off the mangled spindle assembly. The car had apparently hit the wall squarely on the right front tire. The fender was crumpled up, but not so badly it couldn't be quickly hammered back out. Most of the damage was centered on the wheel, the A-frame, and the controlling arms.

"Ow!" Johnny yelped, shaking the hand he had just burned. "That thing is still hot!"

He pulled on some gloves and finished taking off the bent wheel, then tossed it aside so they could get a good look at the real damage.

"I don't know, Bubba. She's pretty chewed up in here."

Bubba studied the mess and nibbled on his lower lip.

"Well, we got to fix it anyway for tomorrow in Maryville, if nothing else. Let's hustle with it, guys. If we can fix it in a hurry and do a little on the toe-in and camber, we can run with it a few laps here and maybe we'll know where we stand for tomorrow."

Bubba stooped down and stuck his head into the fender well. He winced at the sight of all the bent metal. He came back out, shaking his head, but quickly got everyone working on the damage.

As they worked, they would look up occasionally to check the scoreboard or watch as another damaged car was towed in next to them. Joe stayed in their pit watching the progress of the race and making notes for the next time they would face these same cars and drivers. Petty was clearly dominating. Only Bobby Isaac could hang on the same lap with him. Everyone else was already laps down to the two of them.

With still about forty laps left to go in the race and its outcome already decided, Jodell pulled the Ford back out on to the track. Catherine and Joyce rose and screamed wildly, jumping up and down as he went by as if he was leading to the checkered flag. They were surprised to see quite a few others in the crowd do the same, fans who where clearly happy to see their favorite driver back out there even if only to circle and finish a hopeless race.

When the checkered flag finally fell, Jodell was admittedly glad to see the night end. He was hot, tired, and disgusted. He knew they would hardly cash a big enough check to buy the gas to get back home, much less pay for all the tires they wore out and the parts they had used up. It was especially frustrating since the Ford handled perfectly after they had fixed it and he had gotten back out on the track. He found he could run with Petty and Isaac easily and knew he could have had a chance if they had not missed the setup and had not had the blowout.

He watched Petty head to victory lane while he sadly pulled his own Ford down to the truck. He slowly crawled out of the car and flopped down on the ground beside it, too tired and irritated to begin getting it ready to haul away.

"Here you go, Joe Dee. Maybe this will help."

Bubba draped a cold, wet towel around his neck and handed him a paper cup full of ice water.

"What a night!" Jodell said, shaking his head as he crunched noisily on a piece of ice. He poured some of the water down the back of his racing suit and then shivered, but it felt wonderful.

Before long the gates to the infield were opened and a swarm of fans, Catherine and Joyce among them, crossed the track and descended on the drivers and their cars. As Jodell and Catherine talked quietly, a little boy came up and thrust a program and a pen in front of him. Tired as he was, Jodell smiled at the boy and politely signed his name on the page where his picture was.

Before long there was a steady stream of autograph

seekers and he patiently sat and signed for all comers.
The victory lane celebration ended and the Pettys started
moving equipment down to their truck, which had been
parked near where Jodell's was.

Richard himself finally came walking down after doing all the interviews and picture-taking that went with
being a race winner. A seemingly endless line of fans,
many calling his name and thrusting their programs and
pens at him, trailed along behind him, but he was good-
naturedly talking and signing as he walked, no matter
that he was likely exhausted, too.

Jodell stepped over to congratulate him and soon
found himself swarmed by the fans as well.

"You better take yourself a seat, Joe Dee. We might
be here awhile," Petty said, showing his famous grin and
settling down on the tailgate of his pickup truck.

Two hours later they were still sitting there signing
autographs, even as some of the other racers' trucks had
long since departed the speedway.

"Richard, how do you do this? Don't you ever get
tired?" Jodell asked as they finished up with the last of
the fans.

"Sure, I get tired. But remember one thing. These cats
are who pay to come out and see us run. If not for them,
we might have to get real jobs!"

"But they don't seem to care that I finished in the
bottom ten tonight."

"Look, they know you gave it your best. And don't
forget, you're living a dream a lot of them have, being
out there driving a good race car and having a chance
at winning. You got a lot of folks who pull for you and
a lot more who would swap places with you in second."
A kid with a flattop haircut, likely not more than ten
years old, stepped up bravely then and handed Richard
a program to be signed. "And there's a lot more that
would love to grow up and be just like you."

"I like you just fine, Mr. Petty," the kid said, right on cue. "But I'm a Jodell Lee fan. You're the best, sir. Don't worry. You'll do better next race."

Jodell thanked the boy, patted him gently on the head, signed his name, and then added the "green flags" note with a happy brandishing of the pen.

Suddenly, he wanted to see his own kids in the worst way. And he noticed that Catherine was standing there next to him, smiling, likely reading his mind. He gave her a hug and they walked arm in arm back toward where the crew was loading up his car, ready to head out for the next chance to win.

The late August heat had laid its heavy-handed claim on Chandler Cove, Tennessee. There was no hint at all that autumn was less than a month away, despite the promise of the numbers on the auto parts store calendar that hung from a nail on the wall of the Jodell Lee race shop. The doors had been swung wide open since early morning, hoping to capture even the slightest breeze, but so far it had only admitted dusty heat, the occasional stray chicken from Grandma Lee's coop, and a wasp or two that had lazily buzzed in.

But the open doors also allowed an awful lot of racket to escape from inside the place. The clamor of a hammer banging on bare metal echoed off the nearby buildings and, in the still air, even found its way along the finger-like hollows and up the mountainsides.

The commotion didn't seem to be bothering Pit Stop, though. That was the blue tick hound that belonged to

Jodell's son. The pup ignored all the noise, twitching slightly with his rabbit-chasing dreams, otherwise sleeping peacefully in the shade of the shop building.

Inside, in the middle of the metal-banging bedlam, Billy Winton was sprawled on his back beneath the front fender of the race car. It was the racer that they had most recently been running on the shorter tracks. The car looked most like a smashed soda pop can. It had been swept up in somebody else's wreck a couple of nights before. The front end had been almost torn away and now Billy was doing his best to finish the job, to clear the mangled mess away down to the frame so they could start all over. His muscles tensed with each blow with the hammer, his shirtless chest shone with sweat, and his long red hair whipped from side to side as he forcefully pounded away.

Bubba Baxter was all the way across the shop, lovingly inspecting a car that was in far better shape. The bright glare of the overhead lights glinted off the sheet metal and the sun spilling through the shop window cast a glow like a spotlight on the spanking new car they had just finished building. Unlike the disfigured hulk Billy was whacking away at, this racer was slick and clean, freshly painted with primer, almost ready for her birth on a racetrack.

She looked sleek, feline, ready to run, and Bubba could almost imagine he could hear her purr as he ran his hand over her smooth lines.

"I hope you're ready," he told her. "They're gonna be runnin' them new winged Dodges down at Talladega and if you ain't ready, you may get yourself dusted right off that big old track."

And from what he was hearing about the amazing new track that had been gouged out of the red East Alabama clay, it might have been more appropriate for them to have put wings on the Ford instead of fenders. The place had been an old Air Corps base, after all. Word was that "flying" would be the order of the day once the drivers showed up with their big-track cars and set them free on the impossibly high-banked turns.

Bubba had spent most of the morning inspecting every inch of their car, deliberately listing out on a clipboard all the things that still needed to be done to get it ready to his satisfaction for its first race. He had poured his heart and soul into this car, using everything he had learned in their years of running Charlotte and Daytona, the only comparable tracks to the one they expected to encounter in Talladega. But even then, he couldn't be certain if he was on target or not.

This course would be different territory, unlike any place any of the drivers had ever seen before. Bubba's plan was to take the car down to Alabama in two weeks and see what they had wrought. Only by actually taking her out for a spin on the massive track would they know for sure if they had built a jet or a crop-duster.

All the talk they'd been hearing over the last couple of months about the giant track was that it was going to be big, wide, and lightning fast. For that reason Bubba had decided, with Joe and Jodell's immediate concurrence, to sell the Daytona car and start building them a brand new racer to take to Alabama. The months of hard work were finally beginning to pay off. The new car stood there, almost ready save for a few more coats of paint and the insertion of her engine, her body shining in the hot afternoon sun.

Lately, there had been other more disturbing news from the new track. Tire wear was far worse than anyone had ever seen before. Most everyone was certain, though, that the tire manufacturers would solve the problems before the week of the race. Somehow, they always managed to find the right compound to match the speeds and the surfaces of the tracks.

Since it was located only fifty miles from his home base near Birmingham, Bobby Allison had tested at the track in late July. He was very popular among the drivers at the next few races as they tried to glean information from him. He had given Jodell and Joe a detailed run-down, and one comment from Bobby stuck in their minds:

"She's rough. Just ground the tires up like hamburger meat. Rough. Real rough."

Some of the other Ford teams had tested a couple of weeks later and their comments had been much of the same. At a hundred and eighty miles an hour, it wasn't hard to keep the tires under the car at all. But when the car was pushed up to the limit, when the speeds exceeded a hundred and ninety miles per hour, the rubber beneath it was simply chewed away in only a couple of laps.

"You mean a couple of dozen laps," Joe Banker told the driver bearing the disturbing news.

"Nossir. A couple of laps. Right now, by the time you do two laps to qualify the car, you're gonna have to throw the tires away."

Joe shook his head.

"Goodyear and Firestone will work something out," Jodell said hopefully. They had to come up with a solution. They couldn't race on a track that was that rough on tires. And there was most definitely a race scheduled at the new Alabama track. "You can't have a race and not run the car as hard as it'll go. That ain't a race at all. They'll fix the tires!"

"What if it's the track and not the tires?" Joe countered. "What if they can't come up with a tire that'll last? What if we simply can't go that fast?"

"Just remember back to when we went to Daytona for the first time. Remember all the things people were saying about the track down there? That you couldn't keep a car as heavy as what we run on a track that fast? That the speeds would scramble our brains? Don't worry, they'll get it fixed."

Joe was still not convinced. But since it was his cousin who drove the car, he hushed, not wanting to put any doubts in Jodell's mind that might make him hesitant during a race.

All the tire talk failed to faze Bubba Baxter. He did what he always did when they built a new car: tried to make it the fastest car he legally could while making certain it was the safest machine possible. They had all put hundreds of hours, plenty of sweat, and innumerable busted knuckles into getting the new car track-worthy. And finally, Bubba Baxter had pronounced it to be "fast as a saber-jet," a winner for sure in the inaugural race at Talladega.

"Hey Bubba, when you get through admiring your handiwork, can you come over here and give me a hand?" Billy Winton had stopped whacking away at the wrecked car's front end and was now lying on his back on the cool cement floor, resting for a minute.

"Yeah, just hold your horses," Bubba answered, all the while scribbling on a sheet of paper on his clipboard. He had gotten as bad as Joe Banker with his eternal checklists. He, too, felt unprepared if he didn't have pages of checked-off items to assure he had not over-looked something crucial.

"We just gotta get these parts stripped off this after-noon before Joe and Jodell get back with the new stuff."

Bubba knelt down beside the mangled fender that Billy had been wrestling with for the past hour.

"All righty. What you need?"

"Grab this ear and pull back on it while I try to get this bolt loose."

"Got it."

Bubba smiled. He was pleased with the way Billy

Winton had fit into the team and what a valuable member he had become. He had been a lucky find, all right.

"Got it? Let's see what I can do."

Billy grunted as he struggled with the stubborn bolt. With the angle the metal had been bent, it was difficult to get serious leverage with the wrench.

"You need me to come under there and give you a hand?" Bubba asked as he watched Billy strain at the wrench.

"Naw, I can get it. It's just tight. Hang on. I think I'm getting it." He let out one more groan while Bubba gave a powerful heave on the disfigured fender as Billy cranked away on the loosened bolts. Working it back and forth, he was finally able to break the piece loose with a loud snap.

"Got it!" he said as he tossed the twisted metal off to the side. It landed on the cement with a resounding clang. Junior's puppy dog didn't even flinch. "I'll have to hand it to Jodell. He sure tore it up good this time."

"He did smack that other car a ton, didn't he? We're going to end up ripping off the whole front end it looks like. Good thing we got a couple of weeks to get her fixed before Hickory."

"Yeah and a good thing we already got the car ready for Darlington, too, or we would be in trouble. I don't want the Talladega car to even touch a racetrack until we drive it off the trailer down there."

"I'm still amazed at what all there is to be done around a race shop," Billy said, pausing to wipe the sweat from his face. "I figured you just changed the oil and put in some gas and went racing. And I never thought about keeping different cars for different kinds of tracks."

"Was a time, and not so long ago, we did most of the work on the single car we had while we were at the tracks, in motel parking lots, or on the side of the road somewhere. Any flat place we could find. Heck, me and Joe changed out an engine by flashlight in the parking lot at North Wilkesboro one time 'cause we were there too early for the gates to be open yet."

Billy remained amazed that, with all the races they had run and all the travel they had done between tracks, they had still managed to fix the damaged cars, get the other cars ready to race, and yet had found time to build a brand new car from the axles on up. Granted, they had managed all the accomplishments primarily by working eighteen and twenty hour days when they were at home in Chandler Cove and by always fixing as much of the damage as possible on a wrecked car at the track.

"Ow!"

Billy had gotten a wad of his long red hair caught between two pieces of metal and it had yanked it hard when he loosened the bolt holding one of them.

"Why don't you cut that stuff off, Billy? If that car don't snatch you baldheaded first, you're gonna get us whipped up on by a bunch of rednecks one of these nights. You know they don't care for hippies."

"I ain't no hippie, Bub. And most rednecks have more hair than I do these days."

"I know you ain't one of them Beatniks, and you know it, too, but what I'm saying is that with all that hair you got, some redneck somewhere is gonna mistake you for one. And then we're going to wind up having to prove you ain't into peace and love and such. And you know how much I hate to fight."

"Well, okay, but I still don't see what my hair has got to do with this," Billy said, but he was laughing. He'd seen Big Bubba fighting within an hour of their first meeting, and he had seen him in the midst of more than one dispute already at various tracks they had run. "I'm wondering if it ain't just jealousy on your part."

Bubba instinctively put a hand on the recently developed bald spot on the crown of his head. He usually kept it covered with a baseball cap. He gave Billy a mock scowl.

"Aw, hush! You just keep all that stuff tucked up under your hat so I don't have to start a new career as your bodyguard. Understand?"

"You got it wrong, Bub. I want to become *your* bodyguard! And I've had some practice at it already."

They jawed good-naturedly at each other as they worked on the car. It was clear that they had become fast friends in a remarkably short period of time. Bubba Baxter was a typically clannish mountain man, suspicious of strangers, slow to welcome anyone into their inner circle. But somehow, Billy Winton had won him over quickly.

It was late afternoon but still stifling hot when Jodell and Joe finally returned with the parts they needed. Bubba stood in the doorway waiting for them to ease on up the driveway, arms akimbo, covered in sweat, dirt and grease.

"Glad y'all could join us. You sure you don't want a cold drink or a nice nap in the shade before we get to work?"

"Hey, Bubba. If you would kindly open me up one . . ." Joe grinned as he began unloading the parts from the pickup.

Then Jodell, Bubba, and Billy dived in, working hard with the torch and wrenches, gradually piecing the maimed car back to health. Working with the torch in the ovenlike barn only made it hotter and the three men were quickly sweat-soaked, going to the cooler often for drinks. But slowly, the hunk of mangled metal once again began to resemble a race car as they banged, hammered and tightened down the new pieces on the car's front end.

Meanwhile, Joe had his own project underway. He

was putting the finishing touches on a motor in the side room where they usually built and tested the engines. As he labored, he sang quietly to himself, oblivious to the hissing torch, metallic hammering, and the cussing and banter that drifted from across the way where the others worked beneath the short-track car.

He had his work cut out for him. Joe Banker was up to his elbows in a big chunk of metal that hung from chains wrapped around the barn rafters. He was building the race motor for the Talladega car and he was calling on everything he had learned so far in the racing game. If he fulfilled his mission, this one was going to be his masterpiece, powerful, dependable, and perfectly capable of pulling the new car around the track at whatever speeds necessary for them to capture the first race on that breathtaking new track.

Joe was finally in his element with the big four-hundred-plus–cubic-inch engines that they were running nowadays. He relished the way they vibrated the whole car when their fuses were lit, the way they caused his body to tremble in response to their explosive power. It bordered on sensuality, and Joe Banker loved the big motors every bit as much as he had ever loved a woman.

Sometimes, he felt as if he was some kind of modern Dr. Frankenstein, breathing life into a dead mass of cast iron and machinery. It was the closest to fathering a child as he had ever come and sometimes he wondered if it would be the only parenting he would ever do.

Of course, that also explained why he took it so personally any time one of his engines expired. As exhilarating as it was when one of his creations pushed across the finish line ahead of all the rest, his mournful feeling when one died was just as deep.

He had to admit that it sometimes bothered him when Jodell would get all the credit for winning the races, as if the driver could have come in first without a motor that would get him there. But occasionally, a particularly knowledgeable sportswriter would mention him and his winning engine in an article. Or a savvy fan would run him down after a race and congratulate him on the great engine he had built. Or other teams' crewmembers would grudgingly admit that he had the better mill that day, just before they tried to find out from him what he had done that they hadn't.

He tried not to be jealous. And to be fair, Jodell always mentioned him and the rest of the crew when he made his victory speech.

But now, he might finally get his due. The engine appeared to be everything at a track like Talladega. The driver was simply along for the ride, his only chore to keep his foot to the floor and try to steer where nobody else was.

Yes, it would be the engine at Talladega, more important than ever before. And Joe Banker couldn't wait to unveil this one for the sportswriters, the fans, and the other teams.

He sang even louder now as he wiggled the fingers of both hands like a surgeon about to pull on his rubber gloves, grab a scalpel and some sutures, and start to work. He couldn't wait to get back to his latest creation.

Days and nights seemed to merge together end-
lessly over, the next few weeks. They were so
busy trying to get done all they needed to that
they lost all track of time, not even noticing if it was
daylight or dark outside the shop. The only break was
the Labor Day trip down to Darlington, South Carolina.
There had been no trouble telling night from day there.
The late-summer sun had been relentless, a wilting fire
in the sky that seemed to suck the air right of a man's
lungs as he worked in the engine compartment of a race
car. Or to seek him out, even when he hid in the shade
beneath the car, leaving him sweat-soaked and dehy-
drated.

"If hell's any hotter than South Carolina, then I certainly don't want no part of it," Jodell had said as he
wiped his grimy face with his bandanna.

"Shoot, this heat has done about ruined my appetite,"

Bubba had declared, and everybody had been too de-
flated to even jump on so obvious a straight line.

But stifling heat or not, the Southern 500 on Labor
Day Monday was still one of the premier races on the
circuit. And it carried special meaning for Jodell Lee and
his team. True, it had been the site of the first Grand
National race they had ever run, but it had other histor-
ical significance, too. It had been in Darlington, at one
of driver Curtis Turner's legendary parties, the first one
they had attended before their first big-time race, that
Bubba had met Joyce, his wife-to-be.

As Jodell loved to relate to anybody who would listen,
Bubba would likely have missed her altogether had he
not been camped out on the back steps of the tourist
court in a very strategic position. He had found him a
spot where he could keep a steely eye on a pig that had
been roasting on a spit nearby. He had wanted to be
ready to claim the first slices of barbecue when it was
finally fit to eat. Joyce had sat down next to him on the
steps and, when she found he was part of a crew that
would be running in the race the next day, she had struck
up a conversation about her newly acquired love for the
sport. The next thing he knew, Bubba had forgotten the
succulent pig altogether and he had fallen hopelessly in
love. Now, quite a few years, a wonderful marriage, and
two delightful kids later, Darlington was still Bubba's
favorite stop on the circuit.

It wasn't just the personal history that made it so,
though. Baxter also loved the Darlington track itself, the
way it required the best setup, the most intense driving,
the utmost skill of crew and driver combined to ever
hope to conquer its narrow turns and lightning fast
straightaways. No other track demanded as much from
men and their equipment. And that's precisely what
Bubba Baxter thought racing should be all about.

The Sunday parties, which sprang up spontaneously

on the unusual off-day between Saturday qualifying and the race itself on the Monday holiday, made the stop even more fun, all the heat, dust, and hard work notwithstanding. By now, though, the festivities were nothing like what they had once been. Curtis Turner and his usual sidekick, the legendary driver Little Joe Weatherley, had been the ones to proudly hold court over the brawling soirees that had run on for days.

They had been seemingly endless parties that had only reluctantly abated long enough for the race itself to be run, almost as an afterthought to some. And then, after the race, they'd catch a second breath and resume again where they had left off, win or lose, taking the form of wild victory celebrations.

Jodell had never cared much for the parties themselves. He saw them as more of a distraction from the job at hand: winning a very important race. He almost always attended them, though, spending most of the time pumping the crewmembers and drivers who were there for information on the track and how they planned to run it. The free-flowing liquor usually made tongues loose and valuable intelligence would be there for the taking.

Jodell had to admit, though, that over the years the get-togethers at Darlington and the other tracks gave him a rare chance to relax and spend time with the closest thing he had to a family when he was away from Chandler Cove. The barbecue was usually good, the drinks cold, and the fellowship just as refreshing when he could spend time with others who shared the same hardships of their adopted sport. Sometimes, he felt for all the world like some of the other drivers were the brothers he had never had. It at least kept him from missing his wife and children so much when the competition prevented him from being home for weeks at a time.

But then, despite all their hard work and anticipation,

the race at Darlington had been a frustrating one for the team. Early on, they had gotten caught a couple of laps down when the caution flag came out shortly after they pitted to change tires and take on a couple of cans of gasoline. It was a familiar story at the mythical track. Even though they had a race car that was competitively fast, luck simply seemed to have turned her fickle back on them.

Lee Roy Yarbrough, driving for Junior Johnson, went on to take the win. David Pearson and Buddy Baker finished on the lead lap.

It had been a tough race for practically everyone else, but that was small consolation for Jodell and his crew. Afterward at the shop, there was no time to lick their wounds. They had to hustle to get the short-track car ready for the race in Hickory, North Carolina, on the fifth of September, then on to Richmond two days later. Since they planned to show up at the new track at Talladega on Monday, September eighth ready to start testing, they only had about three days left to make sure both the short track car and the new superspeedway car were ready to burst from the chute. There would be precious time to tweak once they were in the thick of competition.

They limped into Chandler Cove after the drive up from Darlington, easing into the clearing in front of the barn shop in the wee hours of the morning, too bushed to do much unloading. Grandma Lee had left a freshly baked chocolate cake on the shop bench and a gallon of milk chilling in a bucket of ice on the floor, but they had been too tired to truly enjoy it. They had eaten quickly, hardly talking at all as they did, then had sleepily dispersed to their various houses for what little rest they could get before the sun was up and it was time to go back to work.

Only a few hours later, they were back in the shop,

trying to hang the fenders on the shorttrack car so it
would be ready for Friday night's race at Hickory. Like
Darlington, the track in western North Carolina had special meaning for Jodell, Bubba and Joe. It had been there
that they had captured their first major victory in the
sportsman race years before. It was one of the tracks
where Jodell always felt he would win, even before the
green flag sent them sliding and skewing around its tight
four-tenths-of-a-mile orbit.

Bubba, Johnny, and Jodell were busily laboring over
the short-track car, putting the last touches on the sheet
metal and setting up the front suspension based on hard-
won experience at Hickory. Joe, meanwhile, worked inside one of his engines. Billy Winton was putting the
final coats of paint on the speedway car. The fumes from
the sprayer had quickly filled the inside of the shop with
a blue, noxious haze.

Johnny Holt had been carefully lining up the measur-
ing tape so they could cut a piece of metal for the fender.

"Man, that paint is giving me a headache!" he howled.
"Can't we open up a door and get some air in here?"

"Nossir," Bubba said without hesitation. He was covered with sweat and his eyes were watering and he was
sneezing from the fumes himself, but he shook his head
determinedly. "It's too windy out there. We don't need
nothing spotting up the finish on that car. It's got to look
good."

"Once it gets a bunch of dents in it like this car it
won't matter a hill of beans, Bub. My head's about to
split wide open and I think I'm gettin' high as a kite."

"It matters a whole bunch to me, so shut up."

"I feel like I been smokin' some of that LSD," Johnny
growled, faking a staggering, wild-eyed swoon.

"You don't smoke LSD, you moron."

"I don't have to with Billy over there giving us all

brain damage. I bet you the inside of my lungs is done painted blue as that car is."

"Y'all bickering like a couple of old women is giving me a worse headache than the paint fumes ever could," Jodell interjected as he stood and stretched, still working out his kinked muscles, a legacy of the long day at Darlington. "Listen. Why don't we take a break and y'all can go outside and breathe for a minute before I have to take off my belt and whip both of you. Behave and I'll walk over and see if Grandma Lee will make us a pitcher of lemonade."

Jodell sensed they were starting to seriously tread on each other's nerves, that the team's patience was stretched about as tight as it could be without something snapping. Sometimes, such tensions were far more difficult to overcome than a flat tire or a broken part on the car.

"I could use some air. And some lemonade. And reckon she's got any of them teacakes with the chocolate icing? You know the ones?" Bubba asked hopefully.

Before the day was over, in the middle of yet another silly squabble that had broken out in the suffocating heat of the shop, Jodell Lee stood suddenly and marched to the middle of the big room. He put his hands on his hips and glared at the group as they stared back at him cautiously, wondering what he was up to.

"Okay! Listen up!" he finally said sternly. "I think it's high time we cooled you hotheads off."

Then he loudly ordered the whole crew to lay down their tools and follow him. He turned on his heels and stomped out of the shop. They looked at each other pointedly, clearly wondering if the heat or the paint fumes or the perpetual pressure to win had finally addled poor Jodell Lee's brain.

He stopped his march long enough to collect his and Bubba's two older kids from where they were playing together, making racetracks in the dirt in Grandma's backyard. He took one of their little hands in each of his and led them past the old chicken coop and through the rickety gate in the rusty barbed wire fence at the back of the house. With puzzled looks, the rest of them all trailed along behind their driver like a platoon of soldiers, blindly following their leader as he led them down a hardly used footpath that wound through the thick weeds of what had once been a cow pasture.

As they approached a line of trees and bushes at the far end of the field, Jodell suddenly raced ahead and began peeling off his shoes and socks and jeans and T-shirt, stripping down to his skivvies. And then, with a fairly authentic Tarzan yell, he suddenly disappeared into the bushes, dropping out of sight immediately.

Joe Banker let out a loud war whoop and was not far behind, then Bubba and Johnny did the same, and finally the kids followed, giggling and squealing the whole way as they shed their clothes down to their birthday suits. Billy Winton had stopped in his tracks, staring in disbelief as the whole bunch of them seemed to completely lose their senses, become semi-nudists, then dive into the underbrush and drop off the edge of the earth.

But he could now hear more laughter and shrieks of joy and the sound of splashing water coming from where they had all disappeared. As he stepped closer, he saw the bunch of them, frolicking gleefully in a deep, clear-running stream, diving and ducking and splashing each other.

It didn't take Billy but a moment to strip down and join them in the chilly mountain water of the creek. He yelped when he first dove into the cold water, but it felt wonderful and soon he was in the middle of the play.

Jodell would later remark that the impromptu dip in the old swimming hole had likely prevented somebody from murdering somebody else before the day was over. None of them would disagree.

By Thursday of that week however, it was obvious that someone was going to have to stay behind to finish the prep work on the speedway car and get everything else ready for the excursion down to Talladega. Since they were expecting to spend six days at the Alabama track, there was more than the usual amount of prep work that needed to be done. Billy volunteered to stay behind and he was the logical choice. He was now responsible for most of the work that remained to be done on the car. And besides that, he was not essential to them at the shorter tracks. It was a luxury to have another wrench, but they could do without him while he completed more critical work back home.

Finally, the truck pulled away, headed for Hickory. A confident Jodell rode shotgun while Bubba drove. Joe and Johnny followed in the car, which had been stuffed with coolers filled with food and drinks as well as the equipment they would need.

Billy had spent the morning helping them get loaded up. He had admitted to Jodell that he felt a twinge of disappointment at not climbing aboard and going across the mountain with them.

Jodell had pulled him aside.

"Billy, you've earned your way onto this team," he said with a serious face. "You're a valuable member of the crew now. That's why we trust you to stay back here and get things ready for Talladega. That race is far more important that the ones we're about to run. We want to win 'em all. But we got to win the first race down there."

Then, with a sincere pat on the back, Jodell climbed into the truck and they all waved as they pulled away. Billy certainly felt better, as much a full-fledged member of the Jodell Lee crew as he had so far in their short time together.

Whistling as he worked, Billy spent the afternoon putting the numbering and lettering on the car. Randy Weems and Clifford Stanley were expected to show up to help after they got off work from their shifts at the mill. Bubba had left a three-page checklist of things that needed to be prepped on the car, along with another list of tools and equipment that would have to be checked, packed, and stored. It would be their jobs to attack those lists. And whether they were unpaid volunteers or not, it was expected that they would have it done by the time Bubba and the rest of them swung back by on the way to Talladega.

Billy was whistling "El Paso" as he sat on a stool, carefully painting the large number on the side of the door panel. He used a steady, practiced hand to get the lettering exactly right. He had lost all track of time as he concentrated on the meticulous job he was doing.

It was the creaking of the large door to the shop that ultimately intruded into his deliberation.

Darn wind, he thought, putting the final touches on the margin of the number before he had to go close the door.

But suddenly something wonderful-smelling drifted his way, wiping out the ever-present odor of paint fumes. There was Grandma Lee, coming his way, carrying before her on a tray a huge steaming plate of meatloaf, turnip greens, mashed potatoes, and a pone of cornbread the size of a hubcap. There was also a large glass of iced tea.

"My, my, Mrs. Lee. Did you hear my stomach growling all the way up to the house?" Billy asked, beaming at the sight of the heaping plate.

"You been in here all day by yourself, working so hard, Billy. I figured you might need a little something to eat by now." She handed him the tray and pulled a fresh napkin and silverware from her apron pocket. "I hope you don't mind if I sit and visit while you eat."

" 'Course not," he mumbled through his first big bite of meatloaf.

They talked for awhile about racing, the boys, how hard they all worked. She told Billy briefly about Jodell's father, about how he had been lost at sea during World War II, and how his mother had gone to California, lost in her grief, leaving Jodell behind to be raised up by his grandparents.

"You never heard from her?" Billy asked.

"Not after awhile. We're not sure if she is even still alive or not. Jodell had hoped she would read about him in the papers when he had first gone out West to race at Riverside, but he never heard from her. Not then nor with all the visits since. Jodell never talks about her. Except once he said he thought little Katie had his mother's eyes. At least from the one picture he still has of her."

Then she related how Jodell had first begun to drive for his grandfather's whiskey-making operation and how good he was at dodging the revenuers' roadblocks. And how he had gotten serious about racing after Grandpa Lee had died, after the whiskey business had perished with him. She told the story of the North Carolina bootlegger who gave Jodell the seed money to field his first race car. And how Jodell and Catherine had later talked a soda pop company into coming aboard as a legitimate sponsor and how they had virtually lived on the soda for most of their first year of serious racing.

Billy listened with interest. He had heard snippets of the stories here and there but now he thought he understood better what drove Jodell Lee to seek excellence in the racing game. He had never met anyone as determined to finish first as Jodell Lee was.

Finally, Grandma Lee told of how she had accidentally discovered Jodell's racing career way back when

by seeing a photo in the local newspaper. She had reluctantly given him her blessing, then had seen him have
a hard crash in the first race she attended. Even now,
she said, she had her reservations, worrying mightily
about her "racing boys" when they were gone on some
distant trip to Florida or New York or California, running around in those old fast cars.

"I got to admit I miss the boys when they are off
racing somewhere," she said. "It's hard for me to believe
they're all grown up now, some of them with children . . ."

As if on cue, a whirling dervish of a kid burst through
the half-open door at a full run, followed closely behind
by his baby sister.

"Hey! Young man," Grandma Lee said sternly, pointing a warning finger in Bob Jr.'s direction. They both
skidded to a halt near where their great-grandmother sat.
"Y'all get back out in the yard to play now. Your daddy
catches you in his shop and he'll take a switch to you.
And why do you have to run everywhere you go, Bob
Jr.? Slow it down before you run headforemost into a
tree."

The boy stared, wide-eyed, at the new race car while
the little girl, bashful in the presence of Billy Winton,
tried to hide in the folds of Grandma's skirt.

Billy set his now-empty plate down, took the last swig
of iced tea, then stood and stepped over to where Bob
Jr. stood transfixed by the car. He gently took the boy's
hand and led him closer to it.

"See the number I've been painting on the side here.
And your daddy's name we've painted here above the
door. 'Jodell Bob Lee.' Same as yours, except we'd have
to put a 'Jr.' after it."

The boy's eyes shined and a big grin split his face.
He clearly liked the thought. Bob Jr. was tall for his age,
clearly taking after his father, but he still had to stand

on tiptoes to try to peer inside the cockpit of the car. It was obvious, too, from the look on his face that the child was already imagining what it must be like to pilot one of these machines like his dad did. In the last few months, everyone had noticed that he had begun to take more interest in the races. Sometimes, when he accompanied his mother to the track now, he would pause in his play to actually watch with interest for awhile the sparring going on out there around him. Or he would perk up from the morning cartoons he liked to watch on the television when he would hear one of the race cars cranked up down at the shop.

Billy swung Bob Jr. up onto his shoulder and walked him around the car. Then the boy made driving and screeching-tire sounds as Billy finally toted him back outside where Grandma Lee had already taken little Katie.

"Okay, Mr. Speed Racer. Down you go!" Billy laughed. Bob Jr. grinned, then took off at a full run again, headed for the tire swing in the big oak next to Grandma's kitchen window. In no time, the boy was in the swing, pretending he was driving and that his sister was his pit crew.

Later, Billy was working on the lettering for one of their new sponsors they were taking on the car while he waited for his helpers to show up. It was painstaking work, getting the script of the letters exactly right, and that, along with breathing the vapor from the paint, had left him with a dull headache.

He heard them long before he could see them. Their old jalopy wheezed and rattled and backfired all the way up the long driveway. The muffler had long since rusted away and the car squeaked and clattered fiercely as it slid to a stop in the dusty driveway. Billy carefully put down the paintbrush and met them at the door.

"Well, if it ain't Goober and Gomer!"

Those were the names he had coined for them and they fit perfectly.

"Hey, Billy boy! What ya workin' on?" Randy asked, stumbling clumsily right on past him.

"Doing a little painting, but watch . . ."

"I'll say! Clifford, look at that lettering."

He reached out with a finger as if he wanted to see for himself if the paint was dry yet on the intricate work Billy had been doing.

"Aiyeeee! Don't you dare touch that!"

"What?"

"I said don't touch that. That paint is still wet."

Billy grabbed Randy by the galluses of his overalls and jerked him backward, out of reach of his handiwork.

"Sorry. You don't have to be such an old sore-tail about it, though," he said, already looking around for something else to get into.

"Just don't touch the paint, okay?"

"Right, chief!" the two men said in perfect unison.

"Y'all can take Bubba's checklist for the rear end over there on the bench and get to work under the car. Put on the right set of springs and shocks that he's got marked down. And double-check everything you see."

"Don't worry about us. We know how particular Bub can be," Clifford said.

"And we don't want him takin' a tire tool to our noggins," Randy added, pantomiming getting whacked on the head, then staggering around as if addled from the blow.

"And whatever you do, don't put your grimy paws on the fresh paint!" Billy ordered, trying to hide a grin at the slapstick routine the two boys carried on continually.

Despite their rube exterior and silly ways, Clifford and Randy were darn good mechanics and tireless workers. Otherwise, Bubba and Jodell would never have allowed them to touch their race cars in the first place.

It was near midnight Sunday night when Jodell and Bubba pulled into the dusty yard after the long drive back from Richmond. A seventh-place and a tenth-place finish along with a virtually undamaged race car towed back behind them had helped make the trip more bearable than some of the other recent ones where they had not fared so well. After all the trouble the past few weeks, it was good to actually bring the car home in one piece and to have won enough money to pay all the expenses, with a little left over.

Billy was sprawled on the cot in the back of the shop, dead to the world, and didn't even hear them when they rolled in. They had worked on the Talladega car all the way up until ten o'clock before his helpers had left to get some rest before another day at the mill. Billy had proudly polished the car one last time before the fatigue had finally claimed him, too, and he had been asleep as soon as he had stretched out on the cot.

Jodell eased the truck to a halt, then backed the trailer to the shop door. He tried to be quiet, to not wake Catherine or the kids or Grandma Lee. No danger of disturbing Bubba Baxter, though. He snored solidly in the passenger seat next to him. Jodell had driven all the way back, knowing that he could nap on the way down to Talladega the next day but Bubba would have more than a full day's work to do. Joe and Johnny had taken off shortly after the race and gone straight home. They needed to get back earlier and get some sleep, too, and would be over the next day to finish up and start for Alabama.

"Wake up, Sleeping Beauty."

No sign of life. He poked the big man with a finger.

"Empty in all the gas . . . all the gas," Bubba mumbled, clearly running some race somewhere in his dreams.

"I said wake up. We're home. I've done listened to

you snore for five hours and I'm ready to do a little log-sawing of my own."

"What time is it?"

"Around midnight. We may as well get it done."

"I guess."

They climbed out of the truck and began untying everything that had been strapped down for the ride home. They each grabbed a load and headed for the shop door.

"I hope Billy and the two clowns got that car close to finished," Jodell said. "We'll be in a heap of trouble if they didn't."

"Billy got it done. No problem," Bubba said with solid conviction as he leaned on the heavy door to shove it open.

The overhead lights in the shop still blazed brightly, just the way Billy had left them when he had stumbled to bed. He knew the returning warriors would need the light when they arrived. Jodell hurried in with his load, Bubba close behind him.

"Whoa!" Bubba said, pulling up short and staring at the sight directly ahead of them.

"Yes!" Jodell added emphatically.

Before the two men sat what was, to them, a bona fide masterpiece. The Talladega car. It gleamed and sparkled beneath the daylight brightness of the overhead lights, its deep colors and glistening lettering shimmering almost as if it might be something alive and breathing.

The car was stunning. She looked powerful, sleek, ready for the racetrack. Jodell began breathing again, then carefully sat down the tool boxes he had been carrying. Slowly, admiring the paint job all the way, he ambled over and ran his fingers across her smooth, silky surface.

"Honey, you are going to be one fine, fast race car if

looks have anything to do with it," he told her lovingly. "I can just feel it."

Bubba touched her skin, too, proudly taking in her beauty. Now if she only ran as fast as she looked like she ought to be able to, they would be just fine.

He couldn't help it. He pictured how great she would look sitting in the winners' circle, surrounded by fans, the press, and the other teams, the winner's trophy resting on her deep blue roof and the checkered flag unfurled across her bright, shiny hood, all while Jodell stood next to her, acknowledging the praise of the thousands who had come to watch him take the race going away.

Only then did Bubba realize he still carried a duffel bag filled with spare parts that had to weigh a hundred pounds. He turned to make sure Jodell had not noticed how lost he had been in his latest dream. But his driver was still standing there, too, his hand still on the Ford's freshly adorned fender, lost in his own musings, a broad smile on his tired face.

Bubba smiled, too, and headed for the door. He would allow Jodell to finish his own victory lane dream while he went back outside to get the next load off the truck.

RED CLAY AND HIGH BANKS

A bright, relentless sun beat down on them as they passed pine thickets and red, plowed fields and old dilapidated barns that had long since been gobbled up by the gluttonous kudzu. Now that they had left the U.S. highway, there was little traffic, just an occasional pulpwood truck meeting them or another race team headed for Talladega behind or in front of them. Farmers on tractors in fields along the road and the few cars they met along the way all, to a man, threw up their hands in a friendly-enough greeting. Banners that had been hung from signs at filling stations and stores all along the way welcomed them to town, to the races.

While Bubba and Billy had taken turns driving, Jodell had gotten as comfortable as he could in the truck cab and tried to catch up on missed sleep. Jodell claimed the seat in the truck was as comfortable to him as his bed at home and, considering the sack time he had logged there lately, it might easily have been the truth. The plan was to let Joe and Johnny come on down at their leisure, then meet up with them later that evening at their motel over in Anniston, about ten miles from the track. They had all covered a lot of ground over the last four days, not even counting all that Jodell had tallied on the racetracks. Taking all day to drive from Chandler Cove down to Talladega was considered a rest day, a rare luxury during the season.

An escalating argument over the best place to stop for a late lunch finally roused Jodell from what had been a deep sleep

"Will you two stop it!" Jodell said drowsily, squinting in the bright sunlight. He tried to find some landmark. "Where are we anyway?"

"We are just about in Talladega proper," Bubba reported. "The speedway ought to be somewhere on the other side of town."

"According to the map we should be getting close," Billy said, a finger on a snaking blue line on the map that led between the red blobs that marked Birmingham and Atlanta.

"Okay then. Pull into that market over yonder. I'll settle this food argument for you right now," Jodell ordered.

He was admittedly hungry, too, and he would be glad for the chance to stretch his stiff, sore legs. It seemed that lately a rough week of racing left him more stove-up than it once had, that the recovery time was longer. It couldn't be age. Maybe he simply wasn't taking as good a care of himself as he once had. True, he didn't work out with weights or jog the way he once had. He would have to consider resuming his workouts. Someday.

"All right, Joe Dee. The market it is."

Bubba was clearly glad the argument had been ended,

that food was at hand at last, and he steered the truck and its tow off the asphalt and into the dusty lot of the small country market. The gravel crunched under the wheels as it rolled to a stop in a spot that would be out of the way of other traffic.

"What about a couple of slabs of baloney and some hoop cheese?" Bubba asked. "Crackers and sodas?"

"Fine by me. I'm gonna walk around for a minute," Jodell answered, and then slid stiffly from the truck cab

He sucked in a deep breath of the hot, humid air. It felt good. And there was the perfume of sweet honey-suckle, too. He stretched mightily, then walked gimpily over to the shade of a big willow tree at the far end of the lot and leaned against a fence there. A gently rolling pasture stretched off into the distance and the summer haze mostly hid what appeared to be a line of tall moun-tains at the far horizon. Not tall mountains compared to the Smokies, but more than he had expected to find in this part of the country. They had made quick trips to Birmingham and Huntsville to run on the tracks there in the past, but they had been hit and run operations with little time to take in the scenery.

For the moment, he was having trouble picturing how a giant speedway could have suddenly appeared here, amid the cornfields and hay meadows and red clay. Such thoughts brought back memories, too, of their first look at the sprawling Daytona speedway which had also been an anomaly, a strange presence that had popped out of the ground amid palm trees and city streets. Their initial sighting of the place's towering banks and the sweeping turns and the long straightaways that had stretched away into the distance had almost overwhelmed them at the time. So much so that they had stopped dead in the mid-dle of a busy street to properly appreciate it.

And this one was supposed to be even bigger!

But like Daytona, this, too, was racing country. Such

a thing should not be a surprise at all. The Allison brothers and Red Farmer and others ran out of Birmingham fifty miles to the west, and Atlanta was only a bit more than a hundred miles to the east. Dirt tracks and tight little speedways were as numerous here as they were in the Carolinas. Jodell knew full well that the competitive spirit would be thick in the air at this place, just as it had been in Daytona, and equally as strong and sweet as the aroma of the honeysuckle.

When Bubba and Billy came out of the store, each man carried two sacks of groceries.

"I thought you were just getting us a bite or two for lunch."

"We did," Bubba said, a puzzled look on his face. "Why?"

"Looks to me like you bought enough to feed Coxey's army."

"Well, I did pick up a few snacks. I can't be running to the concession stand every time I get a little hungry, now can I? We wouldn't never get anything done on the car."

"It ain't ever stopped you before," Jodell said with a wink toward Billy. "Tell you what. Let's drive on over and find the track first, then we'll eat. We can't be more than a couple of miles from it."

"Good idea, Jodell," Billy piped in, joining the barb at Bubba. He set his two sacks in an open spot in the bed of the truck and climbed inside.

Bubba stood there, a pained look on his face, the two bags still under each arm.

"Boys, I think we oughta eat now. We don't know how far . . ."

"Aw, c'mon, big 'un. I'll drive. You eat," Jodell said.

Jodell steered the truck out of the lot and back onto the highway. Bubba was already ruffling through the sacks, collecting the ingredients for a massive baloney and cheese sandwich.

While the big man constructed his masterpiece, Jodell and Billy talked quietly about what they might expect from the new track. Jodell hoped it would be very similar to Daytona, which had by now become one of his favorite tracks. It had been built on a similar plan, only longer and with higher banking, and that promised even more spectacular speeds. From the comments of the drivers who had run the tire tests in July and early August, there was reason to be concerned, though. They all said the same things. The track was big, wide, and extremely rough. The sheer scale of the plant itself was similar to Daytona, but it definitely did not duplicate the smooth ride of the Florida track.

They had driven less than two miles when the dirt mounds that surrounded the track suddenly rose up out of a field like some spectacular geological oddity. They still couldn't appreciate the size of the place, though, until they realized that they had driven awhile without the structure seeming to get any closer. Then, finally, they pulled to a stop at main gate and took in the high banks and the backs of the rows of grandstands, rigged like some gargantuan erector set.

"Whoa! Would you look at that?" Jodell gasped.

"Man, this place is massive," Billy said, poking Bubba in the ribs with his elbow. "Those banks must be twenty stories tall!"

"You ain't seen nothing yet," Bubba said, pausing only a moment between bites of his sandwich. "Wait till you get inside and get a real look at it."

Then they both turned toward Jodell. The driver had a look of pure ecstasy on his face, his eyes wide, his lips with a slight grin, his hands on the truck's steering wheel already in their customary racing position. When he turned to face them, his eyes shone.

"Boys, this place is special. I can feel it. I can't wait to get out there and crack that throttle wide open. Heck, I just want to get inside and see what that thing looks like from the middle! Let's go!"

Less than an hour later they were parked in the garage area in the huge infield, unloading the brightly-polished new race car off the trailer. Sometimes Bubba would look up from whatever he was doing and catch Jodell, standing on something so he could get a better view, staring at one of the broad turns. From the look on his face, it was clear that he was trying to visualize how he would navigate through those wide, sweeping turns to get the best line toward the straightaway.

"Jodell, pay attention and help us get this car unloaded and ready," Bubba fussed. "You'll have practically the whole week to learn how to get around this old monster. The sooner we get her unloaded and everything set up, the sooner you can get a shot at them high banks."

"Sorry, boys. I just can't believe those turns. The pavement up there looks like it is a mile wide. I'll bet you could drive six cars, side by side, through that corner over yonder."

Bubba stopped what he was doing and hopped up onto the toolbox with Jodell. He looked off into the first and second turns where they shimmered like mirages in the late afternoon heat.

"Now that you mention it, I have to agree that that is one wide turn."

For a moment Bubba himself wondered what it would feel like to go sailing off into that broad expanse of track, his own foot rammed to the floor, feeling those six hundred horses pushing him backward into the driver's seat like a giant hand on his chest. Bubba had done a little driving over the years, even competing in a few small track races, but he always felt much more comfortable working on the car than driving it. That did not mean, however, that he couldn't relish the feel of a roaring engine beneath his feet, or that he didn't love the powerful thrust he felt when he punched the gas and the big motor responded to his command.

Just in case the urge ever hit him, Bubba kept a valid competitors' license and would occasionally take the car out himself for a spin during practice. Sometimes, no matter how well Jodell described the situation, that was still the best way to figure out a troublesome setup for a particular track. He sometimes thought he would have liked to run more races himself on the short tracks. The longer superspeedways didn't hold the same appeal for him. He preferred stomping on the gas heading into the turns, then hitting the brakes and feeling the car practically slide through the corners, as opposed to simply nailing down the accelerator all race long on the big tracks.

But every time the urge to compete would rear up, he'd push it back down. His job was to help Jodell Lee win. And he would concentrate on that task. That was his calling.

But now, gazing out at the broad, tilted turns of this untested track, something seemed to reach out and grab him. The wide ribbon of asphalt looked like one of those big interstate highways they were building these days to crisscross the country, roads far more welcoming than old U.S. 78 or U.S. 11. The thought of shepherding a powerful race car at full throttle off into one of those turns was causing his right foot to itch. He knew exactly how Jodell Lee must feel. He, too, wanted to jerk that brand new car off the trailer that instant and put her out there to see what she could do against this monster.

"Hey, Bubba! We gonna to get this car unloaded or not?" Jodell said with a laugh. He knew he was breaking the trance Bubba had fallen into.

"Sorry, Joe Dee. I . . . uh . . . I thought I saw something down there in the turn."

"Ha! I don't believe that. Now if it was Joe, it might be true. He can spot a pretty girl from a mile and a half away. But not old Bubba. Sophia Loren could walk by in a bikini and you'd not take your eye off the toe-in on the front end of the race car."

"Aw, Joe Dee. Quit picking on me."

"Bub, if you want to drive the car, just say so."

"Naw. I was just thinking for a second about what it would be like to run the car wide open around this place. But I'll leave that to you. That's your cup of tea, not mine."

"You know we can always fix you up a car if you want to run. How many laps did you run in practice at Richmond the other day?"

"Aw, fifteen or twenty. But that was just because I couldn't figure out the handling any other way. And it paid off, too, you'll have to agree. You know me. Sometimes I just got to get a feel for the car to understand what you want underneath it, and sometimes the best way to do that is to hop in and take her for a spin."

"Remember Bubba, we're a team. You, me, and Joe. You want to run some then you can run some. It's your call."

Bubba looked Jodell in the eye. It was clear that he was serious, that the kidding was over. He turned back toward the first turn. The sun had just fallen below the wall. The day was getting late.

"Shucks, Joe Dee. I ain't no driver. I'm just a wrench that happens to like to test out his handiwork every so often."

Jodell was quiet for a moment before he spoke again.

"All right. Suit yourself. Let's get all this stuff unloaded so we can go hook up with Joe and Johnny."

They would actually work several more hours before

calling it quits, unloading everything in their assigned slot in the garage area. Bubba and Jodell started going over the checklist for the car while Billy worked on organizing all the tools and equipment.

"Hey, Billy!" Bubba hollered at one point from where he lay sprawled beneath the car. He had to yell to be heard over the roar of a race engine several stalls away.

"Yeah?"

"When you get a chance, how about taking several sets of those rims down there to the Goodyear people and have their tire busters mount us up some? I don't want us to have to fool with them in the morning."

"Got you, chief. I'll head that way in a second."

When he had finished organizing the work area a few minutes later, Billy loaded two sets of rims on the wagon and hauled them down to the tent beneath the big Goodyear sign. There was a short line there already. Several of the teams had had the same idea as Bubba and were trying to get a head start on the next day. Behind the tire busters were stacks of smooth, jet-black racing tires, ready to be mounted up.

Billy talked with some of the other crewmen in line about their thoughts on the massive new speedway. Although it was hard to be heard over the hissing of air hoses and the clanking of all the heavy metal equipment against the hard steel of the tire rims, he still got some impressions. Everyone seemed to have a different idea of what the top speeds might be once the cars got out onto the track and could give it a test. One thing was for certain. This place might still be a mystery, but everyone was certain that she would be a quick one.

Finally it was his turn and Billy wheeled the wagon up in front of the sweaty tire busters, wearing their aprons and covered in dirt and grime.

"Give me two sets to start," he said, as he began stacking the rims beside the mounting machine.

"Gotcha, pal. Two sets, coming up."

"Sure is hot in here. I hope y'all get a chance to get outside and cool off every once in a while."

"Naw, we've been too busy already to take a break. Everybody's wanting plenty of tires mounted up after all the talk about how rough this place is on them," the buster answered. He was already expertly mounting up the first tire of the set.

"Reckon I'd better bring a couple more sets down here this afternoon then?"

"Probably be smart, pal. This place will be packed out tomorrow when all them other teams get in here. Just wait and see."

A helper was already rolling another tire over to him and he quickly hoisted another one of the rims up onto the machine. The tire buster looked more like an old-fashioned blacksmith as he worked, a smoking cigarette dangling from his lips as he quickly mounted and balanced the two sets of tires. In line behind Billy, more crewmen from other teams had come rolling up with their own wagons full of rims, ready to take on tires.

"Here you go, pal. See you tomorrow."

"Naw, I think I'll be back in a few minutes," Billy answered, nodding over his shoulder at the growing line behind him. "I think I'll take your advice. These lines will be a mile long by tomorrow."

"Well then, see you in a few minutes."

With that the burly man effortlessly lifted a tire off the wagon that was being wheeled in front of him and started breaking it down. Billy hefted the last of his own tires up on top of the pile on the red wagon. He had to whip a couple of straps out of his pocket to lash the tires down for the trip back to the garage. The wagon creaked and groaned under the weight as he towed it back across the pavement.

He could see that the activity in the garage had picked

up dramatically, even since he had left on his tire jaunt. There were trucks unloading their brightly colored race cars. And many of the tired crewmen doing the unloading were showing the effects of the race in Richmond the day before and the long drive down to Alabama.

Bubba was still under the front end of their car when he got back. Jodell was standing in the open front fender well of the car, where the front tire usually would be hanging. The Ford rested on a set of jack stands. Both front tires were lying off to the side by the toolbox.

"Hey, the tires are here. Bubba you want me to match up a set or do you want to do it?"

"Naw, you go ahead. Me and Jodell are still trying to figure what geometry we want to put up under the front end."

"Sure thing. Y'all want me to swap out the rear springs or shocks first?"

"No," Jodell answered, trying to turn around in the cramped confines of the wheel well so he could reach a different wrench. "We'll use the set we got on it for the first run. From what I've seen, it ought to be pretty close to the combination we had on the other car at Daytona back in July."

"Check the brake assembly on the back wheels after you match us up a set of tires. If everything looks okay, then go on and bolt them on," Bubba called up from underneath the car, yelling to be heard over the rock and roll on the radio in the garage slot next to theirs.

They made good progress on getting the car prepped and ready that afternoon. All that remained the next morning was to get the car cleared through inspection and it would finally be ready for the track and its first test. They were dog-tired. Even the usually indefatigable Bubba Baxter readily admitted it. A decent night's sleep at the motel would be most welcomed. They had covered a lot of miles over the past three days and it was clearly beginning to wear on them.

Finally, they finished up and started walking toward the gate. They were going to hitch a ride to their motel from there with one of the other teams. As they hiked, Jodell and Bubba studied the track and began their first informal strategy session for how they would attack this behemoth, all the while throwing up their hands in response as they received greetings from other crews along the way.

As they approached the gate that led to the tunnel beneath the section of track between turns three and four, they stopped and turned and looked back out toward the huge infield. It alone was bigger than the whole town of Chandler Cove, and, on Sunday, its population would be five times that of their hometown back in eastern Tennessee. And beyond the infield, where the last glow of the summer sun was finally beginning to fade, they could just see the flags flying and a bit of the outside railing at the tops of the first and second turns.

The conversation had stopped now. They gazed back in silence that seemed almost reverent, worshipful. And Billy Winton was immediately struck by the awed, solemn expressions on both men's faces as they took one more glance back at this cathedral for speed.

And by the fact that the look on each face was identical to the other.

Dawn had hardly broken when Jodell and Bubba climbed from their beds and pulled on their work clothes. Joe and Johnny had pulled in late the night before so they left them and Billy sleeping and walked across the motel lot to a diner for breakfast. As usual, they were eager to get to the track, and especially a new track and a new car to test it with. They had hardly begun attacking their eggs and grits when Billy Winton joined them.

"You couldn't sleep either?" Bubba asked.

"Not with that car out there waiting for us," he said.

They all grinned. They knew exactly how he felt.

Once back in the garage, they set about bolting on the set of tires they wanted to use and made sure the car was ready for the inspection line. They were backing the car out of the spot when Johnny and Joe showed up, sleepy-eyed but eager to get to work. Joe was especially chipper.

"Mornin', gents. Y'all got her all ready for the inspection line or you been goofing off since you got down here?"

"Ready to go," Jodell said as he helped push the car backwards out of the garage slot.

"That was quick," he said, clearly impressed. "Y'all got the setup under her and everything?"

"Finished that yesterday. Billy here and Clifford and Randy basically had her ready to go when we got back to the shop Sunday night. Yesterday it was just a matter of checking things over and getting a glance at this place to decide what we needed to put under the front end."

"Y'all done with that, too?" Joe asked, surprised.

"Yeah, she's ready to hit the track. We just need to get through the inspection and have you jet the carburetor and we'll be ready to go. That is, unless there's something else you need to do with that precious engine of yours that you haven't mentioned."

"I do want to check my motor over good," he said, consulting his watch. "But we have plenty of time for that."

Jodell allowed them to push the car off to the inspection while he visited with some of the other drivers, trying to pick up whatever scuttlebutt he could. He especially wanted to catch up with Bobby Allison. He knew he had tested tires here back at the end of July and would have the latest skinny.

The first driver he ran into was Tiny Lund.

"Jodell Lee, as I live and breathe!"

The man was huge but everybody called him "Tiny." Few even knew his real name was DeWayne. And if they did, they never dared call him by it.

"Tiny, I can't believe you left that old fish camp of

yours long enough to come down here and race."

"No way in the world I would miss this. I'm gonna run the Grand American race and I'm planning on the Grand National as well."

"Heard anything about the track yet?"

"Not much. I talked to Bobby a little bit about it."

"Yeah, I been trying to catch up with him, too."

"From all I have been able to gather, it's one tough ride. They say the track surface is really rough. Not what you would expect at all."

"That is kind of what I've been hearing."

"It's sort of surprising. Just to sit here and look at it out there, she looks smooth as glass," Tiny said, pointing down the short chute toward the sweeping banked turns.

"Yeah, but looks can be deceiving," said Jodell. "I walked out on the pavement in the straightaway yesterday. It looks like it could chew a tire all to pieces in a little bit."

"That's what Leroy Yarbrough said after the Goodyear tire test. But then somebody else said he run five hundred miles around here. It must not be too bad."

"I hope not, Tiny. I don't know about you but there is only one way that I know how to drive around a place like this one, and that is flat-out. You can't be taking it easy 'cause you're scared a tire is gonna come apart on you."

"You and me both!" The big man slapped him hard on the shoulder, hard enough to let him know that he wasn't totally kidding with his next statement. "See you out on the track, Jodell. And I'll wave at you as I go blowin' by."

"Keep on dreamin', Tiny," Jodell answered as he returned the blow to the shoulder, and maybe a bit harder. "Just try to stay out of my way every time I lap you."

Tiny frowned, backed away, drew a fist, then suddenly broke into a loud belly laugh. The fist turned into a wave and Lund turned and walked away, still laughing at the prospects of anyone, even Jodell Bob Lee, leaving him behind on a racetrack.

Jodell moved on down the line, looking over the cars that had been brought to the new track. It was always interesting to see how the various teams intended to attack the track, but especially when it was such unknown territory. There was David Pearson's car and Cale Yarborough's racer. A little farther down sat the blue Ford that belonged to Richard Petty. Several of the crewmembers were working beneath the hood of the Torino. Richard stood off to the side, intently studying some notes on a clipboard. He looked up and waved at Jodell as he walked by, then motioned for him to come on over.

"Jodell, what do you think of this big old place?" Richard asked, waving his hand toward the wide expanse of track that encircled them.

Jodell thought for a moment before he answered.

"I don't know. But I can tell you one thing. I can't wait to get the car out there and see what we can do."

"Same here, same here. Say, have you thought anymore about joining the drivers' organization we're starting up? Did Cale or Bobby talk to you about it?"

"Yeah, Richard. I talked to 'em. I like the idea but I just don't know about this Professional Drivers Association. I still remember what Big Bill did to old Curtis and Tim when they tried to start that union thing."

Drivers Curtis Turner and Tim Flock had been banned from racing for life by "Big Bill" France and NASCAR when they tried to join up with Jimmy Hoffa and the Teamsters to unionize the sport.

"The PDA is not a union, Jodell. It's just an organization to help upgrade things for the drivers and their families at the tracks. Your wife comes to the races all the time, just like mine does. They deserve some decent facilities in the infield where they don't have to deal with all the crazy folks out there. And we need to do something about the purses. Even them out and make sure the drivers get their worth."

"I know, Richard, and that sounds good, but . . ."

"What about insurance if you get hurt? You cats carry any insurance? Or how about retirement? You work for the railroad or for one of the tobacco companies, you at least got some retirement to look forward to."

"Well, I got a little life insurance. Enough to take care of Cath for a little while, maybe. Retirement? Shoot, I got thirty-five more years before I have to think about retiring. Heck, I can work twenty more years after I'm through racing."

"Jodell, you got a couple of kids now, a pretty wife. Think about them if you get all broke up in a wreck."

"I do, Richard, but this is the only way I got to make a living. I was born to drive a race car, not to be in politics."

"Me, too. You ain't gonna ever see me out politicking for office, crazy as this country has gone these days. But somebody has got to get up and take a stand for all of us. Just think about it some more, Jodell. We need your support. We need everybody standing up together or we don't have a chance."

"Don't worry about that. You got my support. One hundred percent of it. I just like to think about things before I do anything about them. I don't like to make hasty decisions."

"I can understand that. You take all the time you want. We just want you on our side."

"Don't worry 'bout me. Good luck with this track."

"Same to you. Better keep a close watch on the tires."

"That's what I'm hearing. Tires, tires, tires."

"At these speeds, it's all about tires," Richard said solemnly.

Jodell could see that the cars were beginning to clear

the inspection line already. The waiting was about over. It was almost time to see what this track felt like from behind the wheel of a race car at speed. The thought of it suddenly made his heart start to beat faster and he thought he felt the blood pumping harder through his veins.

Jodell double-timed it back to their stall to pull on his driving suit. This was what he came to the track for. The monkeying with the engine, cranking on the car's setup, trading small talk with the other drivers and crews was okay, but he came to do one thing: to guide a car around the course as fast as he could. Now, finally, he was about to see what kind of car they had invented for this track and whether they were ready to race or if they still had lots of work to do to keep from getting embarrassed out there.

He climbed up into the cramped back of the truck and slipped on the driving suit, grabbed his helmet and was stepping off the back of the tailgate when he saw Bubba and the others come pushing the driverless car by. They were on the way to the pit road for the start of practice.

Everyone at the initial drivers' meeting had been warned repeatedly to take it easy on the tires to start out. All the drivers had glanced sideways at each other when the subject was mentioned. Everyone, drivers, crews, fans, and the press seemed to be talking about tires or the roughness of the track surface. Jodell was ready to put all the talk behind him now and simply go out there, see how fast the car would go, and then judge for himself. Everything else would take care of itself.

Finally it was time for him to strap himself in and take a little drive. Bubba shuffled around the car nervously as Jodell climbed in through the driver's-side window. He put one of his long legs in the window then swung the other inside, slithering in like a snake, and then settled into the seat. He could still smell the fresh paint inside the car.

Jodell pulled the straps over his shoulders and began to fasten them to the lap belts while Bubba, his head stuck through the window, helped him get settled in.

"I don't know why, but I feel nervous about this thing, Joe Dee," Bubba said as he triple-checked the belts.

"Well, you're making me nervous. Calm down. I got it."

And he tried to wave Bubba out of the way. Bubba would have none of it, though, and grabbed the belts anyway and gave them a sharp tug once Jodell had gotten them locked.

"You get ready to drive. It's still my job to make sure everything is right. Until you get out there on that track it's still my car. And my car does not leave this spot until it's right."

Jodell grinned then and shook the big man's hand. Even after all these years, Bubba Baxter still had the knack for putting him in his proper place.

Johnny Holt circled the car, checking all the air pressures in the tires yet again. Joe Banker stood writing notes in his clipboard, logging all the engine settings, the setup of the springs and the shocks and such, all so they would have a baseline on everything on the car that mattered. Once they began to make changes, they would use this as a reference guide as they worked to build speed into the car over the course of the practice session.

"Ready?" Bubba asked.

"Yeah! I'm more than ready. I wanna see what Miss Katie's gonna do."

He reached over and hit the starter switch. The motor immediately came to rumbling life. It was the same story all up and down the lines of cars as the engines noisily awoke and begged to run.

Jodell listened carefully to the sound of his own en-

gine. As he goosed it up through the RPM ranges, it
sang a beautiful, deep-throated melody. To Jodell Lee,
it was still some of the most beautiful music he could
ever hear.

He pushed the shifter up into gear, held his foot on
the clutch, and waited for the signal to take to the track.
He tried to keep his thoughts on the job at hand, on the
track itself, and how he would attack it. The anticipation,
though, made it hard to focus.

Finally, the cars were rolling forward and he released
the clutch and felt it catch. As he rolled off the pit road
he was shocked to see how high the first turn towered
over the track, blocking out the horizon. The steep banking made it appear a car would have to run up the side
of a mountain to make it through the turn. He slowly
accelerated, trying to feel the texture of the new track's
surface. And he was not surprised to find that, even at
these slow speeds, it felt rough, and he could easily hear
the odd pitch of the noise from the tires, a far different
sound than he usually heard.

Jodell kept it low on the track as he ran through the
sweeping turns the first time. He took the first corner at
slightly less than a hundred miles per hour, half as fast
as he would blast through it if he were going full speed.
When he rolled out onto the back straightaway, he
goosed it a bit, to a little over a hundred, probably, and
as he gazed out ahead through his windshield, the track
seemed to stretch for miles in front of him. He fed Joe's
engine more gasoline and felt an exhilarating surge from
the powerful motor that his cousin had built.

There were cars all around him, cautiously doing the
same thing Jodell was doing, prudently feeling out the
track, trying to get a sense for how the high turns would
effect the car. Just as did Jodell, they all wanted to get
a better feel for the track before they hit it full throttle.

Jodell knew one thing already and he had not even

finished the first circuit. This was most certainly an entirely different track from Daytona, even though it resembled it at first glance. It was made for speed, and the way he was lugging around her high banks was as frustrating as it was necessary.

He took another couple of laps at half speed, then, coming up off turn four, he sensed that it was finally time. With his right foot, he hammered the throttle and the Ford leapt ahead, thankfully untethered, and the force of the sudden acceleration nailed Jodell firmly backward, hard against the seatback. His blood pumped in anticipation of what was about to come. He was finally ready to see what the car was capable of doing.

Jodell rumbled through the tri-oval and across the start/finish line, building speed quickly as the car zoomed off toward the severe banking of the first turn. He sailed into the corner and began to climb the incline. He twisted the wheel and felt the car settle down in the springs as she bit into the turn. He cracked the throttle for an instant as the car approached the center of the turn, then pushed it hard again into the floorboard.

The sense of unbridled speed was intoxicating as the car set off down the long backstretch. But looking straight ahead it didn't seem the car was going fast at all. Out of the corner of his eye, though, the wall and flags and empty bleachers were flashing past in a continual blur. He was flying! Flying as surely as if he had wings and had left the earth behind to race clouds and pass airplanes. And he was stunned at how effortless it was, how easily his car had soared away from the earth, how smoothly he had steered for the stratosphere.

Suddenly, another car came rushing by him on the inside. It startled him for an instant. He had not expected any other aircraft to zoom past him. Then, the other driver had cleared him and had pulled away by several car lengths. He felt his juices start to flow, his competitive spirits begin to rise.

Lord, he hated to get passed! During practice, in a race, or even on the highway that ran from the house down to Chandler Cove. It didn't matter.

Standing on the pit wall, Bubba and Billy struggled trying to follow the car all the way around the track. They could only see her when she was high in the turns and could follow her most of the way down the front stretch. But they lost her much of the time she was traversing the backstretch.

Bubba felt his own heart race when Jodell punched it and started his first hot lap. Now they would see for sure if the car they had worked so hard on would be fast enough to show. It wouldn't take many laps to see if they even belonged with the others on this huge track. Or if they would be so slow they'd slide right off the high banking.

As Jodell rolled by, Bubba clicked the stopwatch he was holding. Joe was off with some of the crewmembers from a couple of the other teams timing the laps from the top of one of the trucks where they could see more. All the crews were anxiously watching the cars, not sure at all what to expect. Most of them held their breath, gripped their stopwatches, and watched with squinted eyes.

Billy and Bubba turned in unison as Jodell headed past them and off into turn one. The hands of the stopwatch spun, clicking off the seconds, as the Ford stayed in the middle groove through the corner then disappeared from view as it turned down into the beginning of the backstretch.

"Well, what do you think?" Billy asked as they watched some other cars pass in front of them. He then turned to look for Jodell to appear high in the third turn.

"I don't know yet. I guess we'll have a better idea in a couple of laps."

"Well, so far, so good."

"Yeah, but he is just now getting the car up to speed. I don't know. The way these cars are bouncing around out there is something else. I'm more than a little nervous," Bubba said, and just then the car showed up high in three.

They followed it on around and, as she came flying down toward the line past the tri-oval, Bubba clicked the stopwatch. He glanced down at the face of the timer and quickly did the math in his head, converting the seconds into miles per hour. The lap had been over one hundred and eighty miles an hour.

"What was it?" Billy asked.

"Fast! Real fast! And he ain't even got it good and cranked up yet. That one was about one eighty-five."

"What do you think it will take to win the pole?"

"I'd say well over one ninety. Likely one ninety-seven or one ninety-eight. Let's just pray these tires hold up going that fast."

"Lose a tire here and you're going to tear the fence down."

Or worse, Bubba was thinking. What would one of these things do if it blew a tire going that fast? The possibilities didn't appeal to him at all.

Jodell ran each lap a little harder than the one before as he began to get a better feel for the track. The wide banks made for flat-out, unfettered racing. He reached a point where he was hardly letting off on the gas at all as he steered the car through the center of the turns. In time, he felt he could probably run full-throttle all the way around the place, and he could only guess what the maximum speeds would be. This was his favorite kind of racing now, and he was loving this amazing new track.

Ten laps in, Jodell began to look for the best ways to attack the track. He found the car liked to take a higher line, allowing him to keep the torque up in the motor. That gave him the best run off the corners as he sling-shotted into the broad, long straights. The case of nerves he had suffered at the start of the practice run had quickly faded as he was now lost, concentrating on get-ting the car around the track the fastest possible way.

But now he could feel the ruggedness of the track in his arms, vibrating up through the steering column and right into his body. The car was bouncing, too, with all the speed he was maintaining across the rough surface. All the patching that had been done on the track over the last few weeks had left slight bumps all the way around the speedway and it felt at times as if he was driving across a rutted field instead of a high-speed race-track.

Next time around, Jodell got a good run off turn four and set his sights for the tri-oval. He could still feel the power in Joe's motor as he closed in on a group of slower cars running in front of him. A drop of sweat trickled down the side of his face as he peered through the goggles, concentrating on the back of the first car he would have to pass. The heat had quickly built up inside the car, but Jodell was too busy steering to really notice.

He quickly approached the first slow car and effort-lessly went on past on the inside as they approached the tri-oval. Jodell almost nicked the grass as he cut the cor-ner as closely as possible. Once past, he took the car back out toward the wall.

That was easy, he thought. The Ford had asserted her-self and went where she needed to go to get past the other racer.

And that's where he suddenly felt a sharp vibration from somewhere near the right front.

For an instant, he thought of continuing hard into the

first turn to feel it out, but his better judgement won out. He pulled down to the inside, out of the groove, and came gently out of the gas. He knew anything sudden would likely send the car spinning, as if it was running on ice. As the car slowed, the vibration did not go away. It actually seemed to get worse as the Ford rolled a bit more slowly through turns one and two.

At the slower speed, the wheel began to jerk violently and the right front began to shake and shimmy. Jodell brought the car slowly around the track, trying to get her onto the pit road before the tire or whatever it was that was causing the vicious vibration tore something up in the front end. He ran her on around the apron of the track, limping slowly through turns three and four. Then, Jodell could see the entrance to the pits, but it appeared to be miles and miles away. He wondered if he could make it all the way down there without the car shaking all to pieces.

"Katie, hold on. We may have to pick up all your parts with a dustpan!"

"Slowed down," Bubba shouted as he saw the car suddenly decelerate as she headed into turn one. If he were merely slowing to come to the pits, he would have done that out of four, not one. Something was wrong.

Johnny jumped up on the wall with them as they watched the car lose speed dramatically and then slip too low on the track for them to follow anymore. They all turned as one and watched for Jodell to come out of four and head their way.

"Blow an engine?" Billy queried.

"Naw, I don't think so. I didn't see any smoke," Bubba answered.

"It's the tires," Johnny offered with certainty.

"I hope not, 'cause we ain't hardly got ten good laps on that set. They should be fine. Something must have broke or he ran over something," Bubba said.

Tires didn't go bad in ten laps, and especially not when the car was not even pushing the envelope on speed as it circled around the track. Bubba could not bring himself to believe that the tires were the problem, despite all the talk at the track so far.

Jodell rolled the car to a stop, easing in front of where Bubba stood waiting on the pit wall. They could already clearly see the right front wheel bouncing, pumping up and down violently from the vibration as the car made its way slowly down the pit lane. Jodell was struggling to hold onto the shimmying steering wheel. Smoke rose from the right front of the car as it came to a stop.

Bubba hopped down from the wall with the jack already in hand and walked around to the right side of the car. He could see that the tire was a blistered mess of smoking rubber even before he jacked up the car. Billy and Johnny started to change the other tires and take the temperatures on their surfaces. Even the right rear was badly worn. Bubba banged on the roof of the car and signaled for Jodell to climb out. Something wasn't right with the car and they had to find out what it was before they would allow him to go back out there.

They all scratched their heads, trying to figure out what could cause the tires to get chewed up so quickly. Johnny went in search of one of the Goodyear engineers to come and look at their tires, but he quickly learned that other cars were coming in with similar problems. Up and down pit road and in the garage area everyone was buzzing about the badly blistered tires that were being pulled off the race cars.

Bubba strung the car, checked the toe-in, double-checked the air pressure, and looked at everything else he could think of that might be causing the problems with the tires. They finally bolted on another set and Jodell took the car back out on the track once again.

This time he was very careful as he cautiously brought the car up to speed.

The pavement was rough. There was no doubt about that. He could feel it as he drove. But he'd been on a lot worse track surfaces over the years. That was what made the situation so puzzling. It had to be the combination of the surface, high speeds, and the steep banking. There was simply no other explanation.

He ran every lap as if he had an egg between the sole of his shoe and the gas pedal. Every sense was tuned into the sensations he was getting from the track and the car. He stared intently at the raceway ahead, but he concentrated all his attention on what the track was telling him about his car. Driving so skittishly made him nervous, kept him on edge, and he did not like the feeling.

Jodell Lee showed up to run fast. That's the reason he raced. He wanted to run faster than everyone else on the track so he could come in first. He didn't want to drive scared, afraid to push his car to its maximum for fear it would fly apart on him. This wasn't racing. It was surviving. Waiting for disaster. The exhilaration he had felt on those first few laps at full speed had now been replaced by a dull disappointment. What was the use of running if you couldn't run fast? You might just as well be out on a Sunday drive with the wife and kids.

After about fifteen laps, the vibration was back, once again shaking the car violently. This time he had not even pushed the car close to the edge, and had certainly not approached the magnitude of speed that would likely be necessary to win a race at this place. Yet the tires had still failed. This track was definitely not ready for racing. He pounded the steering wheel in frustration as he pulled the shuddering car back into the pits.

Bubba could only shake his head as he looked at the nearly new, blistered, worn tires. Jodell climbed from the car while Billy and Johnny changed them out yet again. All around them, the pile of worn tires was building. They weren't the only ones, but that was hardly a comfort.

"Bubba, don't look like they were kidding about the darn tires," a frustrated Jodell Lee exclaimed as he looked over the most recent set of ruined rubber to have been pulled from his car.

"This track is chewing them up like a grinder. I don't think I've seen anything like it since way back when we used to try to run street tires," Bubba offered. He rolled the right front tire around so they could all see the severe wear.

"Somebody is going to get hurt if they don't get this solved quick," Jodell added.

"Well. Let's don't give up just yet. Let's do some adjusting and see what we can come up with."

"All right," Jodell said quietly, his heart clearly not in it.

Joe came strolling up then banging his clipboard on his thigh as he walked, the stopwatches dangling from around his neck. From the look on his face, it was obvious he was bringing bad news. He glanced down at the ruined tires and shook his head sadly.

"It ain't just us, boys. Everybody that's runnin' at all is in the same fix."

They all stood there silently, staring at the dead carcass of the tire for a full minute as if mourning its loss. It was Bubba who finally broke the spell.

"Well, we can do one of two things. We can pack up our grips and tuck our tails between our legs and admit we're beat and go on back home. Or we can get busy and see if we can figure out some way to whip this damn place."

And the purposeful way he turned on his heels and headed back for the garage told them all which way Bubba Baxter's vote would fall.

THE WALL

T
hings didn't improve appreciably for them the next day. The tires were still the chief topic of conversation wherever two or more gathered. The things simply were not going to hold up at the speeds they were running and under the stress the track's surface and banking was putting on them. Nobody had found the solution yet. Nobody. And that was unusual in itself. Normally, one or two teams would come up with a fix and before long, everyone else had found the answer, too. That's one of the things that made this sport so great. Once somebody found a way, everyone else dug until they, too, had found it. Not this time, though. This brand-new track had them all baffled, and the frustrations had caused tempers to run as hot as the August sun.

There was another subject being chewed over in the garage, too. The Professional Drivers Association was being forced into the spotlight now, what with all the concern about driver safety in the face of the tire situation. Suddenly, many of the drivers who had been non-committal about the organization or reluctant to make a stand were having their minds made up for them.

Jodell Lee was one of them.

He had watched the way things had been deteriorating between the drivers and their crews and the people who were running the race. Despite his earlier reservations, he had slowly come to the realization that the only means for him to look out for his own interests was to team up with the others, to show a unified front. The other issues could take care of themselves later. Right now, for safety reasons if nothing else, it was clear to Jodell that he should stand with Petty and Allison and the others. It wasn't as if they were holding out for more money or for vacation time or a pension like some labor union might do. The PDA had now gone from an organization that was merely trying to boost the comfort of the drivers and their families at the races to something far more important. It was trying to make sure none of them got seriously injured or killed on a dangerous racetrack.

Still, most of them wanted to run the race. Everyone in the garage was pushing for some type of solution to the tire and track situation. Most of the drivers, including Jodell, felt the best option was to postpone the race for a few weeks, only until some changes could be made to the track surface. And to give the tire manufacturers, Goodyear and Firestone, time to come up with a rubber compound that could withstand the stress.

None of them was afraid of speed. They simply wanted no part of suicide.

From the point of view of the track officials and the sanctioning body, postponement was not an option. The crowds were already showing up at the track to watch practice, to camp out in the broad fields that surrounded the place. Motels were already becoming filled as the fans flocked from all over the Southeast, tickets in hand, primed for two-hundred-mile-per-hour racing. It would be difficult to tell them to go home for awhile, to maybe come back again a few weeks later.

No, there would have to be a race.

There were also rumors of other pressures on the officials to run the event, that construction loans were coming due within the week, that refunding ticket money already in the bank would squeeze the owners dry, maybe doom the track altogether. That scuttlebutt was quickly denied in hastily called press conferences and with well-placed whispers to key writers. But the talk swirled around the place as surely as the red dust whipped up by the hot wind.

Whatever the truth might be, the frustrations and fears of the crews and drivers were simmering to a boil. And the first-ever driver boycott of a major stock car event was looking more and more like a possibility.

But no one had left the garages yet. There was still hope as the cars prepared to qualify for the race that might never be. Jodell had managed to turn a lap at a tick over 194 mph. He felt he could go faster yet, but he had begun to pick up a vibration on his second qualifying lap and had slowed a bit. Even then, with so few cars having run, those laps were still good enough to put the Ford in the top ten to start the race.

Jodell had actually begun to get comfortable with the giant track, even though he still tended to grit his teeth and keep his muscles tensed the entire time he was practicing out there. Every time he tried to make a long run at speed, he would begin to feel the slight shake in the steering wheel. Then he would know it was time to bring the car in and have the boys inspect the blistered tires. After the first warning from the telltale vibration, it only took another lap or two before the tire would be pushed to the point of failure. He relied on his own experience to sense when a tire was about to let go. Then he could bring the car in before it finally blew, before he found himself in a sudden trip to the fence and the inevitable violent stop once he got there.

The piles of blistered tires were piling up in the garage area in almost direct proportion to the rising tempers. Drivers and crew gathered in tight, angry knots, talking over the situation, first in whispers, then in voices loud enough for anyone to hear. Richard Petty, as president of the PDA, was forced to take a leadership role and had become the *de facto* spokesperson for the drivers.

Big Bill France, as president of the sanctioning body, was likewise being boxed into a tight corner. He had even suited up and had taken a few runs out on the speedway in a race car to prove his contention that the track was as safe as any other on the circuit was. But several of the drivers pointed out the blistered tire on the right front of France's car once he was back in the pits. That didn't help his argument.

Jodell Lee had found himself a shady spot in the garage where he could rest before the next practice. He had admitted out loud that he would be happy when this week was over. He came to a track to race, and most of what he had found in Talladega so far had been politics. He had seen plenty of riots and demonstrations and peace rallies on television, but he never thought such rancor would be a factor at a stock car track. Boycotts and shouting matches belonged at political conventions or in the streets of Birmingham or Nashville or Chicago, not at a racetrack. But as he swigged a cold soda, he had to admit to himself that it was inevitable that the times in which they found themselves had to ultimately affect them, too.

What had Billy Winton said?

"If you can keep your head when all about you are losing theirs and blaming it on you, then you'll be a man."

He knew it was from some poem he had studied back in high school, but Jodell agreed it certainly applied to all that was going on in 1969, and especially in Talladega, Alabama, in August.

The car waited patiently for him, sitting there high on jack stands while her tires and front end drew even more attention than usual. Bubba, Billy and Johnny stood there in front of her, scratching their heads, trying to devise a setup that would not chew the tires right off the rims. Joe Banker had found himself his own cool spot and dozed as he leaned back against one of the toolboxes. He had made a new best friend already, a rather stunning brunette with a molasses accent and the shortest shorts any of them had ever seen, and he had been spending lots of time with her the last couple of nights.

The Grand American cars were on the track now, roaring around, preparing for their Saturday race. Bubba walked over to where Jodell rested, then squatted down so he could be heard over the cars.

"Jodell, we think we got an idea for something we want to try. We're gonna make a few changes for the next practice and see how she does."

"Bubba, I appreciate it, but how many times do I have to tell you that there's not a blamed thing you can do. It's the tires, not the car. You got the car set up perfect."

"I realize that Jodell, but it galls me to sit around and whine about things. If we got time, then I'm gonna try to use it to see what I can do to make the car go faster or drive better."

"I know, and I appreciate that. But the way these tires are blowing out, I can barely drive the car as fast as it wants to go, much less push it to the limit like I want to do."

"I guess you're right," Bubba said, then stood and stretched himself to his full height and puffed out his chest. "But I'll tell you one thing. I'm gonna put Jodell Bob Lee in the best and the fastest car on the track, come hell or high water. I ain't lettin' no tire problems keep me from doing that."

"Okay, okay. Make your changes. We got several more sets of tires we can grind up and we sure ain't goin' nowhere else 'til Sunday."

And besides, he was thinking, it'll at least give me something new to test when I do get out there.

"You heard him! Let's get to work, boys!" Bubba cheered. He clearly had far more enthusiasm for tweaking than the rest of the team did by then.

The heat and the stress in the garage were beginning to wear on all of them. Only Bubba seemed immune.

"Billy, would you mind handing me that three-quarter-inch socket and drive?" Bubba yelled as he banged away under the racer.

Billy handed him the tool and stood there with his hands in his pockets.

"Thanks! Now if you would, hold that bar in place over there while I tighten her back up."

Billy took hold of the bar, then Johnny strolled over to help, too.

Jodell watched as they reluctantly went back to work. Normally he would jump up and help, too, but with Billy now on board, there was little room for him under the car. And besides, what with the smothering heat, he supposed it would be best that he save his energy for wrestling with the car once he was back out there.

But he hated sitting still. He spied a pay phone across the way and there was nobody else using it at the moment. He had a sudden urge and began digging in his jeans pockets, looking for some change.

"Hey, Jodell! Where you goin'?" Bubba cried out as

he spotted him walking away. As he worked, he had already been thinking of asking Jodell to fetch him something to eat. Maybe Joe Dee was headed in the general direction of the concession stand. Maybe there were some hot dogs in his future.

"Just over to the pay phone," Jodell answered, pointing.

"What for?"

"To use the phone, of course."

"Who you gonna call?" Bubba asked. Who in Alabama did Jodell know well enough to call on the telephone?

"I just have to make a call. Is that all right with you, Mother?"

"I guess. I just didn't think we knew anybody round here to call."

"Who said I was calling somebody here?"

"Oh," Bubba said. It never occurred to him that he might be calling somebody long distance in the middle of the day. "So, who you calling?"

"None of your business. Say, weren't you dying to work on the car just a few minutes ago?"

"Well, yeah. I guess."

"I'd appreciate it if you'd get it tightened back up before the start of the next practice then."

"Okay."

Bubba shrugged his big shoulders and went back to work. It was a small thing, but Jodell had been acting strangely the last few days. Like talking with Petty and Allison and them about the PDA. That was so unlike him.

Jodell ambled over to the pay phone and began feeding it coins. It was hung on the side of the building in full sun and he felt the heat of it beating on his shoulders as he dialed the number. He could hear the pulse on the other end of the line as it rang once, then twice, and finally a third time. He stood there, whistling tunelessly, waiting impatiently for it to be picked up.

Catherine Holt was busily typing up a court brief that had to be finished and filed by that afternoon. She was in the office all by herself, her boss off to lunch with someone. It had been a beautiful day so far in the East Tennessee mountains. She had planned to take a long walk during her own lunch hour, just to enjoy the sunshine, maybe look at the new dresses in the window at Barlett's Department Store, then give Grandma Lee a call to check on the kids, as she usually did. But first, she had to get the typing done.

That's when the telephone on the desk next to her began ringing again. The silly thing had been interrupting constantly all morning, the people on the other end frantic about this legal crisis or that or wanting to chat amiably while her work grew cold. Seems like it was far too often trouble, though, when the thing pealed.

She had almost decided to let it ring itself out. Whoever it was would assume she had gone on to lunch. They'd call back. And she could finish this job.

But something told her to go ahead and answer. She marked her place on the page she was working from and reached for the handset as it was chiming for the fourth time.

"Law office," she answered dryly, impatiently, and then noticed the unmistakable hum and static on the line that signaled it was a long distance call.

"Hi, honey."

The voice was wonderfully familiar. But before she could even answer, the roar of a race motor revving up in the background erased any doubt about who it was and from where he was calling.

"Jodell!" she yelled, then realized he had never called her in the middle of the day before. Her stomach turned over. "What's wrong, honey? Are you okay?"

"Of course, I am. I was just sitting here, bored to death, waiting for the next practice. Then I saw the telephone and decided I wanted to call you and hear the sound of your voice."

He could hear her sigh of relief all the way down the telephone line from Chandler Cove.

"Well, I'm certainly glad you did. It's such a pretty day that I was just about to go for a walk. Now I'll have something to smile about."

"I miss you, Cath. I can't wait to get home and see you and the kids."

He had no idea what had made him say that. For some reason, he had felt the need right then to tell her he missed her. And what was wrong with that, anyway? He could love racing and still miss his family, couldn't he?

"I can't wait to see you either. I wish I could come down for the race."

"If there is one. I guess you've heard what's going on down here."

"Uh-huh. There was a story in the paper yesterday." She felt a quick twinge in her breast. She had been trying to put the dour articles she had been reading out of her mind. "You're being careful, aren't you?"

"Of course. Can't win a race if the car is busted or the driver laid up."

"Are you going to run, Jodell? I know some of the others are saying . . ."

She couldn't imagine Jodell not driving if there was a race to be run. And it would be unlike him to join something like the proposed drivers' boycott. Still, she hoped he'd have sense enough to step away from the edge of a slippery slope.

"Honestly, I don't know for certain. We've got a few more things we want to try with the car and we're in the top ten for the race, so I hope we can. And I got to think the tire folks will get something worked out. But don't worry. I won't do anything silly."

"Thank God," she thought, then realized she had said it out loud, into the phone. He laughed softly.

"Don't worry about me. I'll be home late Sunday night either way. How are the kids?"

"Fine. Bob Jr. and that pup of his decided to go wading in the creek this morning, looking for 'fishies,' he said. They tracked mud into your grandmother's house and she threatened to move him and the dog out to the barn from now on."

"That's my boy!" Jodell said, laughing. He had gotten chased out of the house many times for similar transgressions. Even now, he sometimes got a broom to the butt from Grandma Lee if he tracked in sawdust from the shop.

"I apologized for him but Grandma Lee told me not to worry, that keeping up with him and the baby and Joyce's kids keeps her young."

"Well, honey, I guess my time is about to run out. I just wanted to call and hear your voice. I'll call tonight anyway."

"Okay. Do good in practice but be careful. I love you!"

"I love you, too.

Catherine gently placed the phone back into its cradle. She leaned back in her chair, smiling. It was such an unexpected joy to get the midday call from him, and especially when she knew he was having such a tough week at the track.

She settled back and resumed typing the dry legal paper she had been working on. But somehow, it was almost impossible to concentrate on the document. After another half hour, she stopped, decided to leave it until after her lunch break. She needed that walk now.

As she stepped outside into the warm sun, she felt

another twinge shoot through her. Something was nagging at her, something she couldn't quite put her finger on, something about Jodell's unexpected phone call.

She walked along in the clean, fresh air, following the tree-shaded sidewalk that bordered the street. She couldn't help thinking about the phone conversation. And then it hit her.

Why had he really called her in the middle of the day? He never did that. It was a small thing but it was not like Jodell Lee at all.

Maybe the tire situation was even more serious than he had let on and he was truly worried about what might happen. Or maybe he was simply tired and frustrated. He had been so looking forward to running the great new track and now there had been so much controversy and disappointment that it had surely taken some of the edge off for him.

She nodded at several folks she met along the way, answered in a few words their questions about how Jodell would do on Sunday. But as she stood finally in front of Barlett's, looking at but not seeing the display in the windows, she tried to remember everything she could from the brief talk she had had with her husband.

How had his voice sounded? What had been his real mood? And why had he actually called her?

She knew he was fearless on a racetrack. Going fast didn't frighten him. In fact, *not* going fast was one of his greatest fears. The speeds down there wouldn't be bothering him.

Why was she so put off by the call? He had actually sounded fine, almost cheerful. So why was she still so unnerved an hour later when she got back to the office and to the unfinished job that waited for her?

Her fingers flew on the typewriter keyboard and she tried to blank everything from her mind except for the words on the pages in front of her. But the uneasiness lingered.

Jodell walked back across the pavement toward where the car sat on its jack stands. He had a broad smile on his face.

"What's got into you, Lee?" Tiny Lund yelled at him as he passed by. "You look like you just won Daytona."

Jodell dismissed him with a wave and kept walking on over to the race car. The crew was still tweaking the setup under the car. Jodell ambled on over and kicked Joe Banker's outstretched legs to wake him. He needed for him to check the setting on the carburetor jets one last time before they took the car out for the next run.

Joe came awake in a surly mood.

"I hope when you die, the opossums burrow into your grave," he growled as he shakily stood and rubbed his eyes with the backs of his fists, like an ill child.

"And a wonderful good morning to you, too, cousin!" Jodell offered cheerfully enough.

When it was finally time to push the car up to the line, Bubba slowly lowered her while Billy pulled the jack stands out from beneath. They strung down the sidewalls of the tires on each side of the car once again to check the wheel alignment. Bubba took a wrench and went in the front fender well to make a final adjustment before he announced his satisfaction.

Jodell slowly climbed into the hot driving suit while he tried to get himself mentally ready to take the car back out onto the track. With all the tire and track problems, he knew he had to be even sharper than usual every time he pulled out of the garage. At these speeds there was even less room for error.

"Ready to go here," Joe pronounced as he closed the hood on the big engine. He fastened the hood pins, giving each a solid yank to make sure they would hold. "You ready, Joe Dee?"

"Ready as I will ever be. I want to get out and try to draft with some of the other fast cars if we can."

"Look for Petty, Brickhouse, Cale, Leroy, Pearson, or Allison. All of them have been real fast on the watch."

"I'll look for them and hope a couple of us can get hooked up. Billy, why don't you run down to the Goodyear tent and see if there is any news on that new compound they were supposed to be working on?"

"Right, boss," he said as he placed a handful of tools into the toolbox.

"See if they're gonna fly some more tires in here tonight. If they are, then we might have to play around a little with the magic setup that Bubba's just put under the car."

"I'll check it out and let you know. "

"What I wouldn't give for a set of tires that could run at speed here and hold up!"

"Wouldn't we all, boss? Wouldn't we all?" Billy replied with a smile as he turned and headed out of the garage. Bubba Baxter shook his head and echoed Jodell's and Billy's sentiments.

"Joe Dee, don't you know how much I would love to see what my car could really do flat-out around this place? Just sailing along wide open?"

"Well, sir, let's just pray they get some tires in here tonight with the right compound so we can see what we can really do."

"Just run it as fast as you can in the meantime. Don't take no silly chances and mess up the car. Wait 'til we come back next time. They'll get this place fixed up right and you'll love it as much or more than you do Daytona."

"Let's rev her up and see how we do."

Jodell helped them push the car back out of the garage

stall. He swung his long legs in through the open window and settled into the seat while Bubba helped him get buckled in. Then he fastened on his helmet while Bubba wiped at the windshield with a rag he had fished out of his back pocket.

"I'm gonna check these tire pressures one last time," Johnny said, grabbing the tire gauge from his pocket and bending to the left rear tire.

"Make sure they match these," Joe said, handing him a slip of paper with the latest tire pressures being recommended by the Goodyear engineers.

Joe stuck his head in the window and pretended he was about to kiss Jodell on the cheek. He dodged a mock right hook from his cousin.

"I'm gonna go on and see if I can get up on that platform over there to time these laps. I want to try and get some times on Petty, Pearson, and some of the others to see if they've found anything we ain't."

Johnny finished with the pressure check and, satisfied they had the recommended pounds of air, he leaned lazily up against the side of the car. Bubba pulled up the window net and snapped it into place while Jodell reached over and flipped the switch on the starter.

The engine rumbled beautifully. Jodell gave the gas a tentative couple of punches with his right foot, listened appreciatively, then kicked in the clutch and reached for the shifter. Bubba gave the window net one last tug then bent down and instinctively reached in and shook Jodell's hand. While they performed that ritual every time before the start of a race, it was a bit unusual for a practice session. Jodell flashed Bubba the thumbs-up sign anyway and reached over to shift the car up into gear.

Johnny slapped the side of the Ford as she pulled off. Jodell gunned the car, chirping the tires as he pointed her out toward the track. Johnny and Bubba hustled off to their usual perches on the pit wall.

"How do you really think she'll run, Bubba?" Johnny asked. He knew Bubba had an uncanny ability to predict lap speeds to within tenths of seconds.

"Hard to tell 'cause he's gonna go out and try to run a couple of good hard laps first, then try to gauge how the tires are doing. If they hold up, he's gonna try to draft with some of the other fast cars at a race pace. We got to figure out pretty soon who he can run with come race day."

"I'd say it will be the usual suspects," Johnny said. "Add in Brickhouse to that bunch, too."

"We'll see here in a minute."

They stood on the wall and waited for Jodell to bring the car around for the first time. Bubba took his rag and wiped his forehead as he studied some of the cars already running on the track.

Meanwhile, coming off pit road, Jodell gunned the Ford and pulled it out onto the apron of the track. He ran quickly up through the gears and took the car through turn one at the bottom of the track until he had built up enough speed to stay out of the others' way. He twisted the steering wheel back and forth to make sure the tires were clean as he shifted the car down into fourth gear. She sailed off down the backstretch, gathering up speed all the while as the big motor did its job without complaint.

But even then, a pack of cars came flying up from behind him and passed him going into turn three as if he was parked. He tried to use their draft and tuck in behind them but he wasn't going fast enough to latch on. Jodell took the low line through that corner and began to lay out in his own head how he was going to run the next lap.

The strategy was to push it as hard as he could so Joe

could get a good time on the lap. With fresh rubber beneath him, he needed to see where they stood with their speed before he worried about tire wear and setup.

Coming off of turn four, Jodell pushed his accelerator foot all the way to the floor. He reveled in the way the thrust of his mighty motor shoved him backward into the seat, sending his helmet hard into the headrest. Pure, raw, unadulterated speed. That was what he loved better than anything else about big-track racing.

The car came roaring by the start/finish line going full auger. Bubba beamed broadly as he saw the beautifully polished car he'd spent so much time and sweat building go flying by their position. She looked beautiful in the bright sunlight. The engine was not missing a beat either. Bubba could sense that this was going be a really fast lap.

Joe stood high up on the crowded platform, working his stopwatches. He'd click one, then the other, and then he'd scribble something in his indecipherable chicken's scratch on the clipboard. And he'd do it all without ever once losing sight of the cars he was timing.

Jodell now focused on the towering first turn shimmering in the afternoon heat down beyond the front-stretch tri-oval. The car did feel good underneath him. Maybe Bubba's adjustments had done some good after all. He'd have to compliment the big man when he got back to the garage. And he was beginning to get used to all the little nuances on the track's surface, too. This trip, for some reason, he felt calm and confident. He focused in on the white line at the bottom of the track and began sighting the groove he would follow through the turn ahead.

He could feel the gentle vibrations coming up through his foot that was plastered to the floorboard. He looked ahead now to the group of cars that were running a couple of hundred yards in front of him. He wanted to try to close in on them to see how the car would react in their draft as the aerodynamics actually sucked a trailing car along behind the lead machines.

He glanced at the gauges before he got too close to the cars ahead, making sure the temperature was coming up and the oil pressure was holding. Another quick glance in the mirror confirmed he was clear of any trailing traffic and then he looked back at the rapidly approaching turn, ready to take it once more, but this time on his terms.

He held the car down low against the white inside line until the moment he knew it was right to let her start to drift up toward the second groove as it reached the center of the turn. He used the banking to his advantage to get a good run coming off the second towering turn.

"Come on, Miss Nancy! Come on!" he half-whispered as he pushed the car down the back straightaway without ever once lifting his foot from the accelerator. If anything, he now pushed his foot down a little harder, trying to coax another half a horsepower out of Joe's motor.

Jodell tore down the back stretch, purposely drifting down a bit from the outside wall. He set the car up to take the line he wanted through the third turn and sailed into the throat of the corner at over two hundred miles an hour. Jodell sawed at the wheel, trying to keep the car down on the low line around the track. The ride was rough but Jodell could tell it was going to be a good, fast lap.

And those were the best kind. Fast laps that you could drive away from and leave behind.

Bubba watched him come off the fourth turn and streak down through the tri-oval. He stretched his frame to its full height so he could see how the car was positioned when it exited the transition from turn to straightaway. He held up his own stopwatch he was holding and clicked it as Jodell flashed by.

"Whew! Man alive! Joe Dee smoked that lap!" Bubba exclaimed. "One ninety-five or a shade better. I told you those changes would work."

"He was flying, Bubba. Now that he's got a good head of steam, this next lap ought to be even faster," Billy agreed as he turned slowly, following the car off into the first turn.

"Come on Joe Dee! Dig it! Dig it!" Bubba screamed as they watched him drift high into turns one and two. Tire troubles, PDA, boycotts . . . they were all forgotten in the excitement of watching their car sail around this magnificent new track at such breathtaking speed.

The high line through the turns had allowed Jodell to keep the RPMs up in the motor and that had let him get a better run down the backstretch. He didn't need a stopwatch to tell him he had just run a superb lap, or that this one was shaping up even faster. The car still felt good under his seat.

He glanced up into the mirror then back through the windshield at the cars in front of him. He had almost caught them, was within about a hundred yards or so of their trunk lids, and he knew he would catch their draft most likely in the next turn. That would allow him to tuck right up on their rear ends and let them pull him for a bit. With so few laps run here so far, he could only imagine how the powerful draft would be here compared to Daytona.

Jodell set his line in turn three and felt the car start to set down on the springs, exactly the way she was supposed to. The tires got a good grip and he was able to hold his line, even at this higher notch of speed. He could feel the draft off the front cars as he dove into turn three, exactly as he had suspected. The car started to rapidly close in on the group as she drifted up slightly.

Jodell glanced in the mirror for an instant just as the car started to exit the turn, simply to make sure nobody had slipped up on him from behind. A tap in the rear at this speed could lead to a wild and wooly ride.

Nobody there. Good. He could draft or he could pass these guys, then go look for somebody faster to team up with.

But before he could decide which, the steering wheel suddenly jerked hard to the right, as if someone in the passenger seat had reached over and tried to grab it away from him. Before he could even begin to react, the car swerved hard up what was left of the turn, as if she had stubbornly made up her own mind to go somewhere else besides where Jodell wanted to go.

But there was nothing up there in that direction but a solid concrete retaining wall.

Hard lick coming! Jodell thought as he instinctively went for the brakes and tried to twist the wheel to the left, to try to veto the car's foolish intent.

But it was far too late. At practically full speed, the car plowed headfirst into the wall. Hard lick, indeed. It was the most stunning impact Jodell Lee had felt so far in his driving career. The blow brought the car to an instant halt, then she bounced a couple of times before slowly spinning back toward the inside of the track. The hood had been crumpled back practically to the windshield and gas and oil and coolant were already pouring from beneath what had once been the motor.

Jodell was briefly aware of having hit something that did not move. He also recognized that the safety belts had done their job well or he would have been catapulted through the windshield to have his own personal collision with the retaining wall. But he also sensed that the belts had ripped the breath right out of his lungs and that something in his chest that wasn't supposed to give had done just that.

And in the split second before a welcomed gray darkness washed everything away, Jodell Lee was aware of his body flying all over the cockpit. Or at least flying as much as the belts would allow. And of some parts cracking hard against the inside of the car, no matter how diligently he tried to keep them still.

But there was no pain. No hurt.

There was only the precious, warm darkness.

THE TALLADEGA SHOULDER

Joe Banker wore a broad smile. The last lap had been one of the best they'd yet turned in practice, and one of the fastest times Jodell Lee had ever driven. He looked at the stopwatch he was holding and his smile grew even broader. This lap was going to be even better. His driver had found the way around this behemoth in a car that was obviously finally fine-tuned for the monster they were running.

He watched Jodell catch the draft and start to pull in on the pack of cars that were running in front of him. He hoped they would have enough laps left before the tires gave out to allow them to draft awhile with the cars. It would be a good chance to see how the draft worked at this track.

As Joe watched, his grin still frozen on his face, he saw Jodell's car suddenly jerk upward as if yanked in that direction by an invisible force. An instant later it

went head-on *hard* into the outside retaining wall. Even
through the boiling tire smoke, he could see that the car
had seemed to stop instantly before slowly spinning off
the wall, back down to the inside of the track, and then
out of his line of sight.

"Jesus!" Joe said, dropping his stopwatches. He
watched for another minute to see if Jodell might have
gotten the car underway and had somehow managed to
come on around, but he instinctively knew it was futile.
The car had hit the wall solidly and at full speed and
Joe had seen it happen clearly.

He also kept checking the last spot where he had seen
the car drop out of his sight, watching for fire and black
smoke. Thankfully there was none yet.

"Do you see him?" he asked the man standing next
to him, a crewmen from David Pearson's team.

"Nope. It looks like the blue car clobbered that wall
and that thing's gonna be about half as long as it was
before."

"I know. That's what I'm afraid of."

Joe climbed down from the platform and sprinted
across the garage area toward where Bubba and the others had been standing, wondering why their driver had
not come on around. And whether he might have gotten
caught up in the crash that had brought out the yellow
flag over the practice.

Bubba and Billy had lost sight of Jodell as he raced
down the backstretch out of turn two, then they had to
strain to pick him up again in the center of the third turn.
They watched him grab the draft off the bunch of cars
in front of him and begin to pull in on them like a mag-
net. Their view was partially blocked as the cars came
off turn four but they could certainly see the tire smoke
and a car spinning slowly downward on the track.

"Somebody is in the fence!" Bubba said, trying to get
a good look at the car. "Can you tell who it is?"

"I can't see for all the smoke and dust. I don't even know how many cars it is. Looks like one of them hit the wall pretty hard, though," Billy answered as he squinted, trying to see what had happened and to whom.

The group of cars that had been directly in front of Jodell came streaming by their position at full song. The flagman in the flag stand was showing them the yellow flag and they were already slowing. As Bubba watched the cars zoom by, he quickly realized which car was missing and he felt his stomach sink.

"I think it's Jodell, Bubba," Billy said then, having just realized the same thing Bubba had. Bubba stood there for a moment, praying they were both wrong, knowing they weren't. The last time he'd had a feeling this bad had been at the 600 in Charlotte years before when Jodell had gotten caught up in the fiery crash that had cost Fireball Roberts his life. Jodell had come out of that one okay, though. Surely he was all right this time, too.

But the speeds they were running here had Bubba powerfully worried. Anybody hitting a wall in this place would be hitting it deadly hard. Maybe it had been a glancing blow, a quick, smoky kiss, and his driver was out there now, kicking the wreck and cussing his luck.

Billy started to say something else but when he looked up, Bubba was gone.

"All right, we better get all this stuff back to the garage," Johnny said matter-of-factly. He knew they would have a lot of work ahead of them trying to get the car fixed for the race. If they still had a driver to run it, that is. He started stacking tires on the wagon.

"Yeah, I guess we better. That car is going to be all torn up," Billy agreed and he started grabbing up some tools.

Joe came running up then.

"Where's Bubba?"

"He took off like he usually does. He went to make sure Jodell is okay," Johnny told him.

Joe didn't say anything else. It was obvious that they had not seen what he had seen, how hard the car had hit and how much damage it had sustained. He wasn't going to tell them until he found out for sure how Jodell was.

The first of the rescue trucks pulled up to find the crumpled car smoking, steam hissing out the flattened front end. Jodell was slumped over the wheel and he was not moving. The safety workers jumped out of the back of the truck and quickly ran to the car, their first responsibility to check on the driver. One of them was calling for the ambulance even before they got the window net down.

One of the workers dropped the net while several more of them quickly went to work on Jodell, trying to stabilize him. He had a weak pulse but he was clearly struggling to breathe. They avoided doing much to move him until they could check his neck and back. A small tongue of flame licked at something combustible underneath the smashed engine compartment. Fuel from the busted line fed the flames and that forced the safety workers to make a quick decision on getting Jodell out of the car. Fortunately, the ambulance and some of the medical workers pulled up then.

A fireman directed a fire extinguisher up under the hood to try and get to the blaze but the crumpled metal kept most of the retardant from reaching the base of the flames. That made it imperative for them to get the driver out of the car quickly. One of the medical people slipped a neck brace on him while the others worked to get his belts cut away. Finally they got him unhooked and out of the car and placed him gently down on a stretcher.

Just then, with a blast from a larger fire extinguisher, the flames beneath the hood were finally smothered.

With the driver safely out and the fire extinguished, the crews could go to work getting the wrecked car out of the way and the track cleared so the rest of the drivers could continue to practice.

By the time Bubba had made his way down the back of the pit road and had climbed the fence to get out into the infield, running past beer-swigging fans and security personnel who would stop him, he arrived just in time to see the safety crew loading a motionless Jodell into the back of one of the ambulances. The medical personnel were working on him, trying to help him breathe easier.

Bubba stopped in the middle of the grass and looked at the race car. He felt as if his heart was going to stop. The front end was pushed in almost all the way back to even with the windshield. The driver's compartment was intact but it was obvious the car had taken a wicked ride into the outside wall. Now, the ambulance pulled away, headed for the infield hospital.

Bubba turned and walked slowly back to the garage, his head low. From what he had seen, he fully expected the worst. The big man ignored the greetings from all his friends in the garage as he walked slowly past on the way back to their stall. He felt as bad as he'd ever felt in his life. The sight of his best friend being pulled out of the car and being placed, unmoving, on the stretcher kept getting replayed over and over in his mind. He shuffled along, oblivious to everything around him.

Then he felt somebody grab him by the arm. He tried to shake them loose and keep walking. Then, when they would not let go, he jerked away and turned, his fist drawn, ready to throw a punch.

"Bubba!" Joe said, shaking him. "Did you hear me?"

"What?"

"I said come on. We got to get over to the hospital and check on Jodell."

"I don't need to check on him," Bubba answered slowly. "I saw him when they pulled him out of the car. Joe, he wasn't moving."

"He was probably just knocked out cold. Now come on."

The two of them sprinted off toward the hospital area. The ambulance had beaten them there, of course, and had already unloaded its patient. The security guard at the door checked their credentials before waving them on in. They found Jodell on a gurney surrounded by a team of medical personnel. They had cut away his driver's suit and were probing all over his body.

Jodell was awake but obviously very groggy. He kept trying to get up, saying over and over that he was all right, that the race was going to start without him. A couple of the medical folks kept him pinned down to the examining table. Someone told Bubba and Joe to wait in the other room.

After about twenty minutes, one of the doctors came out to talk with them.

"You boys part of his team?"

"Yes sir," they both answered in unison.

"Does he have any immediate family here at the track, by any chance?"

"Me," Joe spoke up promptly. "I'm his first cousin."

"Well, that will have to do. We need you to sign a release. We are going to have to send him over to Birmingham to the hospital."

"Hospital?" Joe asked, his eyes growing wide.

So did Bubba's. Elated at the sight of Jodell actually talking and trying to get up, Bubba now felt the gloom begin to descend on him once again.

"He's taken a nasty lick to the head and we think his leg or knee is broken. He's also dislocated his shoulder. We just want to get him somewhere with the proper equipment and some good bone doctors so they can check him over good."

"Is he going to be okay?" Joe asked.

"All we know is that he's taken a hard shot. One thing's for sure. He's not going to be driving a race car again anytime soon."

"Can we ride with him in the ambulance?" Bubba asked. He had to struggle to clear his throat so he could get the words out.

"Suit yourself, but you're going to have to hustle. They're getting ready to send him on. Sign here."

Joe scribbled his name as Jodell was wheeled past them out to the waiting ambulance. He didn't seem to recognize them now. His eyes were closed and his face was ash white. They followed him out and Bubba hopped up in the front with the attendant. Joe climbed into the back with Jodell. The ambulance took off immediately as soon as the rear doors were closed.

Only an hour or so later, the two of them paced nervously back and forth in the waiting room. Finally, they decided they needed to call home and Joe suggested Bubba call Joyce, tell her, and let her break the news to Catherine so somebody would be there with her.

Joyce picked up the phone on the fourth ring. One of the kids was screaming in the background and that made it hard for him to hear her.

"Hi, baby. How are you?" he asked.

"Bubba?"

"Yeah."

"What's wrong?"

"What? Oh. I'm fine."

"No, what is wrong?"

She had sensed immediately that something was not right. She knew her husband's voice. Something was very wrong.

"Uh. Well. I . . . uh . . . well. We . . ."

"Bubba Baxter! Tell me! What is it?" she yelled.

"I'm at the hospital and . . ."

"Are you okay?" she asked, cutting him off, the fear apparent in her own voice.

"Yes, I'm fine." He took a deep breath. "There was a wreck. We are at the hospital in Birmingham."

"We? Who all is hurt?"

She first thought of an accident on the highway. Nothing really bad had ever happened to them on the track.

"Just Jodell. He had a bad wreck in practice."

Then it hit Joyce what he was talking about. She could feel her heart leap into her throat even as the tears started to flow down her cheeks.

"How bad is he, Bubba?"

"Pretty bad. He just about destroyed the car. The doctor said his leg is probably broke and he took a bad lick to the head. They ain't talked to us in a while so we ain't for sure exactly what is going on."

Joyce and Bubba talked quietly for a few more minutes then she hung up the phone. She pulled herself together and ran over to the neighbors' house to see if they could watch the kids until she got back. Then, somehow, she drove into Chandler Cove to the law office where Catherine Lee worked. She parked the car and tried to hold herself together as she stepped inside. Catherine sat at her desk sipping on a soda.

"Joyce, what in the world are you . . . ?"

Then she saw the look in Joyce's eyes and she froze. Something was terribly wrong. The kids? Grandma Lee? Joyce swallowed hard before she spoke.

"Catherine, they had a bad wreck this afternoon in practice."

Jodell!

"Is he okay? Just tell me he's going to be okay."

"Bubba said he's in a hospital in Birmingham."

"But is he okay?"

"I think so but I don't know. I couldn't get Bubba to tell me much. I don't think they've been told much either."

The two of them hugged, then sat and cried together for a minute. Joyce drove Catherine home as they waited to hear more news. In all the confusion, Bubba had left no number or even the name of the hospital where they were, so they could not call back to check on Jodell.

Finally they started calling every hospital in Birmingham, trying to find which one Jodell was in. On their fifth call they found the right place but they would only tell them that he was stable but in serious condition, that that's all they could divulge over the telephone. They did get the number for the pay phone in the waiting room for the trauma unit and finally got back in touch with Bubba.

"The doctor just left. He's got a jammed knee, possibly a broken leg, a dislocated shoulder and a concussion. That's all we know right now," he reported. "They say the leg and knee are the worst. The shoulder is going to be sore for a while. They're checking his concussion right now. At least he's hard-headed."

That did it. Catherine and Joyce would leave the kids with Grandma Lee and start for Birmingham right then.

Back at the track, Johnny and Billy had begun the difficult task of loading everything up by themselves. Once they found out that Jodell was on the way to the hospital they did what they had to do. They went back to work. When the car came in on the wrecker, they couldn't believe the damage. What had been a beautiful, shiny new race car looked now as if it was fit only for the wrecking yard.

Some members of Junior Johnson's team helped them get the mangled car up on the trailer. Over the years,

Johnny had gotten to know several of them quite well. He had even spent some rare off-weeks over in North Wilkesboro with them, helping them work on their cars and swapping stories.

Finally, late in the evening, they finished loading everything up on the truck. Bobby Allison, Tiny Lund, and many of the others stopped by to check on them and see if they'd gotten any updates on Jodell. Once they learned that Catherine and Joyce were on their way down, they knew there was nothing more for them to do but go on home and wait there. They slowly pulled out of the garage about an hour after dark and started the long, sad trek back to Chandler Cove.

Fans waved and gave them the thumbs-up sign as the truck wound its way through the throngs of people who'd made the trip to Alabama to see the new speedway. They grimly waved back.

Ironically, they were only the first team to leave the track that weekend. On Saturday afternoon, they would be followed by dozens of other teams who simply weren't prepared to deal with all the risk and uncertainty the tire situation had thrown into the mix.

Jodell Lee had been spared the decision of whether to run or not.

The incessant banging and clanging sounds spilling from the racing shop behind Grandma Lee's house were familiar and somehow comforting over the next few weeks. Life was, indeed, going on. Bubba, Billy, Johnny and Joe were hard at work, trying to get both the short-track car and a new superspeedway car ready for the next few races. With the upcoming schedule the way it was, with Charlotte, Martinsville, and North Wilkesboro lurking ahead like rough spots in the road, there was plenty of work to do in the shop to prepare.

The Talladega car, the one they had spent so many hours on, sat forlornly in a corner of the shop. Once they pulled the engine out, they could see how truly staggering the damage was. The whole front end would have to be replaced, as would most of the sheet metal on the car. It would be months before this piece of machinery would see the track again.

A week after the wreck, they were working away one morning and had just taken their first break when they heard the shop door creak open. In hobbled Jodell Lee on a set of crutches. His lower left leg was in a cast from ankle to mid-calf and his knee was still swollen to the size of a grapefruit. He could hardly limp along on the crutches because of the pain in his left shoulder and he grimaced with every step.

"Hey, Hopalong!" Joe cried. "You ain't supposed to be up and around on that knee yet. What are you doing off the couch?"

"I figured I'd come out here and see if y'all needed any help."

"Catherine finally got sick of your butt and throwed you out of the house is what you mean," Johnny laughed.

"Joe Dee, the doc said for you to take it easy until the swelling goes down," Bubba fussed.

"Yeah, but I can't see the race cars and watch over what you boys are doing when I'm all cooped up in the house like some kind of poor, pitiful shut-in."

"We got things covered here. You need to rest and heal up if you're gonna race again this season," said Joe.

"I figure I'll be ready by Wilkesboro."

All four of them snorted in disbelief.

"Wilkesboro? You idiot! That's just in a couple of weeks. Doc said it would be months before you could drive a race car again."

"Aw, come on now. A doctor might know something about medicine, but he don't know anything about racing. Heck, if I don't race for months, we ain't gonna have a race team left. We got bills to pay to keep this thing going."

"We'll get someone else to drive until you're ready."

"Yeah, who? Joe, I'll be ready just as soon as I can get this gimpy leg strong enough to push in the clutch and this shoulder tightened up enough to steer. Give me a couple of weeks when the swelling goes down and I should be able to manage just fine."

"And what does Catherine have to say about this?" Joe asked.

"It doesn't matter. She leaves the racing to me. Now, are y'all gonna keep yapping or are you gonna get us a car ready to race?"

"Listen, y'all leave Joe Dee alone!" Bubba interjected. He had done just enough driving over the years to understand how intoxicating it became to a man, how hard it was to stop doing it once he had had a taste of it. And that was truer of Jodell Lee than anyone else he had ever known. The man lived to race. If there ever came a time he couldn't, Bubba figured Jodell would simply lie down and die. "When he says he's ready to race, then old Bubba here is going to give him a race car that is capable of winning. Joe Dee will know if he can go or not."

Then Bubba seemed to have another thought. He waved for Billy to come follow him. A few minutes later they were back, toting the flowered couch from Jodell's den between them. Jodell grinned broadly and slapped the big man on the back with his good arm, then settled down onto the couch and propped up his bum leg. It took him awhile to adjust everything so it was comfortable but then he sat back and sighed happily.

Although it was tough for him to watch them get a car ready that he would not be piloting, he could, at least, once more feel that he was part of the team. He wished he could grab a wrench and go to work alongside them, but this was the next best thing.

He spent the better part of the next couple of weeks sprawled out on the couch watching them prepare the car, first for Martinsville then North Wilkesboro. Then, when the time came to tow it over for the race the first week, he demanded to be allowed to ride along with them. He wanted to observe the entire process from a perspective he had never had before: outside the car. But Catherine won out and he had to stay home and listen to the whole mess on the radio.

They tried a young driver there who supposedly had a lot of experience on the flat, narrow track, but it had been a disaster. The kid looked as if he had never been inside a race car before and they barely won enough money to cover expenses. Even more importantly, they were lucky to bring the car home with all the fenders still attached after the way the substitute had pounded away on everybody else.

Listening to the debacle had only made Jodell that much more determined to climb back into the car as soon as his leg and shoulder would let him. And he especially wanted to do it the next week at North Wilkesboro.

The Thursday afternoon before that race they were still working frantically on the car, getting ready for the short trip over the mountains. The event was to be on Sunday and they had to hustle to be ready. Plenty of friends and family were likely to be there from Chandler Cove and they would love to have a car running that they could be proud of.

It had not been easy, though. They had been forced to re-brake the car since their sub driver had literally burned them up the week before. The transmission was grinding, too, and it took Johnny the better part of a day to replace it, along with the worn clutch pad. Joe spent all week working on the motor. He could only hope that the kid hadn't over-revved it one too many times. They needed this particular motor to finish several more races before they rebuilt it. Billy worked all week beating out the rumpled fenders and repainting the car, and he would need most of Friday to re-letter it.

They all hoped silently that Jodell would be able to drive the race, too, for several reasons. Of course, he would be far less likely to tear up the car than a substitute would be and, besides, he would have a good chance of actually winning on this, one of their favorite tracks.

But Jodell's own frustration with his slow healing was also beginning to wear on the crew, too. He tried to help as much as he could but Bubba would have none of it, sending him back to the couch every time he tottered over to show how something should be done right or to question an adjustment on the machine. He had finally resigned himself to watching from over there, but still offering his constant suggestions and criticism on everything that they were trying to do. They tolerated his orders and remarks silently but still gritted their teeth and called him ugly names under their breath as they did.

Even though the swelling in his knee had gone down some, it was still stiff and virtually useless, the heavy cast was in the way, and he still wore a harness to keep his shoulder in place. No one talked about how it would be possible for him to drive the car at Wilkesboro, especially when Catherine was within earshot, but everyone on the crew knew it was Jodell's intention to drive the race, no matter how badly it hurt. She was not happy that he was even planning on making the trip to this race either. If she had had any inkling that he might actually be thinking about climbing into the race car, she would likely have tethered him to a tree in the backyard alongside Pit Stop the puppy.

Bubba and Joe had mixed feelings on the subject. They knew he hurt, and he was a long way from being ready to manhandle a race car at speed. But it was not the same racing without Jodell there, and especially without him in the car. The experience at Martinsville had shown that they were only marginally a team without him.

Billy Winton had especially noticed the change in the dynamics of the group, how everyone seemed on edge, directionless. He could tell that the team had fallen apart once its leader had been sidelined. He had seen the same thing happen in battle, and he pondered once again the similarities between pressure competition and all-out war. As he sat sprawled on the shop floor of the shop and banged away on a dented fender, he wondered how he might be able somehow to help restore the unity they had had before the wreck at Talladega. He had done it in Vietnam, under far more deadly circumstances. Or was the only answer simply to get Jodell back in the car as soon as they could?

Finally loading up and getting ready to head out for the track seemed to help everyone's mood. Catherine had reluctantly relented and had given her blessing for Jodell to go along with them, but she had issued a long list of marching orders they all had to promise to obey. He never gave her any indication that he actually planned on driving. It was tantamount to a lie, the first he had ever told her. He knew it and felt guilty about it, but he also knew that if he even so much as hinted that he might run a lap in the car, she would have hidden his crutches and strapped him to the bed.

Neither Joyce nor Catherine planned to make the trip over since they had been gone so much lately and wanted to give Grandma Lee a break from the kids. Besides, they assumed there would be somebody else in the car anyway. Now, with everything set for the trip and their departure imminent, there they were, with Grandma and the kids lined up on the porch, waiting for the convoy to emerge from the barn for a proper farewell.

Jodell dreaded having to get past the goodbyes without giving away their plan. He figured the maneuver would surely be as treacherous as the first turn at Darlington.

Bubba was busy, checking the trailer fastenings, stalling leaving the shop as long as he could, when Jodell hobbled up next to him and poked him with the tip of one of the crutches.

"Come on, big boy. There ain't no use putting this thing off. Just be cool and calm like we practiced and we'll get through this fine."

"I don't know, Joe Dee. Joyce can see through me like I'm invisible or something when I try to stretch the truth."

"We're not gonna tell them any lies. We're just not gonna give any extra information, that's all."

"Okay, but I don't like this one bit."

"You want that kid back in your race car this week, tearing it all up?"

The look in Bubba's eyes answered that question.

"I'm just afraid you and me both are going to be in a peck of trouble before this weekend is over."

"Thanks for the positive attitude, Bubba. Now come on and let's get this over with."

Jodell found a seat on the back of the trailer and they eased the truck up the short drive, pulling to a stop at the porch steps. He carefully slid off, climbed back on his crutches, and eased up to kiss Grandma Lee first, then hugged and kissed each of the kids. They all gave hugs to each of the "uncles," too, while Jodell embraced Catherine and held her as close and tight as his shoulder and sore ribs would allow. He tried to watch Bubba and Joyce out of the corner of his eye to see how that was going.

"Well, I guess we better be on our way," he finally announced and kissed her deeply once more. Lord, he hated to mislead her this way! But what could he do?

She held him away from her then and looked him full in the face, a worried look in her eyes.

"You are going to behave aren't you? You strain that leg hobbling around that racetrack and you'll be that much longer being able to drive, you know."

"Yes ma'am." He tried to manage a grin and hoped he looked sincere as he let her go and started back toward the truck. "We'll see you Sunday night, honey."

"We'll have a late supper ready when you get home."

He felt another stab of guilt. Joyce didn't help his feelings at all when she let go Bubba and stepped over and gave him a careful hug, too.

"Jodell, you sure you feel up to going? Bubba and Joe can handle things at the track, can't they?"

Bubba made a face neither wife could see but he jumped right in to help.

"Now, baby, I don't know. If he stays away from the racetrack for another week I don't know if we can stand being around him anymore."

"I know what you mean, Bub," Catherine agreed. "That's the only reason I'm letting him go. I may divorce him if one of you boys don't take a tire iron to him first."

They all laughed and the two men took advantage of the moment to head for the truck. Catherine followed to help Jodell up into the seat without twisting his knee while Joyce gave Bubba one more lingering hug. The rest of the crew pulled away in the car while Bubba gave a honk of the truck's horn and acknowledged the waves and shouts from all those assembled there.

They weren't even out of sight before Jodell turned to Bubba and gave out a happy whoop.

"I think we did it, Bub!"

"Yep, I believe we are home free."

He found a good song on the radio and both men sang

along as they eased out onto the highway and pointed the truck toward the mountains and the next race.

Back on Grandma Lee's front porch, Catherine and Joyce stood and waved as long as they could see the truck with the race car following along behind it. Then Catherine turned to Joyce and grinned.

"You'll be ready by eight Sunday, right? We don't want to miss the start of this particular race."

"Yep. You see the look on Bubba Baxter's face?"

"Can you imagine? They really thought we'd believe Jodell Bob Lee was going to go over there and sit in the pits and watch that race?"

"Men!" they said together, and then broke into giggles as they gathered up their flock of puzzled kids and headed for home.

DRIVING HURT

The car sat there on pit road, perfectly ready to go out and begin practicing. That was far more than could be said for her jockey. Jodell had gone through a long, painful maneuver to shoehorn himself through the window, then ease himself down in the seat and try to get settled in. They had slid the seat back as far as they could to try to allow him to keep his left leg as straight as possible. Once in, he tried to work the clutch once or twice and thought he could manage to get it pushed in for the shifts. It didn't seem too awkward or painful at first, but he was having trouble reaching the gas pedal now and he seemed too far from the steering wheel. Still, he went through all the movements he thought he might need to make in the race and tried to find a happy medium.

Richard Petty strolled by as he rehearsed inside the car.

"Jodell, you silly cuss! What on earth are you trying to do? You can't drive one of these blame things with a broke leg. I'm wondering if that crack on the noggin ain't still bothering you."

"Aw, Richard. I know you've driven hurt before. I can manage. It feels pretty good now."

Never mind that his knee was throbbing like a toothache with each heartbeat and it felt as if Billy had taken his sheet metal pounding hammer to his calf bone.

"How you planning to shift the gears? What about the vibration from the car? You don't reckon that's gonna hurt a right smart? You're one crazy cat if you try to get out there the way you're all broke up."

He spoke the last words as he turned and walked on toward his own pit, shaking his head.

Bubba had a grim look on his own face when he reached in to help get him buckled up. Jodell cinched up the belts carefully. His ribs still were sore from where the belts had grabbed him in Talladega and the shoulder that had been dislocated in the crash now ached in perfect rhythm with the knee. He motioned for Bubba to give him a cup of water from the cooler on the pit wall and he used it to chase three or four aspirin tablets.

The big man gave the belts one more gentle tug to make sure they were as snug as he could get them. Jodell caught his breath sharply and grunted.

"Sorry, Joe Dee."

"Aw, it's okay. Everything's just a little tender, I guess."

"How about the seat? You comfortable?"

"It don't feel right sittin' this far back but it does help the leg. We'll see in a minute."

Bubba reached over and snapped the window net into place.

"It'll be better when you get to high gear and can stay

there. We got the setup you like under the car to use as a baseline. Tell us how she feels."

Jodell nodded and fired the engine, then awaited the signal to take to the track. The official at the head of the line finally began to wave them past. Jodell waited 'til the car in front of him began to roll before he pushed in the clutch and shoved the shifter up into first gear. But when he lifted his foot to ease out on the clutch the cast slipped off the pedal and the car stalled with a shudder.

"Dang it!" Jodell spat, then tried to ignore the sharp pain that shot up his leg when he again lifted the heavy cast and put his foot back on the clutch.

He re-fired the engine and finally got the car rolling as the impatient official waved frantically at him. The car seemed to bounce around much more severely than Jodell remembered as he took his first slow lap around the half-mile track.

"Just let me get to speed and I'll be all right," he said out loud to no one in particular.

On the start of his second lap, he jammed the accelerator down hard with his good leg and felt the powerful engine clear its throat and dig in. The torque of the motor pushed him hard back into his seat, but the exhilaration of actually being back in the cockpit of the car and feeling the tingle he always felt when he first punched the gas helped him ignore the twinge of pain that shot through his shoulder. That became harder to do when he took the first turn at speed and the centrifugal force pulled him hard against the lap belts and seemed to twist the cast on his leg. He tried to put it all out of his mind, though, as he concentrated on hitting his acceleration points smoothly, finding his line through the turns, and feeling how the car's initial setup matched the track.

Joe, Bubba, and Johnny stood together in the pits watching him maneuver through those first laps. The look on Joe's face as he read the truth from the stopwatches told the story. Even if the setup had been off considerably, the car should have been turning better times. Whether he was aware of it or not, Jodell was taking it easy out there.

"Boys, he's not close to where he should be," Joe reported.

"It'll take him a couple of laps to get comfortable with the way we moved the seat back," Bubba said.

"No, he's doggin' it."

"He's okay. He's just a little rusty," Johnny joined in.

"Rusty, my rear end! He's hurtin'!" Joe said as he waved the watches under their noses.

Indeed, inside the car, Jodell Lee was struggling. His leg felt as if it had lost all its strength and he dreaded having to lift it to the clutch again when he slowed down and had to shift. He gritted his teeth against the pain in his knee where the cast was rubbing with each little bump on the track, and from the shoulder where the belts were biting hard all the way around each lap. He was having trouble focusing on making the car go fast, while sweat was already pouring off his forehead.

He could tell that other cars were whizzing by him on either side but he seemed to be having trouble making his racer go. What was wrong with the thing? Why was it so hot in here?

Bubba pointed as Jodell suddenly pulled down off the track at the entrance to the pits and eased the Ford over to where they were waiting. All three of them trotted over to meet him. Bubba yanked down the window net as Jodell angrily ripped off his helmet and flung it into the floorboard. His face was deathly white, his driver's suit soaked in sweat, and his eyes looked dull and bloodshot.

"Car not right?" Bubba asked, almost hopefully. Springs or front end he could fix.

"Naw. She's close, I think," Jodell said dejectedly as

he unbuckled and began trying to raise himself up from the seat. It took Bubba's big arms to lift him out and half-carry him over to a seat on the wall. Johnny offered him a drink of water but he doused the whole cupful on his head instead. Billy came rolling up with a wagon full of tires and stopped cold when he got a look at their driver.

"What's wrong?" he asked as he dropped the handle on the wagon and squatted down next to Jodell.

"It's the cast. It keeps getting in the way. We're going to have to cut the blame thing off, I reckon."

"Maybe we can get rid of the bottom part and it won't get hung up in the pedals," Bubba suggested, instantly feeling better about the situation. The cast he could fix with some tin snips. He wasn't so good with fractured bones and misplaced shoulders.

Joe Banker took a quick look at his cousin's wan face and thin lips.

"Why don't we let Bubba take a spin in the car to see what he thinks?"

Jodell hesitated, but only for a moment.

"Yeah. That's a good idea. I'm not gonna be good for a lot of laps before Sunday and there's no use wasting them on getting the setup right."

Joe turned quickly to Bubba before Jodell could change his mind.

"Big 'un, you got your driver's suit?"

He always did. He needed it for those occasions when he would take the car out to feel for himself some irregularity Jodell had reported.

"What about Jodell? Shouldn't he run some laps?"

"He will soon's we get the car dialed in."

Bubba changed quickly and hopped into the car. It looked odd to Billy Winton to see the big man climbing into Jodell's racer. He'd seen Bubba taking a few laps at Richmond a month back, but that had only been to figure out a tricky setup. And he had also heard tall tales, mostly from Bubba himself, about his conquests in the several dirt and small track races in which he had actually competed. He couldn't help but grin when he saw how Bubba filled up the inside of the car as compared to Jodell and how he tried to cram his big head into Jodell's helmet.

"Like trying to shove a watermelon into a thimble, ain't it?" Joe Banker asked with a laugh when he caught Billy staring.

But Bubba boldly fired the car up and steered it right out onto the track as confidently as if he did it every day. The three men stood by, anxiously watching as Bubba quickly worked the car up to speed. Jodell sat on the wall, wiping his face with a towel as he shifted around, trying to find a comfortable position. Within five laps he had the times into the range they were expecting from the start. He brought the car in a time or two so they could make minor changes underneath the car.

Jodell ignored the entire process. Finally, he pulled out his pocketknife and began to saw away on the heel of the cast. He slowly removed all of the parts of it that he thought might catch on the pedals. At least it gave him something to do while his car, without him inside it, ran off laps out on the track. It didn't seem right somehow, but then, he couldn't remember a time when he had hurt so badly all over his body as he did at that moment.

Slowly but surely, it was dawning on him that maybe he had no business being in the car at all, that he was hurting their effort by being so dadgummed stubborn about it. That realization hurt him almost as bad as the bum knee or the damaged shoulder. Still, throughout the rest of the afternoon, he tried another couple of times to give it a go and kept his options open for the race itself.

It was near the end of the last practice of the day when

Jodell hobbled over on his crutch and climbed into the car for one last shot before they qualified. Bubba had just brought the car in and had pronounced her to be "right." Joe confirmed that opinion with the undeniable truth of the stopwatch.

There were only a dozen or so cars still out so Jodell ran a couple of laps as quick as he could. Before he knew it, he had closed in on a couple of rookies running side by side in front of him, already engrossed in their own private race, slipping and sliding all over the place. Jodell looked for his spot to try to work his way around the dangerous duo but they succeeded in blocking the track, likely without even noticing they were holding anyone else up. After a couple of laps behind them, Jodell had begun to grow impatient, ready to get some good out of these painful few turns around the track. How could he tell what the car had for qualifying if he was jammed up behind these two goofballs? Finally, Jodell pulled up and gave the Chevy on the inside a slight tap on the rear bumper, using the old "chrome horn" to let them know someone was taking seriously these final few minutes of practice.

The so-and-so in the Chevy didn't seem to care, though, and the two drivers continued to skirmish with each other. Then suddenly, the car on the inside started to slide up the track, leaving Jodell a slight opening. But just as he was about to dive for it, the outside car bobbled dangerously and the two cars in front of Jodell slammed into each other hard.

"Uh-oh!" Jodell said as he jumped on the brakes hard. Instinctively, he jammed his left foot hard on the clutch to keep from stalling the engine. A sharp stab of pain shot all the way up his leg and he yelped in agony. But he kept the motor cranked and headed on for the pits while the two drivers who had caused the near disaster climbed from their wounded race cars and went at each other in the middle of the track while the other practicing cars steered around them.

Bubba helped him from the car once again when he came in.

"You okay, Joe Dee?"

"Yeah, I think so. I just bounced around a little bit when I hit the brakes hard." He quickly changed the subject. "Feels like y'all have done a good job on the car." Then he headed for the cooler and something cold to drink before Bubba could get a good look at the pain that likely showed in his eyes.

Joe walked to where Bubba stood.

"Are you sure he's okay?"

"You know how he is. If he didn't think he could win this race then he wouldn't be in the car trying."

"I don't know. I bet if his head was cut off, he'd find a way to get it propped up so he could drive."

Half an hour later, Jodell managed to get back in the car, get strapped in and get himself set to qualify. He pushed as hard as he could but only managed the thirtieth fastest time, much to everyone's disappointment. It had been awhile since any car driven by Jodell Bob Lee had been that far back to start a race.

Jodell went straight back to the motel after qualifying. He'd driven a total of thirty-five or forty laps during the day, but when he stretched out on the narrow bed in the room, his body felt as if it had been a thousand trips around. Bubba brought in a big sack full of barbecue but Jodell hardly felt like eating any of it. He spent most of the time icing down his knee and shoulder while the rest of the crew ate the sandwiches, onion rings, slaw, and beans. Later, he fell asleep in the middle of a silent, violent argument with himself. Would he hurt the team by trying to drive when he was far from his best? Or would he hurt them more if he were too feeble to go and they had to put the kid back in his seat?

When the wake-up call came from the front desk, it jarred Jodell awake from a dream in which he was trying to run through a swamp. But no matter how hard he tried to run fast, he kept getting bogged down in quicksand. Then, when he tried to slide off the bed, he found his leg and ribs and shoulder to be far more stiff and sore than they had been. All the pushing he had done the previous day had clearly set him back.

When he looked at himself in the bathroom mirror, he saw his eyes were sunken and weak, his skin pale. He splashed cold water on his face and tried to wake up.

Later, as they discussed how they planned to run the race, Joe suddenly turned to Jodell and asked, point blank, the question the whole crew wanted to have answered.

"You sure you're good to go today, Jodell?"

"Yeah, I think so. I was pretty stiff when I first got up but I feel better now," he lied. Somebody was twisting a knife in his ribs and his lower left leg was about to explode.

Joe looked at his cousin sideways, then nodded and walked off to check the rest of the entries on his clipboard list. Jodell eased down to a seat on the pit wall.

The next time Bubba Baxter stepped over to get a tool, Jodell motioned for him to sit down next to him.

"You got your driving suit ready, Bub?"

"Huh?"

Bubba's mouth dropped open and his eyes widened. He leaned back and almost fell off the wall.

"I asked if you had your driving suit. I don't think I'm gonna be able to drive today."

"Come on now, Jodell. That don't sound like you talking."

Jodell leaned close and whispered.

"Look, Bub, I'm hurtin' pretty bad. I thought it'd be better after I got some sleep but I think all that driving yesterday just made it worse. I don't need to be out there, tearing up what healing I've done already and risking hurting somebody else."

"You sure?"

"Oh, I'm sure, all right. We need a decent finish here. I guess I've just been trying to convince myself that I'm the only man on the planet that can drive a race car. And now all I've done is get us a starting spot so far back in the field they may make me buy a ticket to the race."

"I don't know about me driving, though."

"Look, you've run better times than me ever since we got here. And I've watched you drive before. You can get the job done a lot better than I can today, Bub."

"If you think I can do it, you know I'll do my best. Let me get the boys working on finishing up and I'll go change. But there's still an hour or so for you to change your mind."

"I won't change my mind."

Bubba patted Jodell on the shoulder—his injured shoulder—and pulled back and apologized when the driver winced in pain. Then the big man hustled off to get ready to try to save the day.

Catherine Lee and Joyce Baxter had gotten up early and left the kids eating breakfast with Grandma. Then, still laughing about their sneakiness, they had set out across the mountains toward North Wilkesboro. The drive had been spectacular, the Technicolor early-October leaf show in full splendor. Joyce had grown up in the Carolina Low Country and she still marveled at the beauty of autumn in the mountains.

When they joined the line of traffic leading to the track, Joyce said, "So, do you really think he'll try to drive?"

"Of course he will. If he's here, he's going to drive."

"How can you be so calm about it? I'm glad I don't

have to deal with that. Bubba's such a big baby when he's hurt or sick."

"Not Jodell. But I'm gonna have the best time acting mad when we catch him driving."

They laughed some more, ignoring the curious stares from the people in the cars around them. But Catherine was worried, too. Banged up as he was, there was no way Jodell could drive effectively. And would his condition make it more likely that he would get caught up in a crash? Why did he have to be so mule-headed?

Once at the track, they ate a quick lunch from their picnic basket, saving plenty, though, for Jodell, Bubba, and the others to have after the race.

Finally, they followed the rest of the huge crowd through the gates and found their seats. Catherine raised the binoculars to her eyes and began sweeping the pit area, looking for Jodell and the others. She quickly spied the car, its hood still raised. It looked like Joe, Johnny, and Billy were up to their waists in the engine compartment, working on the car. She didn't see Jodell or Bubba anywhere. She passed the binoculars to Joyce who continued to search around the infield for them. After only a moment, she suddenly grabbed Catherine's arm.

"I still don't see Bubba but there's Jodell. Over there sitting on that toolbox by the red fuel can."

"Yeah, I see him. And he's got his driving suit on. I told you, Joyce!"

Down on the toolbox, Jodell was beginning to feel better, and he was also starting to question if he had made the right decision when he put Bubba into the Ford. Joe walked over to review the pit stops.

"Where did Bubba run off to? We need to go over this with him, too."

Jodell felt a pang of guilt but decided to wait a bit before he broke the news.

"Let's go ahead and we can bring Bubba up to speed in a little while."

He almost laughed when he realized what he had just said. Bringing Bubba up to speed?

"Dang it! If that lugnut went off to get something to put in that bottomless pit he calls a stomach . . ." Joe slammed the toolbox hard with his clipboard. "How long we got left 'til fire-up? Twenty minutes?"

"Now, now. Calm down. Let's take a look at what you got here."

They began to review the laps on which they would plan to stop. Finally, they were sure they were ready. Joe had one more thought.

"You got any new hand signals you want us to look for?"

"I don't know. You better ask him," Jodell said, pointing to an approaching Bubba Baxter. He was all decked out in his driving suit, Jodell's helmet under an arm.

"All right, what is this?" Joe asked.

"That's the driver of our car. That's what that is."

Joe Banker looked as if he had just swallowed a fly. When Bubba stood there next to him, looking totally uncomfortable, Joe finally spoke.

"I reckon we better go try to get some more horsepower out of the motor if it's got to pull around all that blubber all afternoon."

The big man didn't even smile. Joe started all over on the pit schedule and hand signal discussion, instantly accepting the fact that Bubba Baxter was about to drive their car in a major race. They were still talking when the call came over the loudspeakers for the drivers to go to their cars.

"What the heck is this?" Johnny blurted out as he spied Bubba standing there, all ready to climb into the Ford.

"We're scraping the bottom of the driver barrel now, ain't we?"

"Lordy, Mr. Baxter!" Billy Winton teased. "I thought you just built these things. You drive them, too?"

The kidding was actually helping Bubba. He was so nervous he was afraid he might actually drive the wrong direction around the track once he got out there.

David Pearson happened by on the way to his own Ford. He did a double take as he saw Bubba getting ready to climb into the blue Jodell Lee car.

"What is this?" he asked, pointing to the big man. "I gotta go tell the other guys. We may have ourselves another boycott!"

Bubba grinned and waved him on and began trying to climb in the car's window as gracefully as he could.

Joe stood back, watching Bubba and the looks on the faces of Johnny Holt and Billy Winton. At first, they had thought Jodell might be playing a joke on them. But that wouldn't have been like him at all. This close to the start of a race, Jodell Lee would never have been clowning around.

No doubt about it. Their driver today at North Wilkesboro was to be Mr. Bubba Baxter.

Catherine and Joyce were watching over the crowd, talking with some of the folks sitting next to them in the grandstand. Finally, Catherine picked up the binoculars so she could see her husband climb into his car for the start. But she could see Jodell, standing there beside the car, and he was still leaning casually on his crutches, showing no signs of getting himself ready to go racing.

"Where's Bubba? I still don't see him," Joyce asked. He was usually hard to miss.

Catherine suddenly stopped her sweep of the pits,

pulled the binoculars away from her eyes, blinked a few times, then looked again.

"Oh, my God! Joyce, you're not going to believe this!"

"What is it?"

"Here, take a look for yourself. In the car."

She passed Joyce the binoculars. Her mouth flew open immediately.

"What on earth are they doing?"

"I don't know for certain, but it looks like your husband is getting ready to drive that car."

A voice on the public address system ordered the drivers to start their engines.

"But he can't . . ."

The roar drowned out her disbelieving words as the assembled race cars all cranked up in unison. And it was Joyce's husband who was apparently firing one of them up.

But not exactly. Bubba was so nervous, he almost forgot to flip the ignition on. Why weren't the gauges coming up? What was wrong with the Ford? Jodell had leaned in the window to help him get the belts clicked shut. He pointed to the ignition and gave Bubba a questioning look, and he quickly reached over and obeyed the "start your engines" command.

The motor came to life and Bubba remembered to survey the gauges in front of him again, checking each of them to make sure the arrows stood straight up. The tightness of the helmet seemed to be restricting the blood flow to his head and he felt dizzy.

Jodell watched the look on Bubba's face and smiled as he cinched the safety belts as tight as he could. It occurred to him then that their roles had been reversed. Bubba was getting a taste of what he went through before every race.

The pace car rolled off and Bubba tried to remember how to make the car go. He quickly shifted up into gear and let it slowly move away.

The parade laps helped and when the green flag finally fell, it all seemed to have come back to Bubba. He had done this before. He was hardly a Jodell Lee or David Pearson or Freddy Lorenzen, but he knew how to drive a race car. He smiled as he gunned the Ford and chased after the car in front of him. Slowly, lap after lap, his confidence grew as he felt how well the car was running and he began to pick his way up from the back of the field, passing a car here and there as the laps gradually began to count off. He wasn't driving pretty, but he was driving.

They were three hundred laps into the race before Bubba suddenly realized that he was sweating like he'd never done before. The perspiration ran down his face, behind his goggles, and he was having trouble focusing his eyes on the track ahead. It felt like someone had turned on the oven and he was rapidly becoming well done.

By then, too, the car was suffering. She looked as if someone had taken a sledgehammer to her. Bubba had brought the car from the back of the field to fourteenth position, but he was running several laps down. His driving style had hardly been subtle. Whenever he couldn't manage to pass someone, he simply banged and slammed against them long enough that they either moved over and let him by or managed to find a way to drive away from him.

Finally, the checkered flag waved, but by then, Bubba was ready to run a few hundred more laps. He was still rubbing fenders with another car when he came off turn four to take the checkers. The crowd stood and cheered appreciatively as he finished, the more knowledgeable

fans fully aware of what he had accomplished. The public address announcer had informed them that Jodell was
not inside the car today, that it was, in fact, the team's
chief wrench who had brought the car home in a very
respectable fifteenth place.

Bubba didn't feel tired at all until the cool down lap,
and then he almost didn't have the strength to steer the
car into the pits. He recovered quickly, though. A few
minutes after he had managed to climb out of the Ford,
Bubba was holding court around the battered race car,
like a big game hunter recounting his exploits out there
in the jungle. He was more than willing to describe every
single lap to anybody who was amenable to standing
there and listening.

He was describing a particularly brilliant move to
some other team's members, showing with his hands
how he had shoved aside some poor, unfortunate racer
so he could move ahead. But suddenly, when he looked
up, something he saw caused him to fall silent, his mouth
open in mid-boast.

Ambling his way, her arms crossed and with a grim
look on her face, was his wife.

Bubba could feel the blood begin to drain out of his
face. Later, he would claim that his life passed before
his eyes as surely as if he had been drowning.

"Honey!" he managed to squeak.

"Bubba Baxter! What on earth are you doing?" Joyce
demanded, trying her best to continue to look upset with
him.

The other team members hooted. The look of terror
on Bubba's full-moon face would be the subject of garage talk on the circuit for months to come.

Catherine hid behind the car so he wouldn't catch her
laughing. Watching the scene play out between Bubba
and Joyce, she hardly noticed that Jodell had slipped up

behind her until he grabbed her in a powerful embrace.

"Y'all make a wrong turn on the way home from church?"

She turned in his arms, kissed him, hugged him tightly for a while, kissed him again, then looked into his face.

"Can I tell you how proud I am of you and Bubba? I know how hard it must have been for you to let somebody else drive that car today."

"She's right, Lee." Richard Petty stood there grinning. Neither of them had noticed him when he walked up. "You did the right thing today. You don't have to prove anything to anybody. You'll race again. But I need to talk to you about your substitute. We're probably gonna drop our car off at the junkyard and not even bother towin' it home."

"Now Richard, you know I didn't hit you or anybody else on purpose," Bubba called over from where he was, by then, signing another autograph with a flourish. Joyce had temporarily dropped her mad act and stood there with her arm around her husband's waist as if she might not let go of him.

Petty waved Bubba off and started walking on back toward where his own crew was finishing up. "Just leave the driving to this cat here from now on." He motioned toward Jodell with a thumb, then called back over his shoulder, "You look better under the car than inside it anyway!"

Later that night, as they all circled a table at an all-night diner and finished up platters of cheeseburgers and fries, Bubba was still reliving the day. But he was also forced to deal with the barbs being thrown his way by Johnny and Billy, and still more mock anger from Joyce.

But at the end of the table, Joe and Jodell talked quietly while Catherine sat close by and listened.

"You know what you did today, cuz?" Joe finally asked.

"Became a spectator, I reckon."

"Nope. You did one of the smartest, bravest things you've done since we started this thing."

"What do you mean?"

Joe took a sip of his coffee and looked him in the eye for a moment before he went on.

"Some drivers would have pushed it too far today. Let their ego get in the way and gone out there and likely messed up somebody else's race, too, when they couldn't get the job done. Or they would have just parked the car and not let anybody else drive it if they couldn't, no matter what it cost the team." He set his cup down, reached for Jodell's hand, and shook it sincerely. "I'm proud of you, Mr. Jodell Bob Lee. Proud to be your kin. And I'm proud to be on your team."

Catherine put her head on Jodell's shoulder.

"Me, too," she added, almost in a whisper.

Jodell simply smiled and then pulled them both close to him for a moment in the best embrace he could manage with his Talladega shoulder and bruised ribs. It had been a rough, painful year so far. At times, and especially the last few weeks, he had been doubtful that he could continue. But these people, the ones around this table and a few others, had helped him see it through. It occurred to him that he never took the opportunity to tell them how much they meant to him. Though they fussed and feuded like all families did, they were still a team, still all on the same side.

Bubba and Joe and Johnny. Billy Winton, now, for sure. Of course, Catherine and Joyce. Even Clifford and Randy, who gave so much for no pay and even less of the glory.

Then Jodell seemed to have a sudden thought. He let go Cath and Joe, leaned forward, cleared his throat of the frog that had just taken up residence there, and addressed the whole group gathered around the table.

"Look, I've been thinking about the springs we been running under the short-track car . . ."

Don't be left in the dust!

It's a brand new season
—and a new generation of drivers—
roaring like thunder to the checkered flag!

Young Guns

Book Five in the
Rolling Thunder Stock Car Racing Series

The garage area teemed with activity. The Cup crews were occupied with their early practice while all the Grand National teams were busy preparing their machines for the start of their afternoon race. The grandstands were already brimming over with enthusiastic fans that had come, despite the pervasive heat and humidity, to watch a race. Any race. Cup, Grand National, or wheelbarrow, they didn't care so long as there was wheel-to-wheel competition.

Jodell Lee showed up and took his young protégé, Rocket Rob Wilder, on another of his tours of the tracks he would be driving. As they sauntered back down through the garage on the way back to their stall, Rob thought to himself once more how wonderful it felt to glance from side to side and see the faces of men he had idolized since he was old enough to watch a televised race. Guys like Waltrip, Earnhardt, and Elliott. And Jodell Lee, the man who walked beside him. Jodell noticed the gleam in the kid's eyes.

"You ain't star struck are you?" Jodell asked with a grin.

"Naw. I'd just love the chance to drive against those guys."

"You prove yourself in Grand National and you'll get the shot."

"I don't know. Waltrip and Elliott and some of the others are hinting they might give it up before long."

"Who knows? You may be one of the young guns that helps them make up their minds."

Rob was still thinking about Jodell's words when he climbed in and strapped himself to the car. It would be something to be practicing this afternoon for the race the next day, to plan strategy against Gordon and Labonte and Jarret and Burton and the rest of them. But he also knew he had his own race to run, and before he knew it, he was pulling away with the others, two-by-two, and heading off into turn one. The nerve-wracking hoopla, the endless driver introductions, all the pre-race festivities were finally all over.

Then, before he could even catch a good breath, the green flag was waving, and, with a cloud of dust and a deafening reverberation, they were off . . .